I0822836

ALSO BY W.P. TRUESDELL

The romantic comedy

For Love of Art and Ericka

The Phantom Bugatti

W.P. TRUESDELL

The Phantom Bugatti is a work of fiction. Unless otherwise indicated, all the names, characters, businesses, places, events and incidents in this book are either the product of the author's imagination or used in a fictitious manner. Any resemblance to actual persons, living or dead, or actual events is purely coincidental.

ISBN: 979-8-9910438-0-9

William Prenevost Truesdell, wptruesdell@gmail.com
309-714-1600, www.wptruesdell.com

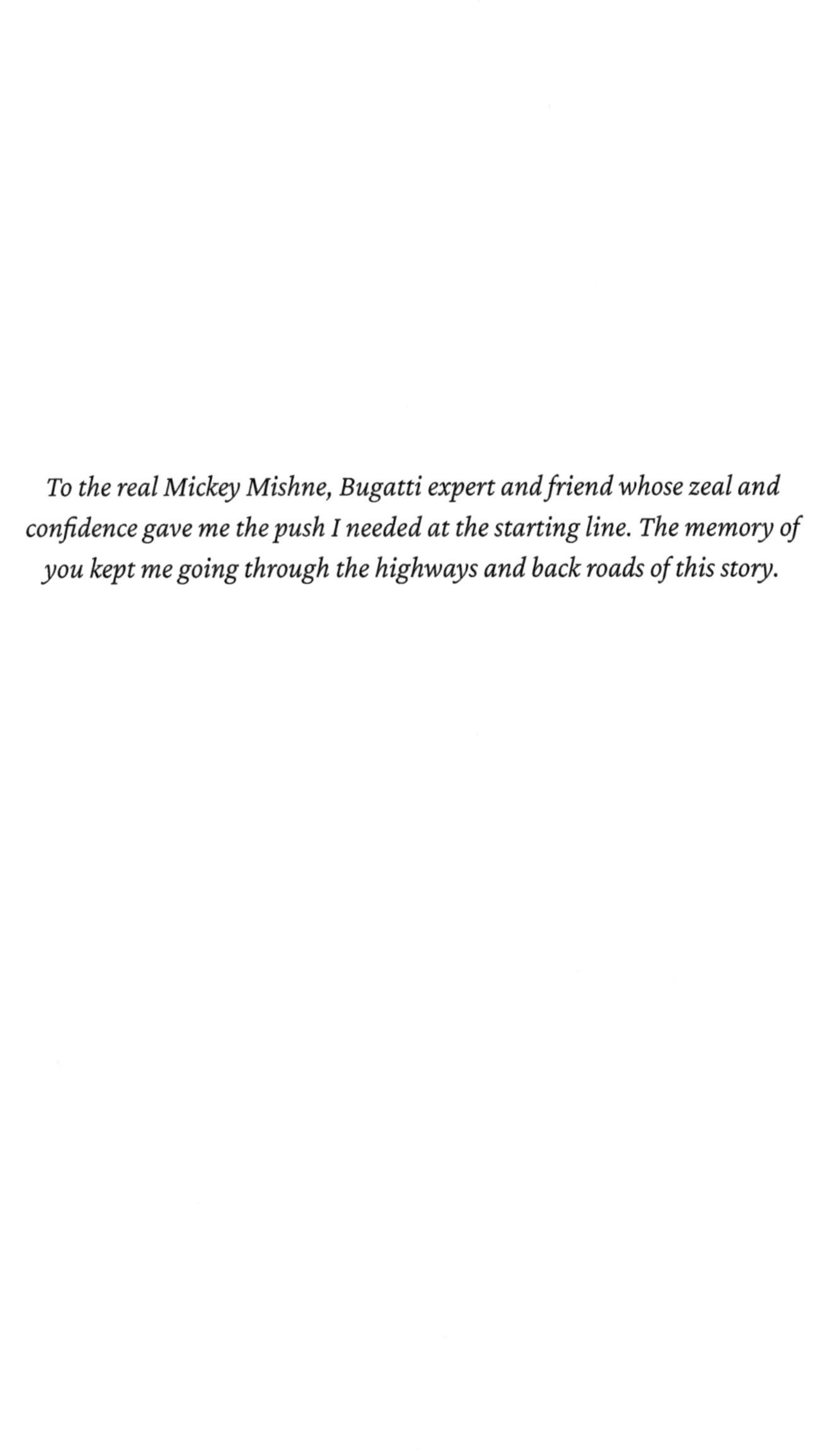

To the real Mickey Mishne, Bugatti expert and friend whose zeal and confidence gave me the push I needed at the starting line. The memory of you kept me going through the highways and back roads of this story.

ACKNOWLEDGMENTS

So many people supported me over the years it took to complete this novel. It began with a few pages written in Cleveland in 1998 to the first draft completed in Indiana at my sister's lakeside cabin. I am grateful for the encouragement given to me by the folks at the Bugatti Trust in England, members of the American Bugatti Club, especially Paul Simms and Evelyn Wilburn, as well as the Auburn Cord Duesenberg Museum.

With apologies to those who I may have accidently omitted, I want to thank the following Roseanne Browne for her support including use of her lakeside cabin which became my writing retreat. Mary Grant and her husband Mike Prenevost for the long nights listening to my words, the proofing countless drafts. Mary Michael for your inexhaustible enthusiasm and support and your beta-reading friends. Bernard Kress, Patrick Peronnet, and Alan Yanowitz along with others who participated in my GoFundMe campaign to get this book over the finish line! And my wife Susan Stiner and our daughter Nicole S. Prenevost for their patience.

The Phantom Bugatti

W.P. TRUESDELL

EARLY 1998

THE FIRST TIME Grandpa drove me to his abandoned remnant of a farm, I dashed from the pick-up down the path to the barn and jumped like a hurdler floating in the air for an instant. It became a ritual with every visit, that vault for an infinitesimal moment of weightlessness. With repetition and time the sensation may have diminished, but my urge to attain it never died.

It's been over twenty years since those halcyon days. Yet today, the memories race through my mind as we head out to that humble house and iconic red barn atop the sloping meadow. My cherished Grandpa Jacque Dreyfus passed the property on to me, as I had hoped he would. A week after he died, a lawyer came to our apartment to deliver the keys in person. The moment I signed for them and the man left, my wife, Sally, asked, "How soon can we sell it?"

We just surpassed the three-hour mark cruising an interstate highway in northeastern Indiana.

With her pink ASICS sneakers resting on the dashboard, Sally flicked the ashes off her cigarette out a crack in the window. "This is a long way from Cleveland Heights, Ohio."

I glanced at her through my aviator sunglasses. "Like I didn't tell you how long the drive would be."

We had been together for nine years, married the last eight. Despite the rust spots, my thirteen-year-old white Civic was holding up better. If only the equivalent of oil changes and lube jobs existed to keep a marriage humming so well.

Sally took a last drag on her smoke and flicked the butt out the window. "Are we there yet?"

I ignored her rhetorical moan. Cher's "Believe" came on the radio, diverting her attention in the journey's third and final full-hour.

Late one night in 1991, after studying for my college finals, she seized my attention at the Circle Bar and Grill. The strawberry blonde served me a draft beer with a Kim Basinger come-hither glance. Lust at first sight. After dating for the better part of the summer, she moved in with me and ditched her barmaid gig to be a sales clerk at a Gap clothing store.

We survived the initial stretch of living together before settling into a groove. Marriage came into our conversations when "safe sex" became the watchword for those seeking carnal fulfillment. So, after my graphic design business became a reliable livelihood, we married. For me, matrimony seemed more like the next logical step into adulthood. Sally coveted the ring, dress, and gifts.

I slowed from interstate speed to that posted for a narrow

country road. The newly sown fields, farmhouses, sheds, and equipment were now discernible in detail. The only businesses in view for miles were at freeway junctions. Decades ago, horses and buggies had traversed these dusty, gravel-covered trails. Then they poured cement slabs mortared together to accommodate the increasing number of motor cars. Asphalt completed the evolution, but eventually, cracks arose at the cement seams and produced the rhythmic thumping inside the vehicle—da-*da,* da-*da, da.*

It pulled me back into the trance, recalling those times with the only grandpa I knew. Mom gave me his name, Americanized to Jack. He taught me how to drive, shifting gears on the column of his old Studebaker and bouncing over the rutted farm lane. I slammed the brakes without clutching and killed the engine near the end. He told me about that sweet spot between accelerating and releasing the clutch.

“It will come once you learn to relax,” he said. “Life comes easier.” Soon I engaged the gears like extensions of my arms and legs without a screech or stutter. His compliments and confidence meant more to me than I ever acknowledged. My daydream reached deeper. His Belgian baritone voice said, “You treasure this farm and it will treasure you someday, eh?”

“Jack!” Sally barked. “Wake up! You just missed the turnoff.”

I pulled to the side of the road to study my MapQuest printout.

“ "You’re right.”

“And I’m not blind, and I can read!”

“Sarcasm?” I bit back.

A dirt road ahead provided an easy turnaround, and the sign in question appeared.

Avilla
Population 1,249

We lowered our windows to get a good look at the houses: a mixture of small clapboard structures with brick ranch styles. The streets looked only three to four blocks deep. One majestic veranda-fronted Victorian with a circular driveway occupied the better part of a block. Then came a tall red-brick Catholic church next to a playground and park, followed by two-story dwellings. Finally, retail storefronts started appearing with some abandoned or empty. A tavern, a beauty salon, and a cute pink café seemed active.

The business district, of sorts, ended before Sally could get out a snarky remark. Residential blocks resumed until we reached the gateway of the Avilla Cemetery. A newer Marathon gas station dominated the next intersection on the opposite side. Further out, a 55-mph speed limit sign signaled the western edge of town.

As I picked up speed, Sally said, “I hope that wasn’t the city you said was nearby.”

“That’s Fort Wayne, further south.”

“And is Fort Wayne an actual city?”

“The metro area is big enough to support a professional orchestra.”

She turned to me and lifted her sunglasses. “And how would you know that?”

“I did some research.”

“And having an orchestra makes it a city?”

“Along with a theatre company and art museum, yes. To some people.”

“Well, let’s get packing!” she said, slapping her thigh.

Three minutes later, I spotted the farm. “There!” I pointed forward to the left. As I slowed to turn, my heart took off, forcing a deep breath.

The dirt pathway extended about a quarter mile. I brought the car to a crawl so we could examine our mini estate. Sally focused on the house with its green shingles and faded red door flanked by two windows. Except for taller trees and abundant weeds, the view matched the grainy image from my memory.

Our windows came down again, letting in the crisp springtime air. The road leveled at the top of the grade, narrowing to faint tracks rolling several yards to the barn.

I parked a few feet from the house, sprang from the car, and stretched. Sally got out, brushing cigarette ashes off her pink sweatshirt with Gap in glitter letters. We observed the panoramic view of the property.

A breeze tossed her shoulder-length hair. She propped her hands on her hips. "So. This is it."

"All nine and a half acres!" I said, spreading my arms over my head.

"You didn't exaggerate. I'll give you that!" I pulled the keys from my jeans as we headed to the front door.

The grass mixed with weeds around the foundation.

I pushed a key into the weathered oak door. With extra effort, the lock turned. I shoved the brass doorknob, and it creaked halfway open. Sally looked over my shoulder without a word.

We stepped inside. Pine-paneled walls and wood flooring gave the room a cabin-like feel. A set of old kitchen appliances lined the west wall with a window above a porcelain sink.

At the center stood a potbelly wood-burning stove next to a structural column. An exhaust duct ran up through a tin-tiled ceiling, which I studied while Sally inspected the stove and refrigerator. A lonely, dark wooden desk and chair sat near the east wall with a front-view window. I couldn't resist checking the drawers and found a faux ivory pocket knife about four inches long.

A raised floor outlined the back one-third of the house. I stepped up on it. "This was the bedroom area." It felt a bit like standing on a stage as I watched Sally approach. For a moment, I saw Grandpa gazing out the kitchen window toward the barn.

"You're grinning like a... I don't know what. Imagining your Grandpa here with us. That'creepy."

I survyed the space. corner to corner. "It all looks smaller than I remember. But I guess that's natural."

"Small is right." Sally noticed a smaller-than-usual door and started towards it. "This must be the bathroom." She twisted and pulled the doorknob. "What the hell?" The mid-day sun flashed in her face and she shielded her eyes.

"Oh yeah," I said. Outside, some fifty feet away, stood the barn. "Watch your step."

We walked out onto the sprouting lawn. Pointing to a molting gray booth with flakes of white paint, Sally asked, "What's that?"

"It's the outhouse. I forgot. So, you were kind of right."

"Why didn't you tell me about *that*?"

"It's been a long time. I forgot some details."

Lips pursed, Sally shook her head. "Now I see why your mother passed on this place." She walked to the car for her cigarettes, lit up, and walked back toward me.

I said, "The property goes north to the ditch along the county road we came from. There's a stretch between those two maple trees where Grandpa grew vegetables. The lane borders the eastern boundary. You can see the neighbor's crops breaking through the soil. That was part of the original farm." I turned around, facing south. "We've got another acre behind the house until the woodland. Don't you love the pines and the white birch mixed in there? The Dalmatians of trees." I pivoted to the west. "It ends behind the barn by those rocks."

Sally went into her thinking position with one hand on her hip, the other holding the cigarette at the ready. She took a drag. "Okay. I've seen enough. Let's get back."

"What? We just got here!"

"I've seen enough."

"But you haven't seen the best part!" I whipped off my Cleveland Indians jacket and dashed toward the barn. When Sally reached me, I had already removed the padlock and opened the double doors. A stale odor of decaying hay, animals, and machinery oil drifted out. "Mm, good old barn smell!"

Sally, pinching her nose, said, "Ew!"

On the left, a workbench dominated the wall. In the middle were several stalls for livestock. I could make out an exit door in the back wall. The dusty floor had clumps of caked dirt and straw fallen from hay bales on the upper deck.

Then, I spotted the built-in ladder to the upper deck next to the back door. "All right!" I started up without the fearless speed I once had. Near the top, I looked down at Sally. "It's not as high as I remember. Come on up."

"No, thanks! But you go ahead. Maybe you'll break your neck."

"Love you, too."

The hayloft floor was about thirty yards deep, half covered by bales and loose straw. Keeping away from the edge, I walked to the eastern wall to peer out a small window. I got a bird's eye view of the farmhouse through the dust and soot. On the way back, I looked down at Sally, and that brought a touch of vertigo. I returned to the ladder and noticed the hayloft door for hauling in bundled field grass.

With both hands around its iron lever, I yanked. Nothing. I jerked harder, and my hands gave way.

Sally laughed below. I looked at her and said, "Glad to amuse you, my dear!"

I'm no bodybuilder but still in decent shape for a thirtysomething. I spit on my hands, gripped the handle, and pulled. "That budged it some!" I took a breath and gave it a final heave-ho, letting out a deep grunt.

The door swung open with an ear-piercing screech. The force of the heavy door flung me onto my back inches from the hayloft's rim.

"Jack!" Sally shrieked.

The heavy dust penetrated my nostrils, making me pinch my nose to stifle a sneeze. I stood up and advanced to the large opening. The blue sky and swaths of fresh sprouting green created a magnificent view to the west. "What a view! Brightens the dullness of the black fields and gray woodlands," I said. "You should come up! It's *Magnifique!*"

"I'll take your word for it," Sally replied.

Near the horizon line, I could make out a car and a semi-trailer on an interstate highway. Gazing into the sky, I whispered, "Thank you, Grandpa."

After I clamped the window shut, I spotted a thick twine rope with a metal hook rigged near the ceiling. It was used to hoist up the bales.

"Jack, I need to pee," Sally shouted. "And I will not use the outhouse!"

"I'm coming down," I replied. With one foot in the hook, I pulled the rope to test its tightness and give. Satisfied, I pushed off the edge and swooped to the floor faster than expected.

Horrified, Sally screamed. I braced for a hard landing inches from her stiffened body, landing with a thud and a slide.

She leaned over me. "Jack! Are you okay?"

I rubbed my aching hip and said, "That didn't go like I remembered."

She rolled her eyes. "You idiot! Thanks for not knocking me over."

Resting to catch my breath and settle my heartbeat, I noticed a faint square outline on the floor of the north wall.

"Jack, come on. I need to go!"

I rubbed off enough muck to see that the cutout measured about three feet by four feet. "Sally, there might be something underneath the barn!"

"Well, check it out later!" She rushed to the car, and I followed.

We were down the lane onto the country road in no time and speeding towards the Marathon station in Avilla. While Sally did her business, I filled my tank. On the way back, I got her to open up more about the farm. Despite my keeping her expectations low, she still felt a letdown.

At least the secret hatch door gave us an unanticipated thrill. I told Sally how Grandpa once kidded me about confronting a notorious hoodlum during Prohibition. He also told me gothic tales of werewolves from his European childhood. While I dismissed those from the old country, I thought there might be more to the gangster remark.

"I hope he left me a distillery down there," I said. "Along with jars of over-aged moonshine."

"Who was that famous gangster from Indiana?" she said.

"Dillinger. One of the FBI's Most Wanted. He staged his greatest escape from the law in Indiana. But he wasn't a bootlegger," I said. "Only robbed banks, I think."

"And killed people. You don't think there could be a body down there?"

"Not that Grandpa would've been part of."

I PARKED near the barn and grabbed a flashlight and screwdriver from the glove compartment. Walking inside, I said, "Of course, a body would be a skeleton by now."

She slapped me on the shoulder.

I used my car key to scrape the grime from the grooves, then angled the flat head under for leverage. After prodding one side, the cover came off.

"What's that?" said Sally. "A secret compartment or a trapdoor to who knows where?"

The screwdriver worked much better than my key. The covering popped up. I said, "When you got the tools, you got the power!" With the flashlight, I spied into the black hole. "Oh, my god! I don't believe it!"

Sally looked panicked. “What? Let me see! No, wait. Do I want to? A skeleton?”

“Not a complete one. Just some bones scattered about like a critter got to the remains.”

“You’re jerking my chain. Get out of the way.” I handed her the light, and she looked in. “It’s a bunch of junky old car parts.”

“There’s a wooden ladder leaning against the wall,” I said. "Going closer for a look." With the penlight in one hand, I stepped down gently. Any step might crumble.

My foot touched down on a dirt floor. I felt the chill of being well underground. Casting a flashlight sweep of the room, I guessed it looked about ten-by-fifteen, with cinderblock walls. Half of the ceiling showed the raw underside of the barn’s floorboards. I could easily reach them, making the height about six feet. A long, waist-high object covered by an oilcloth filled the center. The dusty car parts lying about signaled what I’d see under it.

Sally called out, “What’s down there?”

I lifted a corner of the tarp and saw an ancient, stripped-down car. Holding up the covering with one hand and the light in the other, I stepped to the front of it. My eyes opened wide when I spotted the distinctive red oval-shaped logo affixed to the radiator. “What the hell!”

“What is it?”

I knew Sally wouldn’t get the significance of our discovery, so I didn’t respond immediately. Instead, I dropped the canvas, crept up the ladder, and popped my head out. “A Boo!”

Sally gasped. “Goddamn it, Jack!” She slapped my backside as I crawled out. “You scared me!”

“Those are not ordinary car parts. That’s a Bugatti!”

2

"Hey, Mom. Would you be surprised if I told you that Grandpa was hiding a car under his barn, all dismantled?"

She sighed. *"You know how I feel about you doing drugs, Jack."*

"For real!"

I called her in Arizona right after we returned to our apartment in Cleveland Heights. My mom, Kate, to almost everyone who knew her, had retired there with her third husband, George, whom she swore would be my last stepdad.

I never knew my biological father. His number got called back in the old military draft before my mom knew she was pregnant, and he became a Vietnam War casualty just over a year later. When I turned two, her concern for my needing a father reached the point where she started dating. Mom explained how different things were back then, thinking she needed a provider and a father figure for me. She married a car salesman who turned out to have a cocaine addiction and ended the marriage before their second anniversary. I only faintly recall what he looked like.

Mom took back my father's last name, Reinhart. A few years later, she continued searching for a father-figure type, but because the requirements were higher, the dates were fewer until she gave up.

"Sally saw it too," I said to Mom. "An old car under a tarpaulin in what might have been a storm cellar, but under the barn."

She pondered my words. *"Coming from the old country, Dad did some odd things. But assuming you're not pulling my leg, this one takes the cake!"*

"Not pulling your leg, Mom. Does the word 'Bugatti' mean anything to you?"

"It's an Italian line of handbags and accessories."

"It's a very early line of automobiles made in France."

"Never heard of it."

"Very rare. Think about it and let me know if any thoughts pop up."

"Sure. But enough about cars. How did the farm look?"

"Neglected," I said. "But inside the house wasn't too bad. No signs of vagrants or rats living there. Some weather damage on one wall, and musty as expected."

"What did Sally think?"

"Paraphrasing, she knows now why you rejected the old shack."

"That 'old shack' was your grandpa's haven."

"You know he never had a toilet put in?"

"He stopped going out there after you grew up. About the time I met George. Are you still thinking about selling it?"

"That's on hold until I figure out what to do about that car. Sally would sell it all tomorrow if it was up to her."

After Mom divorced the loser, we all lived together with Grandpa and Grandma. Mom's photo album shows me as a toddler with them. She got a job at a toy store to augment the military's widow's compensation, so we moved into an apartment.

Eventually she became the office manager for an insurance agency in the Standard Oil building in downtown Cleveland. There she met an assistant vice president for the gas station giant. His combination of Texas swagger and gentleman-like manners charmed her. I was in the sixth grade. When she saw how much fun

I had with him tossing a baseball or football, she knew he was the one.

"Your grandpa's memory started fading," she said on the phone.

"My mind was flooded with memories out there. I loved that place."

"Fortunately, Dad didn't forget that."

"You deny it, but I know you had a hand in giving it to me."

"I might have," Mom said. *"Wait! Dad worked for a while at a car factory during the Depression before he moved us to Cleveland."*

"Any chance you remember the name of the carmaker?"

"He didn't talk much about those early years off the boat. Neither did my Mom, who grew up in Fort Wayne."

After the call, I got this image of Grandpa as a vigorous middle-aged man with that ever-present cigarette. And I could hear his heavy French-sounding Belgian accent. He had so little when he passed away, after all the medical costs. He probably hid the farm from the government so that he had something to pass down.

Or was there another reason?

THE BUGATTI OCCUPIED my mind all week. Every couple of hours, I took a break from work to do more research on the Internet.

I discovered The Bugatti Trust in England, a not-for-profit, education-based organization. They were a treasure trove of information and photographs about the car company and the entire family.

The American Bugatti Club, on the contrary, was minimal. When I discovered that membership required owning a Bugatti car, I thought, *Hey, that's me—a Bugatti owner!* Then, like a stone hitting my windshield, I realized I had no documentation. How would I prove the car is mine? Could I? The importance of provenance was something I learned in art school, so I knew how complicated it could get to track ownership of desirable objects.

Back then, Grandpa didn't have the money to buy a Bugatti—new or used. Maybe the car was a wreck he was trying to fix. Or was he holding it for someone else whose plans changed? Or was there a darker reason? Could he have stolen it? *Grandpa, a car thief!*

They had lived in a bungalow in Kamm's Corner at the southwest border of Cleveland, near the plant where Grandpa worked and where Mom attended school. She met my real father in high school, and then they attended Kent State together until the draft took him.

Back then, Cleveland was second only to Detroit in automobile and truck manufacturing. I wished I had spent more time with Grandpa Jacque before Alzheimer's started to erode his memory. Until now, I didn't realize he had buried those events on the farm with the Bugatti.

3

Sally returned from work, mumbling something to herself. Off the vestibule, a hallway led to the kitchen one way and the master bedroom the other. The kitchen provided access to my office and the living room. I was designing a benefit invitation for the Lyric Opera when I heard the thud of her shoulder bag landing on the kitchen counter.

She skipped any greeting. "A lousy ten thousand dollars!" she yelled.

I saved my work on the desktop computer and stepped into the kitchen, where I could see her spread out on the sofa. A counter separated it from the living room.

I decided to take her verbal bait. "What's it about, Sally?"

"The farm. I called a realtor to look into its value. She thinks the house is probably only worth ten to fifteen thousand without doing anything to it."

I folded my arms and leaned against the kitchen counter. "It's a small parcel of scrubland with an old cabin and barn," I said. "What did you expect?"

"I was hoping for more, like maybe a real farmhouse."

"And then there's the location," I added.

"I know, but still..."

"You want a drink before supper?"

"Not here. Let's go somewhere."

When opting for more than fast food we often chose Ravelli's, a quaint family-owned restaurant about a mile east on Mayfield Drive in Cleveland Heights. Along the way, I asked Sally about the realtor she talked with. "Is she one of those part-time agents?"

"Yes, but I trust her."

"The farm market must be very different from the city or suburbs."

"She talked with someone who knew about farms and land who explained how yours is just a remnant. And investing anything into it would be a complete loss."

I thought about that and how installing a restroom would help me if I ended up restoring the old car myself. But I didn't want to bring up the Bugatti despite it being a wildcard in the situation.

We arrived at the restaurant, its storefront slightly wider than the dry cleaner and Chinese joint flanking it. With just a handful of diners, our order was taken almost immediately. The banter with the middle-aged waitress, pretty much capped the conversation Sally and I had going. My work bored Sally, and her job in women's clothing did nothing for me except the occasional incident involving a wacky customer or a teen girl trying to steal something. For amusement, we watched a young couple trying to manage their two squirming toddlers.

Finally, our food arrived. Ever weight conscious, it was spinach cannoli for Sally and I had ravioli. She was on her second glass of wine when she said, "Is there any reason we can't put it on the market right now?"

"There's a lot to consider. Not the least being the Bugatti."

"But isn't it worth something as it is?"

"Why are you in such a hurry?"

"We've been talking about getting a house forever and I'm tired of talking. I want to get what we can for the farm, including the junk car, and put the money into the house fund."

"I know that's what we agreed to, but now we have to consider the antique car. It's a wild card in our planning. It's a potential game changer and will take time to investigate. We'd be fools not to."

Sally's attention went to the children. I studied her pensive face. Her beauty still bewitched me from time to time, and this was one of them.

"That couple will be us someday," she said. I looked over at the family. "And you wouldn't want to raise them in an apartment, would you?"

"You know the answer. Let's not go there now."

"Okay." She finished her drink. "So, what do you want to do about the farm?"

"Seems to me selling it right away is pointless now. It's not something to rush into, especially after what we saw out there."

She surprised me. No wisecrack reply.

THAT EVENING, I got on the telephone in my office to talk with a guy I knew in high school: Doug Flaven. He had been a star linebacker on the football team. His friends often called him "Flatten" for his hard hits on the field.

Even though he flunked out before graduating, I saw him once at a class reunion. His having worked as a car mechanic didn't surprise me. Then he got into construction and eventually became a contractor to start making what he called "serious money." I didn't bother analyzing his meaning. At high school reunions, you expect old classmates to embellish. Everyday jobs became positions with titles, and others came with descriptions. I had my own "advertising and promotions business."

It didn't matter to me if Flaven had any experience with antique automobiles. I needed a guy with muscle and a working knowledge of cars. Someone I could trust. Given the Bugatti's potential value, I didn't want a stranger.

"You've got to be shitting me!" he said.

"Yes, an old Bugatti! No doubt about it once I saw that red and white logo on the front of the radiator."

"Un-fucking-believable!" he said.

"Blew me away! So, here's the thing, Doug. I need someone who knows cars to help me and thought of you. Interested?"

We talked some more. He said the underground space was likely a barn cellar. As a car guy, he knew a restored Bugatti's rarity and potential value. He turned it down, though, when I offered to pay him for his time.

"No need," he said, *"as long as it doesn't cut into my business. I'm happy to help, assuming you'll let me drive the car now and then. It'll be a chick magnet, for sure!"*

The words sounded hollow. When the call ended, Sally asked me about it.

"That was Doug Flaven. You met him at my high school reunion. Kind of tall. Reddish hair." I struck a bodybuilder pose. "Big chest."

"Oh, yeah. The good-looking football player."

"That's him. He's got the mechanical experience and strength I'll need to get started."

"What will it cost if we decide to rebuild it?"

"I'm hoping he can answer that when he sees it."

A WEEK LATER, Flaven insisted on driving us to the farm in his new Ford F-250 pickup. Along the way talked about his truck, his women, and his construction projects, in that order. I learned his pick-up was built in 1996, which made it two years old. With the exception of cheerleaders in high school, where he was a star, the girls he dated seemed the kind who were content with one-nighters for the most part. And his so-called projects sounded more like handyman gigs, but maybe that's how contractors built a business.

Three and a half hours later, we were stretching our legs and walking the grounds at my grandfather's farm. As we surveyed the site, I realized that Doug looked like a contractor—from his weathered leather construction boots to the blue jeans and his golf shirt with "Flaven Construction" embroidered in the corner. I outlined the property borderlines, but unlike Sally, he paid close attention.

We entered the cellar with flashlights. Flaven made humming sounds as he inspected the space, the covered car corpse, and various parts. "Okay," he said. "Okay. We're going to need the lights I brought." Flaven fetched a pair of intense lanterns that plugged into the pickup. Positioned right, they illuminated every corner of the cellar.

Removing the canvas, with the once-slick side now cracked all over, wasn't easy. It seemed almost glued to the car frame in places. I also noticed a foul odor. "Whew," I said. "That better not be the remains of something. Or someone!"

Flaven looked inside and under the car's frame. "Don't see anything. My guess is a combination of moldy leather, rotten wood, and rat shit."

The tires were flat. Body parts had black and red paint peeling away, along with rusty patches. Wooden crates held smaller pieces, like bolts and screws, wrapped in crinkled wax paper.

"Man, this will need much more than cleaning up and basic assembly. It's a major restoration job beyond my grade level," Flaven said.

"For now, I'd be happy just getting all this out of the ground and up in the barn."

Flaven studied the floorboards, then the cement block walls. "It looks a couple of feet wider than the entry to the barn. So, your grandpa must have dug a ramp from the outside, starting from here." He pointed to the far end. "And there."

"Makes sense," I said. We were standing at the front of the chassis. I pointed to the radiator. "Think you can get that off?"

He studied it. "Pretty sure. Let's get a closer look." His eyes grew. "Man, this engine looks ahead of its time. And not just in design but materials... aluminum, brass... God only knows how much horsepower."

"Grandpa knew cars," I said. "His cousin raced cars over in Europe back in the day. And he worked for thirty years at Ford." I stuffed my hands in my back pockets. "Still, it begs the question: Why? What would have compelled him to bury it?"

"Maybe it wasn't him. You said he moved out right after he got married. What year?"

"The early thirties," I said.

Flaven scratched his butch-cut head of hair. "And this property's been unoccupied since then?"

"Never rented, as far as I know."

My mechanical friend started taking measurements of the chassis and the cellar walls. Then we went above, taking interior and entryway dimensions and studying the ground. "For the digging, we're going to need a Bobcat," said Flaven.

"A what?"

"It's a small bulldozer. I can use my contractor's license to get you a good rental price. We'll only need it for a day and it'll save us a lot of time and sweat."

"This is exactly why I asked you to join me."

"You're lucky I have some free time."

"Before we head back to Cleveland," I said, "could you estimate what it would cost to bring the house up to code?"

We headed over to it. On the way, he said, "Looks more like an oversized shack."

"Inside, it looks better. Like a cabin."

"When you say *up to code*, there's a cheap version to flip it for a quick buck. Or, there's doing it as if you're going to live in it. Maybe you and the wife. What's her name?"

"Sally."

"Right. You and Sally might decide to keep it as a cabin in the country."

"No way she'll go for that. Sally wants to flip it."

We circled the exterior. Then he examined the inside, knocking on walls, running the water, and testing the electricity. Five minutes later, we returned to the pickup and started coasting down the dirt path to the highway.

"I'm not a realtor," he said, "but I'll bet you even money that fixing it up for resale is a losing proposition unless you want Home Depot's cheapest way to do it."

"I've been a renter my entire adult life, so I wouldn't know about such things. Is there a cheap way to build a basic bathroom that doesn't look or feel cheap?"

He thought about it. "Kinda sorta, if all you want is functional." We were quiet for a couple of minutes and then he asked, "Is Sally still the gorgeous chick I recall, with that fine, long, blonde hair?"

"Yeah."

"You know, you could do this place right. Make it into a classy retreat with a jacuzzi and have some romantic weekends out here. Recharge your love life."

He had gone into upsell mode. I ignored his recommendation. "I fished out here somewhere with my grandpa when I was little. Even did some hunting."

"There you go! Make it into a recreational retreat!"

Over the next three-plus hours back to Cleveland, I recalled those days when Grandpa taught me how to fish and shoot a rifle. When Doug returned to his improvement ideas, I called a timeout. "All I want is a basic bathroom, as much for you as me, while we work out there."

Perhaps to save face, he dismissed any interest in an extensive upgrade given the distance he'd have to travel.

I NEEDED to see Tom Anderson, another classmate. But he was college level at the Cleveland Art Institute. He had the enviable job of being the graphic designer for the Cleveland Art Museum.

We agreed to meet for lunch in the garden court. Given his promotion to head of publications, he offered to treat me. It didn't take him long to show me pictures of his wedding ceremony at Jacobs Field last fall. He was a true fanatic of the Cleveland Indians baseball team. He claimed his girlfriend had the idea of getting married in the ballpark. I wondered what would happen to them when the team inevitably returned to mediocrity.

His light brown curly hair had grown out, looking like an Afro. After we placed our food order, he asked if I still did any sculpting. I replied by asking him if he still did any painting. He got my point. We both had put aside our artistic pursuits in college to make a living. At least our jobs were art-related. In his case, designing exhibition catalogs for the world-acclaimed museum gave him plenty of personal satisfaction. When I asked if anything special was coming up, he mentioned an exhibition featuring the Bugatti family—furniture, sculpture, and cars.

I had just taken a bite out of a hearty tuna salad sandwich and nearly choked. "What? Really?"

He nodded.

I swallowed. "When's it happening?"

"Next year. It's been in planning for years."

"Bugatti cars in the art galleries?"

"Sure. And animal sculptures, decorative objects."

I knew Tom well enough to trust him with the story of my discovery. To my surprise, he didn't register much of a reaction. "Really? What model?"

I explained that I didn't know yet and needed to find a knowledgeable antique car guy to advise me.

He looked up a number on his cell phone and jotted it down on a paper napkin. "Here's the guy you want to talk to — Mickey Mishne. He's curating the automobile part of the exhibition. Interesting guy. A past president of the American Bugatti Club lives in the area."

"Really? You just blew my mind, Tom."

"You'd be surprised what we've got in this area. Collectors and experts on all kinds of art! And on lost or forgotten works that surface.

"Like my grandpa's buried treasure."

"I'll believe it when I see it."

"Deal!"

Mishne lived near Medina, a sizable town south of Cleveland, where the landscape was a mix of farmland, forests, and golf courses. His smallish white house appeared to have been part of a farm at one time, under a cluster of oak trees. Not far to the west, a half-dozen ducks waded in a large pond.

I pulled into the gravel driveway east of the house. This led me to a gray metal structure, the kind used for tractors and related farm implements. A sign across the top said, “Portholes into the Past Museum” in large block letters.

As instructed, I parked in front of it and walked down the path to the house’s side door. I rang the doorbell and after a minute, a diminutive, sixty-ish man in a T-shirt and blue jeans opened the door.

“Hi, I’m Jack.”

“Call me Mickey.” His name was friendlier than his demeanor. He put out his bony hand and gave me a firm shake despite its disfigurement. A crop of gray hair surrounded his balding top, connecting to a beard. He welcomed me inside, stepping back. The dark glasses propped on his commanding nose cleared, as a photochromic lens will, revealing lines of trifocals.

“Watch your step,” he said, signaling me to go ahead of him

down a set of stairs to the basement. At the bottom, I saw him using a walker to help support his slightly deformed legs.

"Welcome to my library," he said, waving an arm. Six tall bookshelves dominated the large room that was packed with books, magazines, and souvenirs. A slight staleness in the air and industrial fluorescent lighting gave the space a dreary feel.

Mickey walked over to a modest, industrial-looking steel desk with rounded corners. A large calendar covered most of the top with papers, folders, and photographs. A desktop computer rested on a typewriter table, flanking a swivel chair. Mickey settled into it, pushing the walker away with a soft curse.

I didn't know what I expected to see in this avocational historian who had invited me to visit him in his library and study, but this was a letdown.

"Take a seat," Mickey said, pointing to a folding chair beside him. He removed his glasses and studied me. "Now, you say you've found a Bugatti car." He looked me in the eyes intently.

I took a breath. "Yes. Where should I begin?"

"Start with where you found it."

I described the circumstances, the visit to the farm, and about finding the trap door. At this point, Mickey leaned back and folded his arms over his chest. He seemed disconnected as he listened, like a therapist. When I told him how unlikely it was that my grandfather could afford to buy the rare French car, he raised an eyebrow.

"Could it have been a junker from a crash?"

"Nothing crunched up or even a scratch, that I tell."

"You called it a barn cellar. Those a pretty rare."

"It's what a friend of mine called it."

"Then it has a side entrance."

"No. I was goofing off in the main part of the barn and landed on a loose board, which turned out to be a trapdoor. That's how I got in."

"So it's totally sealed off." He rubbed his beard. "Curious." Is it possible someone else put it there after your grandfather listed there?"

"He kept it as a retreat from the city until he got older and just left it."

That triggered him. He leaned towards me and started asking for details like the condition of the chassis, engine, and other parts, even the size and shapes of the fenders, headlights, taillight, and bumpers. On the call to set up the appointment, he asked about the radiator with the Bugatti. That's what got me in the door. Based on the dates I gave for when Grandpa lived there.

When I exhausted everything there was to describe, Mickey wrote a note on a small yellow pad of sticky note paper. "From what you say, it is safe to rule out it being a Type 57. I'd like to see it when you get it out of the cellar."

"Great!" A mechanic friend is going to help with that."

"Put everything in the barn, and be sure to log each part you bring up. That's especially important. Don't forget." His instructions rang out like fatherly commands.

Standing, I said, "Yes, sir."

"The barn needs to be cleaned as thoroughly as possible. The cleaner, the better. That's what Ettore demanded in his factory. It was immaculate compared to most factories. Workers wore white monogrammed laboratory coats. Even the rags were a clean white with his initials: *EB*." The professor paused. "Consider using a tarp over the flooring to prevent bolts from falling between the boards."

Fortunately, I brought a steno pad to take notes as he fired his instructions off.

"Any more questions?"

"Just one. Does this mean you'll help me?"

His face lit up. "Of course! To me, it's like a moonshot or a comet. There are legends about lost Bugattis, forgotten treasures! Bugatti enthusiasts will travel the globe for the next great find. Only ten thousand Bugatti cars were built, including those for Grand Prix racing. This wasn't a Henry Ford assembly-line operation. Ettore Bugatti's obsession with speed and beauty is one reason they're so valuable. The other is the precision and care he demanded of his craftsmen in his factory."

I hesitated to ask my next question. "I don't suppose there's any way to know the car's value, restored or otherwise."

He shook his head with a rueful grin. "Could be a few thousand for the parts salvageable. Or, if you decide to do something with it, a hell of a lot more! I'll have a good idea when I see it."

"How soon can you come out to the farm?" I said, adding its proximity to Fort Wayne.

"I'll let you know. Give me your e-mail address." As I wrote it down, he added, "In the meantime, I advise you to keep the lid on your discovery."

"Don't dig it out?"

"When word gets out, you'll get people wanting to see it or buy it, even steal it for that matter. You don't need any of that until the time is right." Mickey pressed his swollen knuckles on the desk while extending his arms for leverage to stand up. "Now, let me show you what I've got here."

We walked around the basement shelves as he identified various items and publications. Among them were all the back issues of *Pur Sang*, the American Bugatti Club's newsletter. "I've written several articles and edited many more," he said, "as its managing editor. There's always something happening in the world of Bugatti. Most discoveries are in Europe or the UK, so yours is special. It could be an incredibly significant find. Hell, the discovery of certain car parts is news! And we report on activities like car shows and rallies. Articles cover engineering, design, and the Bugatti brand. And not just cars. Ettore built a train system for Paris and designed an airplane engine and even a yacht. We also do stories about his brother Rembrandt, a renowned sculptor, and their father, Carlo, who designed exotic furniture."

"I think I might like to become a club member, but I haven't any proof of my ownership. My grandfather's will didn't refer to it. Grandma is long deceased and my mother doesn't recall it."

Mickey scratched his beard. "You had better ask your lawyer about getting a title. As for the club, it would be premature to join right now anyway."

We went up the stairs and strode through the house to the living room, where he introduced me to his wife, Lori. She was watching a TV game show and flipping through a magazine. She appeared to be in her mid-30s and was plain-looking with bobbed mousey brown hair. The smoke from her cigarette hung in the room. She glanced my way, and I nodded amiably.

Mickey hastened ahead of me through the back door on a path toward the museum building. His eyes were focused straight forward as he spoke. "She's my second wife. I got her pregnant. We have a beautiful daughter."

We walked slower the rest of the way. "I'm the cliché of the foolish old man forced to abandon his family for his secretary." He paused, leaning on his walker to take a breath. "But enough about me. Here's my humble museum and retreat!"

He unlocked the side door of the gray structure. Rows of industrial fluorescent lights high above us lit up. The Bugatti racer grabbed my attention immediately. We circled the main floor display room, which held a 1940s fire engine, a vintage Ford pickup, two motorcycles, and some bicycles. Lastly, we approached the sky-blue antique race car with the red and white Bugatti logo at the top of the radiator screen.

I leaned in toward the front left wheel well for a closer look at a string of nickel-size holes.

"Bullet holes from the Nazis," Mickey said.

"No kidding." I touched one with my fingertips. "Do they add or subtract value?"

"Add!" he said, with particular pride. "A unique characteristic. The Type 35 was the most successful race car Bugatti built, largely because he sold them to anybody who wanted one—not just to professionals."

"Did it win any races that you know of?"

"Not any you'll know of. It's on the label here with the engine specs."

The 3 x 5 notecard on the windshield said the Type 35 B was sold at the Luxembourg races. It was sold to an American Bugatti dealer in 1973 and a few years later, Mickey acquired the car. He ran it in races at Chimay, the Eifelrennan, the Autorennen in Gruenewald, and the first, second, and third Grand Prix du Centenaire Luxembourg-Findel and Zandvoort races.

As I read, he continued. "It's not the original engine, but it still runs. I haven't been able to race it since these legs started folding up on me. There was a time when . . ." He pointed to a shelf against the wall with three small trophies and an old wraparound leather cap with goggles. "Still have some of the soot on the goggles." A grin brightened his face.

Next to the Bugatti was a 1970s Maserati, a legendary brand and undoubtedly valuable. Perhaps because the sleek red-and-black set of wheels was not an antique, he bypassed it.

We moved toward a set of stairs at the back of the room. As before, he told me to go up before him.

At the top, I gazed into a large room with rows of long tables holding open storage boxes, each filled with prints and posters. Colossal movie, theater, and opera posters from their original runs draped the walls. In the boxes were lithographs of art from the many museums he had visited in the U.S. and abroad.

"Henry Hawley, the curator of the Bugatti exhibition, has been through my collection. He thinks I have some that are museum-grade. Except for a few items—the more personal ones—the Cleveland Art Museum can have whatever it wants when the time comes. Neither of my sons shows any interest in fine art."

Mickey started flipping through one container, pointing out some of his favorites. He pulled out an original Toulouse-Lautrec poster.

“I’ll try not to drool on it!” I told him.

“I’ve got others that still need to be verified,” he said, wiping his sweaty brow. Even with two ceiling fans spinning above, the heat was intense.

“That’s generous of you. So, you’ll be putting it in your will?”

“Right after the museum identifies what they want.”

“What about the Bugatti?”

“I’d like to keep that in the family. But my two boys sided with their mother in the divorce and we haven't talked since. I'm not going to hand it down to them if I think they'll sell right away out of hate and for the money.”

Mickey’s face had turned beet red. I couldn't tell how much of it was emotional or simply because of the heat. Drenched in sweat, we headed for the exit.

OUTSIDE, we found shade next to the building where I had parked. A gentle breeze gave us a bit of relief. “Have you ever thought about selling your Bugatti?” I asked.

“I've had offers,” said Mickey. “Fortunately, I’ve never been in a position where I needed to sell off any parts of my collection. As for the Bugatti, there are days when I think, *hell, I’ll just be buried in it.*” He looked at the ground.

I sensed his fatigue. “Well, thanks again for inviting me out and giving me so much of your time today."

"Yes, nice to meet you, too. You've got a whale of a story. No, don't let the Bugatti off your hook!"

"With you as my guide, ain't no way that's happening.”

We exchanged smiles and shook hands. Mickey’s face was still wet but no longer red. As I opened my car door, he said, “I see you drive a Honda. Good cars.”

“And excellent mileage. What’s your everyday car?”

“I have a Ford Contour," He shrugged. "It gets me around.”

“Not like a Bugatti.”

“Nothing in this world is like a Bugatti, my friend!”

As I drove away, I thought, *this guy is an original.* I couldn’t remember meeting anyone more fascinating, and I've got a number of colorful characters from art school and work. Mickey's guyish guardedness gradually melted away in the course of the afternoon. Now I felt like we were old friends. Bonded by Bugatti.

5

SPRING 1998

FLAVEN APPEARED four inches above me, sitting behind the wheel of his black Ford 250 pickup. I rode shotgun. We had loaded it with tools and equipment for the first stage of the project: extraction. Since meeting with Mickey last week, I couldn't wait to begin the restoration.

We started just after six a.m. under a rain cloud. Two hours later, just past Toledo, we made a pit stop at a McDonald's. We had some breakfast and got back on the interstate.

The weather forecast was good for the operation: upper 60s to low 70s with little chance of rain. First we cleared miscellaneous debris on the barn floor. Flaven unloaded things from the truck bed. I picked up an industrial broom and started sweeping the floor, creating a cloud of dust that sent me outside sneezing. Before I recovered, Flaven had put on one of those full-face air masks with goggles that made him look like a man-size insect. He said, "I've only got one mask. Why don't you take the hose and connect it?"

The waterspout was on the south side of the barn. I made the connection and tested the water pressure. Passable. The plan was to water clean the floor after we removed the car and parts from underneath.

When I returned, he had fetched a heavy-duty nail remover from his tool chest and started working it on the thick floorboards at the entry of the barn. Given the physical exertion required, I assumed we'd be trading off. Mine was lifting the planks off and stacking them on the north side of the barn. The former football star took pauses, but never asked to switch off. He had maintained his bulging biceps for more than show.

Two-thirds through the marked section, he appeared winded and stretched his right arm from fatigue. I suggested we take a break. From a cooler in the truck, he took a Coke and I pulled out a Mountain Dew. We sat in the shade of a tree near the house. I put the cold can to my sweaty brow and said, "Man, I didn't think I was that out of shape. And I had the easy job!"

He laughed. "Gettin' old, my friend."

"We're the same age," I said.

"But your job has you sitting on your butt all day. And because you're married, you're probably sitting on your butt at home most of the time."

"She works, too. We split the home chores."

"Just saying. Married men don't get the same type of workouts." Flaven drank and surveyed the scenery. "I like how your property gives you a good view of the surroundings. It doesn't look like you're on a hill from the road."

"Yeah. I hate the idea of selling it, but we need the money to make a down payment on a house."

"Who wants it more, you or her?"

"Sally. But I figure it's a safe investment."

"I've had a fixer-upper for a while now. It's got a metal shed that's perfect for my business." Flaven finished his Coke and tossed the empty in the truck bed. "How long have you been married now?"

"Little over eight years, going on eighteen."

He snickered. "That good, huh?"

"Well, you go through these rough patches. This inheritance is festering into a Duesy. She doesn't like the country. Wants the money it could bring for her dream house. I blame the Good House-keeping channel."

"Good luck with that!" He paused. "She still as hot-looking as she was at the reunion?"

"Yeah. She puts a lot into her appearance."

Back to work. It didn't take long to clear the rest of the boards. Looking down at the hidden treasure brought me back to my original question: What circumstances had made Grandpa go to such lengths to hide this car?

At noon, we dug into the cooler and ate my lunch sandwiches. When we finished, Flaven asked if the house was unlocked so he could use the bathroom.

"Only have the one with cobwebs, buddy," I said. "You forget?"

"Damn! Man, you are getting an indoor toilet next time I come out here."

"Great. And while you're at it, toss in a sink and shower." I said.

"You'd be amazed how little it'll cost you in materials."

"Okay," I said, "but don't tell Sally. God knows how she'll react."

THE MARATHON GAS station at the edge of Avilla had the equivalent of a convenience store. As he refueled his truck, Doug was also bagging some donuts. I poured us coffee. A perky, sixty-ish woman with shoulder-length brown hair streaked with gray, wearing an Indianapolis Colts jersey, stood behind the counter. Her nametag said, "Betsy." While paying Betsy, I asked about places for dinner nearby.

In a raspy voice, she said, "Sure. You got the Pastimes Bar and Grill in town just down the road. Good for a hamburger and fries, fish on Fridays, and store-bought pizzas any time. Basic bar food.

And there's a cafe called Rosie's, although they mostly serve breakfast and lunch."

"Got it," I said.

She added, "You boys new around here or just passing through?"

"Doing some part-time work about two miles west."

She thought for a moment. "Not that little slice of a farm that's been dormant forever?"

"Um, yeah. It belonged to my grandfather, who passed away recently."

"Oh, sorry to hear."

I thanked her and followed Flaven back to the truck.

We were silent for most of the drive until I said, "How soon do you think it'll take the whole town to know about us?"

Flaven looked at his watch. "I'll mark the time."

THE BOBCAT we had reserved sat on a small trailer at the equipment rental store in Auburn. After I charged the fee to my Visa card, Flaven hooked up the trailer to his truck and we headed back. We had almost finished the donuts and coffee when we pulled up near the barn.

I could tell that my partner loved this part of the job by the way he took control of the earthmover. He pumped the gas, popped it off the trailer, and positioned it a few feet before the barn doors. The scoop shovel came down and pushed into the ground. A minute later, I went below to observe the progress inside the cellar. Once he breached the wall, I used a shovel to manage the dirt the Bobcat pressed through.

Flaven explained that a driveway slope grade shouldn't exceed 12%, but on that basis, the opening would need to be three times longer. This wasn't an everyday garage driveway, so we aimed for a 20% grade. When the hole Flaven dug reached well over a car length, he came down for a look and decided we needed double that size to allow the Bugatti to clear it.

As he reached it, it became apparent that more earth was necessary below. He dropped the dirt while I fetched floorboards to provide a hard surface over the dirt foundation. Once aligned, we jumped up and down on them to pack as solidly as possible. Given the angle, I slipped and fell—much to Doug's amusement. Eventually, he was confident enough to test the makeshift ramp with his all-wheel-drive pickup.

When the ramp passed the test, we carried out all the car parts. We started with the larger pieces like the fenders and doors. Given the 20% slope, I huffed and puffed with each carry.

The dashboard received special handling. Its reddish-brown wood veneer had textural outlines in varying black and gray tones. I wondered what kind of tree it came from. Despite its thick surface, decay was present along the edges, so we placed it on a piece of plywood for support. When I opened the small glove box, I spotted what appeared to be a package of cigarettes with French lettering. This might be a clue for Mickey, I thought.

Clouds had come and gone all day, and our outlook to avoid a rain-drenched mess was good. We lined the parts up on the grass along the south side of the barn until all we had left was the biggest and heaviest: the chassis with the engine.

Flaven attached a chain from the truck to the front axle, greased the joints, and said, "Stand by and yell if you see something that shouldn't be happening."

He sat behind his truck's steering wheel and touched the accelerator. The chain connecting the Ford to the chassis went taut. Sensing the weight of the payload, he gave the engine more gas until it started moving.

Locked from decades of idleness, the Bugatti's four wheels dragged initially. When the front tires met the edge of the boards, the resistance jerked the wheel loose with a clunk and a screech. The wheels unlocked, spinning free after decades frozen. The scraping sound repeated with each rotation as the car inched up the makeshift ramp.

Flaven had to give the pickup more gas to continue pulling the one-and-a-quarter-ton chassis up the ramp. The short ramp made more sense for lowering it into the secret tomb but not for pulling it out. Either Grandpa didn't think ahead or he hadn't cared because he wouldn't be the one pulling it out.

When the front wheels reached ground level, the rest of the car came up with less effort. He pulled the mystery vehicle an extra car length in front of the barn onto the grass, applied his emergency brakes, and jumped out.

"Glad I have an F-250. I needed every one of those extra horses!"

The daylight illuminated the details of the ancient chassis. I gazed upon it with renewed awe.

"Beer break!" said Flaven. He reached into the cooler and grabbed two bottles of Great Lakes Ale from a new Cleveland brewery. We spoke very few words as we drank. Except for high school, we had little in common. He reminisced about certain football games, which transitioned to cheerleaders and girls he had dated.

The amber brew tasted great.

The midafternoon sunlight would be gone in a couple of hours and we wanted the job finished before dark. For reinstalling the floorboards, Flaven had a nail gun. Holding it out toward me, he said, "This makes it go fast. You ever use one of these?"

"A nail gun? No, never," I said.

"With these size nails, you could easily kill someone."

I grinned. "Speaking from experience?"

"No, not actually killed," Flaven leered back.

We got to work. I put a board in place and he banged the nails in. The noise was ear-piercing but it sped up the process.

About an hour later, with the floor back in place, we pushed the chassis into the barn, rear end first. Its width and length left plenty of room for the body parts on all sides. By the time I padlocked the doors, the sun had set, leaving only a glow on the horizon.

"Dinner and drinks on me!" I said. "And I know just the place—Pastime's Bar and Grill!"

GARTH BROOKS' "Do What You Gotta Do" played on the jukebox as we walked into Avilla's only tavern. The ambiance appealed to me, from the worn wooden floors to the incandescent light fixtures hanging from the tin ceiling and the mahogany bar. A combined scent of hops, cigarette smoke, and a deep fryer wafted in the air.

The patina of the wooden tables and chairs that were dispersed around the rectangular space enhanced the bar's charm. Parallel to the right wall stood the bar. Four booths lined the opposite side. The kitchen flanked the gaming area in the back, including a long shuffleboard.

A dozen customers were eating and drinking. We planted ourselves on the wooden stools at the bar, which was unlike any I'd ever seen—narrow with a crude surface like someone had chiseled it. It was not the usual high gloss, flat surface here in Pastimes.

A fiftyish guy with ragged red hair and beard sat at the end, slouched over his beer. Most everyone had already shot us a glance, but not him. The bartender, a tall man with a white bib apron covering a moderate beer gut, approached me and Flaven. His long silver-streaked hair was pulled back from a receding hairline into a ponytail. In a resonating, raspy voice, he said, "What's your pleasure, boys? Drinks, dinner, or both?"

Together, we said, "Both."

He handed us a single-page laminated menu and then told us about the Budweiser, Heineken, and Miller Light beers on tap. Something in his face said he had seen much in a lifetime. A crooked Roman nose sat above a thick gray handlebar mustache.

We ordered Heinies and two steak sandwich specials. By the time our food arrived, our beer mugs needed refilling. As we dug in, the bartender promptly refilled them.

Five minutes later, the man asked, "How're the sandwiches?"

With my plate half-empty, I said, "Good." Flaven nodded.

"Right on," said the barkeep. He started washing some glasses in front of us, whistling. "Say, you wouldn't be the boys working out at the Phantom Belgian's farm?"

I froze. "Phantom Belgian?"

"That's what some old timers around here call it. About two miles off the county road west of town. The shack with a faded red barn."

Flaven tapped his watch. I looked at him. We grinned.

"Yeah, it's my place now. My name's Jack. This here is Doug."

"I'm Joe. Nice to meet you." He nodded and continued washing. "I own the joint."

I asked, "How did you know about us, Joe?"

"The wife works out at the gas station."

Joe dried his hands, picked up a remote control, and pointed it at a TV mounted above the bar. To our delight, the channel settled on the start of a Cleveland Indians game and we gave Joe two thumbs up.

When we finished eating, Joe took our plates away and then the mugs, which he refilled. "Compliments of the house, men. Welcome to Avilla."

The beer was cold and the atmosphere relaxed, so we stayed for the game. Most of those who came for dinner left within an hour, replaced by a different, younger group. Several twenty-something merrymakers played darts in the back corner next to the kitchen. Another four in a booth were annoyingly kidding each other.

Two women in their mid-thirties parked themselves at the bar. The one nearest me had brunette hair in a bob with bangs, an oval alabaster face, wide eyes, and a pert nose. Sitting taller, the other girl had similar features, but had long light brown hair tied up at the crown of her head.

"Evenin', girls," said Joe. "Usual?"

The one with bobbed brunette hair wore black jeans and a

yellow sweatshirt with “Loyola University” in bold raspberry letters. The taller of them fit snugly into faded blue jeans. Her light brown hair spilled onto a gray sweater with red speckles. Joe brought a glass of white wine for the short-haired girl and a Bud Light for the other, who lit a cigarette. He moved an ashtray over to her.

The brunette looked at the TV. “What’s the score?”

I turned to her. “Tribe up by three, seventh inning.” Her eyes were brown, and medium gold rings hung from her ears.

In my experience, bar-sitting game-watchers direct many of their comments to the TV as a shared experience with anyone paying attention. On this night I wanted to engage more directly with the sisters, searching for eye contact in situations like close calls by the umpires. I’d say, “Did you see that?” or “He was out! Wasn’t he out?”

“The Yankees stink!” said Ragged Red, looking at us blurry-eyed.

“I’m with you, my friend,” I replied. Flaven chuckled. Pulling for the same team and putting down the opponents offered opportunities to connect with the patrons.

Towards the end of the game, Joe said, “If you boys are still around tomorrow, Rosie here offers a nice brunch two doors over.”

I turned to them. “Which one of you is Rosie?” The short-haired girl raised her hand. “The Rosie in Rosie’s or just a colorful name for a café?”

“Roseanne, officially.” She put her hand out, and I took it. “This here is my sister Diane.”

Before I got a word out to introduce him, Doug shot his right around me to Diane. “My name is Doug. I’m happy to meet you!”

When the game was over, I paid Joe, leaving a generous tip.

“Thanks much,” he said, then added, “Which of you two is driving?”

Flaven put a thumb into his chest. “Me.”

“You’re a big boy,” said Joe. “Ever been a bouncer?

"A couple times," said Flaven. "I liked it but got into too many fights."

"You look the type," said Joe. "Drive carefully now. And come back again soon."

We started for the door. Then I paused and looked at Rosie. "Be seeing you."

She flashed her white teeth at me. "Bye, Jack."

My eyes remained fixed on the white line heading back. Before we reached the farm lane, I broke the silence. "Thanks again for all your help today, Doug. I appreciate it."

"We worked our butts off, all right," he said and paused. "Those girls looked kind of delicious. I would've liked some of that Diane for dessert."

He parked the pickup next to the house. We grabbed our sleeping bags from behind the seats. I ambled towards the front door, looking up and saying, "The stars are marvelous!"

"You're marvelously drunk," he said, nudging me forward.

I unlocked the door, turned to him, and said, "Phantom Belgian?"

6

In the morning I ached from my head to my feet, the effects of the physical labor and the heavy drinking. We didn't waste any time heading back to Avilla and the corner of Main and Second Street, two doors west of Pastimes.

Rosie's Café had a boutique look and feel, with only a half-dozen tables and some seating at an off-white counter. Pink and yellow splashed the walls, which were otherwise dominated by black-and-white checked patterns. Frilly curtains framed the windows. Each table, surrounded by white bentwood chairs, featured a red rose in a tiny vase. A "Welcome" sign hung above a split counter and a mini chalkboard with the day's specials rested on a tripod in a corner.

Diane spotted us as we stood, appreciating the aroma of fried eggs, bacon, and toast. "You came! Be there in a minute." She wore a long white apron and an Indianapolis Colts football T-shirt. She finished taking an order from a senior couple and then turned to us. "Sit anywhere. I'll be right with you."

We chose the counter. Behind it stood a display of baked goods on one side. The other side had a cut-out for passing food. A batwing door gave access to the kitchen. Rosie wore a short cook's hat over the grill and an apron matching her sister's.

Flaven pulled two menus from a metal clamp at the counter's edge and handed one to me. "Kind of a girly place," he said.

"I suppose," I said, looking at the cook.

We perused the menu. A minute later, my eyes were back on Rosie.

"Hey, now," said Flaven. "You're a married man."

"Doesn't mean I'm dead."

Diane walked behind the counter and placed a customer's order on the shelf, saying something about a food request to Rosie. "And look who just arrived."

Rosie looked up, took a beat, and then smiled and waved. I waved back.

Diane picked up a carafe of coffee and two mugs, turned to us, and said, "Coffee?" We nodded. She started pouring. "To be honest, we never thought we'd see you, boys, again. But here you are."

"Here we are," Doug said, flashing his bright white teeth.

Diane returned the grin. "Now, what can I get you?"

We placed our orders and she gave Rosie the ticket. Several more people arrived, so she moved on to greet them.

Flaven continued the conversation we were having before we came into the diner. "A basic bathroom is simple as long as you're already connected to water. I'm guessing your minimum cost in materials would be two to three hundred with a shower."

"And labor?" I said, "I'd want to pay you something."

"Unnecessary. I figure we're doing it together, and I'll need it as much as you."

"That sounds too good to be true."

"Well, I'll figure out a reasonable amount. Adding a bathroom normally improves the value. Although, I'm not too sure in this case." He chuckled.

"We already know there's not much value there. Sally got an estimate. A whopping ten thousand dollars."

"That much?" He laughed again.

"She was hoping for enough to make a decent down payment for a house."

We talked some more about houses and the cost of mortgages. Doug made the case that ten thousand could be enough of a down payment to get a decent fixer-upper. I said Sally wanted a newer house.

I finished my coffee and looked up to see Rosie standing in front of us with our food. "Jack, right?" I nodded. "Which one's yours?" I pointed. She put the plates down. *"Bon appetit."*

Returning her smile, I said, "*Merci.*"

"Je parle l'anglais et le français?"

"Just a *petite,*" I said. "I noticed the acute accent on the 'e' in "café" on your sign and the menu. Nice little logo treatment."

"You know something about graphic design?"

"It's how I make a living."

"Interesting. Sorry, but I—" Rosie dashed back into the kitchen. We dug into our food.

A few minutes later, her sister returned and refilled our cups. As she poured, Flaven said, "I like how you've decorated the place. I dated an interior designer once."

"It's mostly Rosie's ideas. I helped with some sewing, hammering, painting—"

"A regular handywoman," Flaven replied.

As Diane returned the carafe, she said, "You guys heading back to Cleveland today?"

I said, "What makes you think we're from Cleveland?"

"We deduced it from your reactions to the game last night. And Joe's known as a Sherlock Holmes type around here. He noticed your Ohio license plate."

"Joe's bar and detective service?" said Flaven.

Diane leaned on the counter in front of him. "He was a cop in Fort Wayne before he retired a few years back." She looked up from the sound of more customers coming in. "Looks like Church is out.

Here's your ticket." She put it between our two plates and returned to the front.

We finished eating and put down cash for the bill. Rosie came back out in time to see us heading for the door. "Glad you stopped by. Hope to see you again."

Her smile stayed with me back to the barn. I wanted to believe some of it came from a natural connection I felt for her. Or was it simply a polite, business-friendly smile? Sally always looked hassled when I saw her at work. She'd lighten up for a male customer now and then but still never showed any love for the job.

WHILE FLAVEN INVESTIGATED the plumbing and took some measurements for a toilet room, I did an inventory of the car parts. Next, he checked out the electrical in the barn to see about the power load for more lights and for outlets for some heavy-duty tools. He gave his approval.

Early that afternoon, we started back to Cleveland. I appreciated Flaven's deficiency in small talk. Even with his choice of country music on the radio, I could digest all that had happened and plan for the next visit. The unearthing of the roadster was monumental. The discovery of genuine human beings in Avilla was comforting.

For the first third of the trip, the compass pointed northward. The two-hour stretch to the east put the sun at our backs. By the time Cleveland's suburbs became visible, dusk had crept onto the eastern horizon. Flaven decided to listen to his talk radio station. I might have preferred static the rest of the way home.

I thought of how different we'd become, growing into full adulthood. Fortunately, working together has not produced any clashes thus far. But then, this was going to be a long-running project.

Mickey rode shotgun next to me as the Honda hummed along at 75 mph on the interstate toward the farm. Flaven said he'd meet us there with materials to build the bathroom as promised. We had agreed that the exterior construction should be a priority, given the chance of rain before the Sunday ended.

On the road, Mickey changed from a reserved historian to a friendly professor discussing his service time in Germany during the Korean War. Traveling into France whenever possible, he attended a major event featuring art and autos where he first saw Bugattis. That's when his fascination took hold. He also started collecting posters and lithographs.

Mickey drank the last of a can of Coke he had brought along. "Back in the States, I snatched up the first one I could afford and loved racing it. Of course, that was when my legs were in full working order," he said.

"Why would anyone take a chance racing their valuable antique car?"

"The races are more like time trials," he said. "We spread out our starts and tracked each car's performance. And we often used a well-maintained course or an infrequently used road. As for my particular car, it didn't have any big Grand Prix wins or other significance, in which case it wouldn't have... check that. I still might have raced it."

The glint in his eyes told me he had racing in his blood.

A LARGE SIGN told us we had entered Indiana. About a mile further, a billboard grabbed Mickey's attention. "I must be getting old," he said. "Did you see that?"

"What?"

"The billboard back there for the Auburn Cord Duesenberg Museum. That's got to be the car company your grandfather worked at.

"Never heard of Cord cars."

"They were one of the many builders of horse carriages that went into the horseless carriage business. The easy availability of combustion engines made it possible. Indiana had more than its share of them. That's what happened south of here in Auburn, home of a company that made a mark for itself. Besides Auburn cars, they made Cords and Duesenbergs."

"I've heard about Duesenberg."

"There's actually a Bugatti-Duesy connection. The Duesenberg brothers specialized in making engines and cars for the Indy 500 races. When they decided to expand into production cars with a manufacturing plant in Indianapolis, the company struggled, and E. L. Cord bought them out. Duesenberg's design, administration, and sales departments moved to the Auburn headquarters while manufacturing stayed in Indianapolis. It became the top of Auburn's lineup. The three distinct levels of cars were a success, at least for a while. Then the Depression hit."

We exited Interstate 90 and then went up the ramp to I-69 South. A large green sign indicated Fort Wayne and Auburn ahead. Less than an hour later, I turned onto County Road 8 towards Avilla and then fifteen minutes to the farm.

I pulled up just short of the barn. I held the passenger door for him, given his disability. He led with a black cane he brought along. Mickey noticed the soft ground in front of the barn doors where we had dug. "What's this?" he asked.

"It's where we dug the car out."

He looked at the house several yards behind us, then to the south and north and back at the barn. "Well, let's see what you got inside."

Tom had lent me a set of photography light stands, which I pulled from the trunk and set up at opposite sides of the dismantled car. Even on a partly sunny day, the barn's lights would not be enough for Mickey to examine the weathered parts. When I finished, he had already begun circling the inventory of tarnished black, red, and rushed metal parts surrounding the chassis. I flipped on the additional lighting. "Ah. Good," said Mickey

I trailed alongside my expert. He stopped to fix his eyes on the engine. Finally, he turned to me and said, "You've got a Type 50, my friend!"

"Is that good?"

"Yes. And you forgot something."

"What?"

"A floor covering."

"Damn! Sorry about that."

"No harm," he said. "The floorboards look clean and tight enough." Scratching his head under a Cleveland Indians cap, he added, "The plywood is new."

"The engine was separate from the chassis in the cellar below, so we—"

"Clever," he said. "You're lucky it held." Mickey paused his circle around the chassis and parts to study the axle, wheel joints, and transmission. Then, finally, he turned to me. "I hate asking, but have you got anything for an old man to sit on?"

"Crap." I looked around. "Oh, I've got a chair in the house."

"For now, just move that hay bale over in the corner."

"I'll do one better," I said. "I'll drive us to the coffee shop in town. It'll take less than five minutes."

"Sold," he said. "Let me look over a few more things, and then...." The polished wood dashboard caught his eye.

"I've been curious about that wood," I said. "Do you know what it is?"

Lightly sweeping a hand over it, he said, "The exotic olive tree."

"Oh. And this has been puzzling me, too." I opened the glove compartment, revealing the nearly empty package of cigarettes.

"Ah!" he said. "A nice little artifact of the times. *Gauloises Caporal*, the brand of cigarettes the French took with them into the First World War. Did your grandfather smoke?"

"Most of his life," I said. "Camels, mostly."

"Does the color of this packaging look familiar?" He paused, waiting for an answer, but I just shrugged. "It's about the same blue as my racecar and the official racing color of France," he went on. "Some believe that Ettore's wife, Barbara, recommended this shade of blue because she smoked them herself. I'd keep this in a safe place if I were you. Could be a clue about the original owner."

Exiting the barn, Mickey said, "Let's see the north side of this barn." We walked over a few steps to where he stopped and studied the landscape. "Do you recall if there was a vegetable patch nearby?"

"Yes, just over there, down from the front of the house, after the slope."

"That slope probably extended west, at least the length of the barn."

"What makes you think so?"

"Root cellars always faced the north, dug into a hill or mound." He pointed out, "That side of the barn is where they put the opening. Making it easy for your grandpa to drive in the chassis. I'm afraid you boys did a lot more work than you needed to get it out."

We got into my car and started towards the lane. I saw that

Flaven had arrived and parked behind the house to unload materials for the bathroom. I stopped to introduce Mickey to him.

"Hey Doug, this here is Mickey Michne, our expert advisor for the restoration. Turns out he also knows some things about old root cellars." They waved at each other.

"I got a great deal on the bathroom parts," said Flaven. "I should have a good start on it by the end of the day. Tomorrow, I'll work on the plumbing."

"Mickey's gotten a good start, too. Reviewed the car pieces. We going to Rosie's to do some planning over coffee."

"Oh, bring me back a large coffee and some donuts."

"You got it," I said. "Thanks for doing this. Are you saving all the receipts?"

"Hey, you're talkin' to a pro here!" he said.

I just grinned and moved on.

The cafe wasn't as busy as the Sunday morning I ate there with Flaven. Mickey and I were in a booth waiting for coffee when he reached into the pocket of his denim shirt, pulled out a two-inch-thick bolt, and placed it on the table. "Did you know that Bugatti created his own bolt? Here's an example. Found this one at the bottom of a box at your place. From these and other parts, it's likely to have been a new car when they dismantled and hid it for some reason."

Diane placed cups of coffee before us and said, "Back in town long?"

"Just day-tripping today with my friend Mickey." They exchanged nods.

"Where's Doug?" said Diane.

"Out at the farm doing some construction work."

"Tell him I said hi."

Before she walked away, I placed Flaven's order.

Mickey poured cream into his cup and took a sip. "The Bugatti Type 50 you've got has an eight-cylinder double-cam engine. The same developed for Bugatti's 1930 Grand Prix entry. It will be a hell of a ride for you or whoever ends up with it."

"Why wouldn't it be me?"

Mickey shrugged and, with a Yiddish dialect, said, "These things sometimes get complicated."

I drank some coffee, letting that sink in. The words reached deep into my head.

"The last Bugatti like this, in Concours condition, sold for three-quarters of a million dollars. That was seven or eight years ago. Today, it would get a million."

"What's 'Concours' condition?"

"The full term is Concours d'Elegance. Car shows where entrees are judged on specific criteria. Very ritzy, high-class affairs. Often includes a road rally. The goal is a car that drives and looks, inside and out, like it came from a factory or showroom. It's the ultra-expensive way to go because you need original or fabricated parts from original drawings. That level is all about possessing an award-winning prestige machine. Some owners want a high-level investment like an art masterpiece. But most just love their cars and have the means, like Jay Leno and the playthings in his garage."

"Like playthings for the wealthy."

"You'd be surprised by the number of guys who do it in their own garages."

I noticed Rosie delivering a plate of food to a farmer wearing a John Deere cap at the counter. She was a pleasant distraction. "Any idea what my cost would be for just a basic restoration to where I could drive it?"

"Ballpark, fifty to a hundred thousand," said Mickey. My eyes bugged out. "Surprised?"

"Yes and no," I said. "That's quite the range. My wife and I have some savings for emergencies and a fund for a down payment on a house. I could pull a little from here and there and be nowhere near fifty thousand. I'd have to double the clients I have now. And she doesn't make much in retail."

"What about the farm?" said Mickey. "Could you borrow off the equity?"

"That's only ten to twenty thousand," I said. "My wife wants to sell the farm and the car to put towards a house. And she wants to move fast."

"There is a market for Bugatti parts. Yours are worth maybe twenty or thirty thousand. The chassis will bring the most. Hell, I'd make you an offer myself, but—"

"But what?"

"I'm not in any condition to restore it myself. And it's not proper, ethically. You came to me for advice. Besides, I've got too much on my plate with the exhibition and my business."

"At first, I imagined putting it together myself with help from others. I've been told to get a hobby to get me out of the apartment where I live and work. Given the connection with my grandfather, I think this could be more like the adventure of a lifetime. Man, that would be so..." I paused. "You think I'm dreaming?"

"A dream come true was that car falling into your lap," Mickey said. "I don't know enough about you to say if your plan is realistic. But then, as a *working* artist, you seem pretty well grounded to me. Creatively rich but cash poor."

"What would you do if you were my age?"

"You mean, would I sell the car to keep the wife? Or the other way around?" He grinned. "Hindsight is great. I'd have replaced the secretary and kept the car."

AT THE FARM, Mickey pointed out specific restoration issues with certain parts. While I was taking notes Flaven enjoyed his coffee break, often nodding in agreement with the suggestions. With questions and answers, we went for about another hour.

I took Mickey home, arriving before dark as promised. From there, my place was forty-five minutes away. Mulling over all his observations and insights nearly put me into a fugue state. By the end of the road, I landed on a key takeaway from the trip: *Don't let Sally derail you!*

SALLY HAD SKIPPED lunch and I didn't feel like making dinner, so we went to the new Culver's a few blocks away. As we ate, she seemed more curious about my trip to the farm than usual. Was it because the former head of the Bugatti Club of America came with me this time?

After I shared what Mickey had explained to me were the various restoration levels, she cut to the chase: "What's the cheapest one?"

"At least fifty to seventy-five thousand."

"That's more than a good down payment on a house."

"I know."

"You're not going to touch our house fund. It's taken us years to save nine thousand!"

"I know. And I won't. Okay? Let's change the subject."

I took a bite of my cod sandwich. Unfortunately, our conversations too often grew into arguments. She had a grilled chicken salad. I watched some sports highlights on a TV screen hanging in a corner of the place. The silence between us helped my digestion but with my last swallow, the silence ended.

"How long would it take?" Sally asked.

"Six months to a year, depending."

"On what?"

"For one, the amount of money I have to work with. The more I get, the faster it can go. That low estimate is basically me and another guy working part-time." I finished the last of my coleslaw.

"So, if you somehow got the money, say the fifty thousand, how much could we sell the car for?”

“I'm not sure. I’ll check with Mickey."

"Well, it would have to be at least a hundred thousand or it wouldn't be worth the trouble."

"Whose trouble? Not mine. Sally, this is something I really want to do. For myself and for Grandpa."

"Okay, okay. But we don’t have the money and I'm not going into debt for some hobby of yours.”

"Fine. That makes two of us."

In the car heading home, Sally started in about trying to get a big offer for the Bugatti and what that might take. From there, she went shopping for beginner houses. Sally loved open house events as much as shopping women’s fashions. Based on the times I had gone with her to open houses, she seemed to relish most snooping into the lives of others. That was anathema to me.

I told her she should expect to be alone, as I’d need my weekends to work out at the farm.

No problem, she said. Her sister, who already owned a house with her husband and two kids, would be a much better companion.

My takeaway was that she wouldn't get in my way if I went out and raised the money for the renovation, which was a leap from where we were before. Now, how in the hell was a poor, good-looking nerd without glasses like me going to do that?

8

Mickey enticed me to his place to see photos of the cars he had picked for the art museum's Bugatti exhibition. I stood at his desk while he laid down a series of color photographs of the classy cars like he had a grand flush in a poker game. The eight-by-ten photos had small labels detailing the model, year, and owner.

Only six car examples for the major exhibition seemed insufficient. Mickey pointed out that the cars were only one-third of the show and occupied half of the gallery space. Works by Ettore's father, Carlo, and his sculptor brother, Rembrandt Bugatti, made up the other two-thirds. Each grouping of objects would illustrate quality, breadth, and artistic growth.

He talked about why he, as the curator, chose those cars. The Type 41 Royale, Ettore's "Super Car," was the largest and most luxurious passenger car. One of only seven ever built, this spectacular version came from the Henry Ford Museum. All the other vehicles were privately owned.

In contrast, he had a "Baby Bugatti" designed for Ettore's youngest son. The battery-powered racecar for kids became a popular model. Also chosen was a Type 51 racecar covered with a glimmering chrome body. A Type 55 Roadster, black with yellow highlights, shouted pure fun. I imagined a joyride amidst the mountainous California background.

Then he laid down the *pièce de résistance*, the fabled Type 57 SC Atlantic owned by Ralph Lauren. It took my breath away!

"Ah, but there's more," said Mickey. "Here's a 1931 Type 50 Coupe, my friend. That has your car's chassis. Frankly, yours, with its body design by Jean Bugatti, Ettore's son, in that fiery red and black, is going to be a knock-out!"

Holding the photo, I sank into the chair beside him. My body twitched and a sense of dread rose from my stomach. "Something's wrong here," I said.

"No, that's the Type 50," he said, "I assure you."

"I mean, it must have been an expensive car. So how is it that my poor grandpa had one? He couldn't have paid for it. Not in brand-new condition. Salvaged from a major wreck?"

"Not from what I saw in the barn," said Mickey. He paused, then added, "Do you think it might be ill-gotten? That there's someone else who is the rightful heir?"

"Something like that," I said. "Is there a way to find out?"

"Was your grandfather ever involved in nefarious ways?"

"The man I knew worked hard all his life," I said, "and told stories of the old country."

"There you are," said Mickey, collecting the photos.

"What if I take out a loan," I asked, "sweat and toil to restore it, and then someone else comes along claiming the car belongs to him?"

"Ask your lawyer," said Mickey. "You'll need to get a new title for the car. Proof of ownership is something he can address."

"Establishing the provenance."

"That's right." Mickey put the photos into a manilla folder.

We stood up and walked to the stairs. "Those pictures," I said. "Those cars, some considered priceless, are all owned by wealthy people way above my class. Even if it's proven I'm the legal owner, a part of me feels like I don't deserve it."

"Many of these cars were inherited," Mickey said, as we started up the stairs. "Some by young men your age who, believe me, deserve them less." "Have your lawyer contact me if he'd like some sources for the research."

We stepped outside. The late afternoon air seemed too hot for early June. Glad I wore sandals.

He stood in white sweat socks. "Tell him not to reveal your name. The news of your Bugatti discovery will leak from the ownership inquiry. In the Internet age it will spread like wildfire, which you don't want."

"Got it," I said, taking a deep breath.

"As for that other thing," he said, "you're feeling that you don't deserve that buried treasure. Are you Catholic, by any chance?"

I kicked a pebble on the ground. "Once upon a time."

"Between my people, the Jews, and yours, we carry around more than our share of guilt. Try to let it go." Mickey held out his hand. I took it. "Remember, your grandfather gave you the farm and the car with it, regardless. And for good reason."

THE RESEARCH RESULTS came in the mail marked CONFIDENTIAL. My investigator had tracked the VIN from the Molsheim factory in France to the London Auto Show in 1931. My Type 50 had been on view with two other Bugattis for two weeks. The local Bugatti dealer that sponsored the display also coordinated the logistics. They had had the authority to sell any of the three cars.

The newest and most innovative Type 53 lingered with the London dealership until an Irishman bought it. While it had the same Type 50 engine, Ettore gave it four-wheel drive and independent front suspension – the first and only one he made. A nobleman in Essex acquired the supercharged Type 51 racecar, successor to the lauded Type 35 as Bugatti's premier racing car. It won several races in Northern England and Scotland.

The sponsoring dealer had rented my roadster for six months to E. L. Cord, President of the Auburn Automobile Company of Indiana. As a renter, he didn't receive a title of ownership. The amount he paid was equal to the factory price. The motive behind handling the transaction as a rental stumped the researcher. Though uncommon, they found other examples.

Then a fire at the dealership conveniently destroyed documentation of transactions over that period, including the title. Recordkeeping at the Bugatti company was Byzantine at best. The researcher in France hit a dead end in the Molsheim, where paperwork for the London Auto Show indicated the Type 50 was sent.

I learned that Cord had attended the show in London, where he lived for almost two years. Many believed his extended stay was to avoid testifying before a U.S. Congressional inquiry into his complex stock holdings. He held LLCs in more than a hundred companies, most in transportation. Cord's success earned him the cover of *Time Magazine* in 1932, joining the likes of Henry Ford in the automobile field. The publicity may have sounded an alert in the Treasury Department.

The Auburn company got hit really badly by the Depression in the following years, pushing its financial woes to a point beyond recovery. Bankruptcy proceedings were undertaken and its inventory would be liquidated not long after.

At the end came the words I had been praying for. *We have concluded that under Ohio state law, you own the Bugatti Type 50 roadster found on your Indiana property.*

"Yes!" I yelled, punching the air above me like I had just scored the winning touchdown in the Rose Bowl!

I TOLD Sally the good news when she returned from work that night.

"I was unaware of any doubt about us owning the car," she said. Straight-faced, she added, "Why didn't you tell me?"

"I did. I'm sure I did. Remember? Mom said she had no recollection of the car. Then Mickey Mishne advised me to get documentation that the car belongs to me."

"Oh. Well. I can't keep track of everything going on in Indiana. I've got my job and career to think about. Do you remember me telling you the regional office is putting the screws to my manager because our quarterly sales stink?"

Instead of answering, I shook my head no.

"There you go," she said.

Fortunately, I had already poured our cocktails. Sally took hers into the living room, and once she settled down I showed her the lawyer's letter. I remained standing, rubbing the back of my neck, and then drank.

She scanned the document. "How much will this cost us?"

Not wanting all of my lingering joy drained, I said, "The bill is coming separately." In

fact, I had a ballpark estimate of five thousand dollars.

The invoice arrived a week later for $4,500. Among the advantages of working at home was seeing the mail before Sally. I buried the bill in my office until I could confer with Mickey.

When I reached him later that day, he said the price was not out of line and offered to intercede with my permission. I gave him my blessing and soon received a revised invoice reduced by $1,000, reflecting "Mr. Mishne's initial research guidance."

Sally quickly comprehended certain things that I couldn't, like the price of women's fashionable clothes. Legal fees were another matter altogether. Even at the reduced amount, she tore into me.

"You need to consider the fee as an insurance policy on a rare antique!" I said. "This piece of paper will protect us from anyone who claims the car belongs to them. Given the potential return on the car, this is a relatively small amount."

"Okay, but can we bank on it?"

"What do you mean?"

"If I find the perfect house for us next week, what happens?"

"We wouldn't qualify for a hundred thousand plus mortgage on a pile of car parts, even Bugatti parts, as collateral. For that option, we need to make improvements to the farmhouse.

"God knows I don't want our money going into that, either!"

She grabbed a magazine from the coffee table and plopped onto the sofa. I pressed my hands into my hips, watching her shut me out.

I got a drink in the kitchen. While pouring the whiskey over ice, a twinge of futility hit me in the ribs. I took a mouthful and returned. "You're talking cash flow, Sally. If you weren't in such a hurry to get a house, we might have more leeway!"

She lit a cigarette and continued flipping the pages of the magazine. "Look. Why don't we drive to the farm this weekend and visit the Auburn Car Museum?"

"What good will that do?" she said.

I thought, why bother responding if she didn't know?

She continued, "There's an open house I want to check out this weekend. Isn't it about time you went with me?"

"You've not gone out to the farm since that first time, and you're razzing me about not going to this one open house lately? What the hell, Sally! I've been going to those things for years with you. It's been our *go-to* cheap date."

Expressionless, she flicked the ashes off her cigarette and returned her eyes to the magazine. It was her distinct way of telling me to flick off.

9

SALLY HELD me in suspense all week without a commitment to go to the farm. On Friday, I forced an answer from her. She said the only way she would travel all that distance would be to post a "big ass" For Sale sign at the highway turn-off.

I took that as a solid N-O and invited Tom Anderson, framing it as a classic car day trip. He eagerly accepted.

His curiosity about my Bugatti had grown since he had seen Mickey's photos for the exhibition catalog. And visiting the car museum was a no-brainer for him. It's what museum professionals do on their days off.

When we got to the town of Auburn, we lunched at a restaurant near the museum. The management claimed it was a favorite among workers at the Auburn car factory. The pictures of those days posted on the walls made it convincing. It was fun imagining what the favorite dishes were back then.

Two blocks away in the museum's parking lot, we studied the facade of what had been the headquarters for the auto company. Except for the large Palladian windows in the front, the building reminded me of my Catholic elementary school with its four equal sides of brown brick. Upon closer viewing, I noticed faux iconic columns embedded in sections of the walls.

We paid our ten-dollar admission fee to a chatty attendant and stepped into the first gallery. Magically, like Star Trek's Scotty had beamed me into the 1930s, I gazed at the gloriously restored ball-room-size space. Masterfully displayed was an array of sparkling automobiles, delighting me hypnotically. The Art Deco style oozed from the marble floor to the painted motifs on the ceiling, and even the light fixtures were engulfed in amber cones stacked one above the other.

Here was where the company's newest models were showcased to dealers nationwide and abroad. I thought, *where do I place my order?*

Tom stood beside me, equally fascinated by the company's history which was handsomely presented on a display board. The Auburn Carriage Company adapted to the changing world of gas-powered engines by switching to automobiles. The number of car manufacturing startups in America peaked early, with 253 in 1908. That number plummeted ten years later when the First World War created material shortages.

To survive, the company's local owners sold out to Chicago investors who believed they could revive it. They hired an aggressive, entrepreneurial car salesman in Chicago named E. L. (Errett Lobban) Cord. By 1932, he had grown the automaker into the fourteenth largest in the U.S.

Examples of the finest Auburns, Duesenbergs, and his namesake line, Cords, were lit up in the showroom like works of art at the Louvre. Hard to believe that Cord started as a racecar driver and mechanic in Missouri. His staging sensibilities were more like the great Ziegfeld or, dare I say, Ettore Bugatti.

Upon arrival in the small town, Cord took all unsold inventory, repainted the cars with striking colors—some in two tones—and placed them together on an empty city block. He hung "On Sale" banners and attached bunches of balloons to create a festive atmosphere. Every car sold made the sales event a huge success.

Then his cagey investing in related companies netted new

revenues to fulfill his vision for the company, producing what seemed like an overnight turnaround. The most ambitious and audacious change came when he introduced a new luxury line named for himself.

Tom and I zigzagged through the shiny antique autos assembled. We marveled at body styling, color choices, and advancements to more powerful engines. A surprising number of the vehicles resembled Bugattis to me. But then, given that both companies had existed in the same era, it made sense.

The showroom had a grand staircase in the center that divided the two sections. One had Auburns from 1900 to 1924, and the other had Cord's cars from 1924 to 1937.

Unlike most of the competition, Cord's leadership had terrific results. The sporty styles came with superior engines, some achieving new speed records. The pricier Duesenbergs had a certain elegance with the power.

Cord, a salesman at heart, brought a business savvy that included promotional ties with sports figures and movie stars. Tom, who loved baseball even more than I did, was excited by the 1926 Auburn Roadster that had once been driven by Babe Ruth. I favored the bright orange Cord L-29 that Frank Lloyd Wright bought. The placard quoted the architect who said, "The front drive was logical and scientific and that eventually all cars would have it."

"How prophetic was that?" I said, then snapped a photo.

Neither Tom nor I were what we thought of as typical car guys. In my mind they were motorheads first. Style and design were secondary. We were more impressed by the artistic achievement than the engineering brilliance of these vehicles. Tom observed how E. L. Cord and Ettore Bugatti were alike to some extent in their approach to car making. They equally emphasized style and speed. Bugatti saw more in racing for public relations, whereas Cord sought promotions with celebrities.

Midway through the galleries, Tom got excited seeing a curiously displayed Tommy gun. The exhibit told the account of the notorious Indiana outlaw, John Dillinger, robbing the Auburn police station. Tom joked, "As a kid, I loved having a gun named after me."

The label inside the long glass case described an example of the Thompson Submachine Gun stolen and other police artifacts. A yellowed newspaper clipping from the Detroit Free Press recounted the incident. I started skimming the article:

Dillinger Gang Robs Auburn Police Station

> AUBURN, Indiana
>
> Oct. 22, 1933 — The notorious John Dillinger, Indiana's infamous gangster, committed one of his most audacious crimes early this morning when he and another desperado confronted night patrolman and former chief of police Jed Pettinger on the streets of Auburn, Indiana. The gangsters took the chief to the police station, robbing it of guns, ammunition, and bullet-proof vests.

Tom had moved on and called out, "Hey Jack, check this out!" He pointed to a sign that read, *Hall of Excellence and Innovation.* "Think they have a Bugatti?"

My pulse quickened. But no Bugatti red oval logos appeared in my scan. Perhaps as a nod to their home state, they had a Formula One Indy car circa the 1970s. Tom, the museum professional, noticed how incomplete and unfinished the gallery appeared compared to the others. "These cars only grasp the theme rather than tell a cohesive narrative. We should see Mercedes, Alpha Romeo, Rolls Royce of the era, and Bugatti."

We were walking back through the exhibits when I spotted a car I had somehow missed. Squeezed into a corner against a black curtain sat a stunning black and red Duesy that amazed me in its resemblance to my Bugatti. At least, what I imagined my car would look like restored.

Noticing my gawk, Tom asked, "What?"

"You'll see when we get to the farm. This car could be mine." I read the label—a 1933 Duesenberg SSJ. Even the specifications seemed comparable to my Type 50. While taking photos, I said, "How cool would it be to see my Bugatti next to this car?"

My fluttering around the car drew the attention of an elderly museum volunteer. I told him how the Duesy resembled a Bugatti model and asked if anyone had made the comparison.

"Not that I recall. I've read about them cars. Are they Italian?"

"French," I said. "Do you recall any shown here, or at your annual festival?"

"Not to my recollection," the volunteer said. "And I've lived here all my life."

"You have? Does *Phantom Belgian* mean anything to you?"

His deep forehead wrinkles moved up and down as he repeated the words to himself. "Can't say it does. Lots of Belgians settled in these parts back then. Of course, I was just a kid when the factory still operated."

"I think my grandpa worked here. He was from Belgium."

"What was the last name?"

"Dreyfus."

"Huh. Same last name as the famous French racecar driver, Rene Dreyfus. There was a scandal about a Jew named Dreyfus in Paris," he said.

"No, you're thinking of Alfred Dreyfus, who came from a different Dreyfus family line. Someone falsely accused Alfred of being a spy. The trial became famous because the jury convicted him and sent him to Devil's Island until the French President pardoned him. Years later, his innocence was proven."

"Oh, yeah. That's the one I'm thinking of."

"Rene Dreyfus was considered a hero of France by beating the Nazis with a race car."

Our reverse walkthrough took a fraction of the time. We decided to check out the museum gift shop before heading back. I saw the usual swag, some fun trinkets, and books. They had a fabulous pair of art nouveau earrings I considered for Sally, but she hasn't liked any jewelry I've given her.

Instead I purchased a coffee-table book, *The Most Elegant Automobiles Ever Made,* with four pages of priceless Bugattis. Tom bought one, too, as a reference for the Bugatti exhibition catalog.

IN TWENTY MINUTES we were driving up the farm lane. The scene looked much greener. Tom commented that the house looked darling for a derelict.

When I opened the barn and switched on the lights, his restrained countenance gave way to a wide-eyed fascination with the loosely assembled antique auto.

I said, "Imagine it fully restored."

"Don't bother. Just take a killer photo of this, title it *1930s French Car Wreck,* and pass it off as contemporary art."

"Fact is, I am awed standing in its presence, like installation art." I raised my hands, forming a frame with my fingers, and pretended to snap a camera.

That he got my joke made me realize I missed being among art people.

Standing outside the barn, Tom said, "Bet you never thought your attempt at metal sculpture back in the day would come in handy."

How right he was. But thinking back on it now, older and hopefully wiser, I didn't want another false start on something I felt passionate about. I had to go all in for Grandpa's Bugatti.

10

SUMMER 1998

CAR GREASE on Flaven looked fitting somehow. We were cleaning dirt, rust, and mold from the parts of the forgotten car. I didn't think he would make the drive just to do grunt work, and given his experience and the time he'd save me I was glad to have him along.

Then, on the drive, he told me he was hoping for a rendezvous with a particular lady in Avilla. Now, his willingness to tag along with me made sense. Of the two attractive café sisters, Diane seemed the likely target.

We finished our work that day in time to catch the early start of the Indians game that night at Pastimes. Joe greeted me by name and even remembered our choice of brews.

We sat at the front of the bar. Ragged Red sat at the end as before. His appearance was improved today. He asked me how the Indians would do against the Twins.

Then I noticed he wore a faded Cleveland Browns T-shirt. "You're from Cleveland?"

"Born and raised," he said, scratching his snarly beard.

"What's your name?"

"Arnold. Dick Arnold."

"What brought you here?"

"A rusted-out Chevy truck and cheap beer."

I told him my name and nodded. Flaven did the same. Arnold lifted his beer to say, "Gladda meet you." We drank and returned to the game. A minute later the Indians' all-star center fielder David Justice added three runs, hitting a homer with two on the bases.

"Guess that answers your question about the Twins," Flaven said, standing up.

"I'll drink to that," Dick said.

Flaven walked over, clinked glasses with him, and sat down next to our new buddy. "You live in Avilla, Dick?"

"Got a small farm west of here. Mostly cattle."

Flaven could be affable with the right person. When our food arrived, he returned to his stool, and we dug in. He also kept glancing out the front window.

By 8:30 the crowd began trickling in. Picturing Diane with Flaven made sense to me, both in size and demeanor. Mostly, Diane seemed his type, whereas Rosie appealed to me. Jim Thome smashed another homer on TV as the two sisters walked in.

"Hey there, boys!" Diane said.

Flaven turned to her. "Fancy meeting you two here!" he said, going to them. "Why don't we share a booth?"

Rosie looked askance at her sister and then over at me. I shrugged and joined them.

Diane and Doug slid into the last booth available. I paused beside the booth and offered Rosie the inside position, which she took and thanked me. Once settled, she folded her hands and spouted, "My, oh my! What a coincidence seeing you guys being here tonight."

Diane and Doug laughed. Rosie shook her head.

Flaven blurted, "Whatcha drinking, ladies? It's on me."

They told him, and he dashed to the bar.

Rosie asked me, "So, what have you been up to in Cleveland?"

"The usual grind—graphic design work and pursuing new clients. And I had to deal with some legal things that kept me in the city longer than I wanted."

"I hate legal stuff," replied Rosie.

Diane chimed in. "Her divorce was a nightmare! I offered to shoot her husband to make it much easier, but she rejected the idea." Rosie rolled her eyes.

"Seems to me," I said, "that the emotional toll must be the worst."

"And that it lasts so much longer," Rosie said.

The reappearance of women in summer wear is always pleasing. In pink shorts and a white tank top against her tanned skin, Diane looked sultry. Rosie wore a black T-shirt with the Eiffel Tower at night and blue shorts. She showed no signs of being a sun worshiper.

Flaven returned with beverages and began his All-State linebacker pickup banter. It started with favorite colors, beer and wine, and preferred cocktails and bar foods. He tried to segue into nightclubbing.

"Really, Doug?" I said. "How are they going to rate Cleveland nightclubs?"

"I was thinking for or against," he replied.

Diane jumped in with night spots she liked in Fort Wayne. I swear Flaven was making mental notes of every word she spoke.

After Rosie and I forged into the latest Internet websites, Diane took us into advanced themes of dating, relationships, and the always popular sex. I thought Flaven would need a drool cup. Then he plunged into the proliferation of porn on the web and even Diane jerked her head back.

Rosie diverted to the challenges of relationships and marriage. When that fizzled, I brought us back to the subject of our initial banter—the baseball game on TV.

"Bottom of the ninth and all tied up! Are we going into extra innings?"

"For the win, definitely," Flaven said, peering at Diane.

After one extra inning, the Indians broke the tie. The clock ticked towards eleven and the conversation had crested. Now tipsy, Diane's subtle flirtations with Flaven became evident, much to his delight. Rosie and I were looking for closure on the coerced double date.

Then Flaven said, "You girls should come to the farm and see what we're working on."

Applauding, Diane said, "Yes. Oh, yes! Let's go!"

Rosie monitored my reaction—a *what the fuck* glare at the Flattener. But Diane's effusiveness distracted him, so I gave the "time-out" signal.

Doug and Diane saw my disapproving frown.

Diane said, "What? Did I say something wrong?"

Flaven said, "No, I did. Stuck my big foot in my mouth. It's really not my place to invite you. It's really Jack's thing."

"Oh, please, Jack," Diane said. "We've been dying to know."

I turned to Rosie. She shrugged and said, "Don't do it for her, Jack."

"What about you?" I asked Rosie. "Are you curious?"

"Of course. But I don't want to do anything that makes you uncomfortable."

In a Bill Murray way, Flaven pleaded with me. "Come on, Jack. I said I was sorry."

"Like that makes all the difference?" I replied and then tried to read Rosie's face.

She read mine and said, "As long as it doesn't involve moonshine, illegal drugs, or mattresses." The tension in our booth melted away.

Looking at Diane, Flaven answered tongue-in-cheek. "I can't promise you that!"

She giggled.

I said to Rosie, “Nothing gross or nefarious. I promise. In fact, it just might appeal to you given your art background.”

“I'll drive Diane out," said Rosie. "And we promise not to stay too late.”

"I checked my watch and mumbled, "It's already late."

11

Soon after I pulled away from the curb with Flaven, he revealed a tiny vial of breath freshener as if he kept it up his sleeve.

"Dibbs on Diane," he said.

"Duh."

"Just checking, buddy."

"I'm not in the hunt."

He glanced in the mirror on the reserve side of his visor and tried to smooth his curly hair. "Some extracurricular activity might be just what you need."

"Don't push it. I'm not happy about this."

That hushed him the rest of the ride. I pulled up next to the barn, opened the doors, turned on the lights, and prepared to welcome my Avilla guests as pleasantly as possible.

The temperate night air was refreshing after so much time inside. In the sky a scattering of clouds floated in front of the stars, giving the half-moon the spotlight. Creating a noticeable distance from me, Flaven approached the girls' late model Chevy Malibu and opened the passenger door for Diane.

Before letting them inside, I said, "Don't take this the wrong way—but you cannot talk about this project to others."

"What you got in there?" Diane asked. "Remains of a flying saucer?"

Rosie elbowed her. "I promise to pull her vocal cords out later."

I inserted myself behind the sisters, cutting Flaven off. Once inside, he dashed ahead of everyone.

Diane and Rosie froze at the sight of the chassis and strewn parts. Diane said, "I don't get it."

"It's a Bugatti roadster!" Flaven said.

Diane shrugged. "Still don't get it."

"Bugattis were an elite brand of cars made in France," I said, "highly valued as antiques among collectors. That's why our work here needs to be kept under wraps."

"We dug it out from underneath the floorboards," Flaven said, flexing his muscles.

Diane showed her approval.

Rosie leaned in to scope out the array of metal, rubber, wood, and decaying leather. "Did you have any idea it was here?"

"I'm looking for clues to answer that question."

"Looks like you've got a long way to go before it's worth anything," said Diane.

"Yep," Flaven said. "A really long way."

"What makes this a roadster?" Rosie asked.

"No back seat."

"This looks like a very ambitious project," Rosie said.

"I'm lucky I found a specialist outside Cleveland to advise me."

"And me," Flaven said with phony modesty.

We walked around the assembly. Flaven picked up an object and said in a low voice to Diane, "This belongs to the engine's lubrication system."

"Do you know the year of the car?" Rosie asked.

"Nineteen thirty-one," I told her. "The discovery blew me away at first. But then it got complicated, like finding a Rembrandt painting in an attic. Elation, followed by disbelief, then doubt, and even soul searching. Do I restore or sell it as is, along with the farm?

I haven't got anything near the fifty thousand dollars needed for restoration."

"Provenance issues?" said Rosie.

"I don't know yet. You know something about art. And you're smart."

Pleased, Rosie said, "Thanks. I find this more than interesting. Intriguing, really."

She and I stood by the workbench. Diane and Flaven were on the other side of the car, having drifted toward the back of the barn.

"You know that picture game?" I said. "What does not belong in this picture? That's been on my mind since the discovery under these floorboards in April. The Bugatti doesn't belong in this Indiana farm picture. Doesn't fit into any of my family portraits. And my wife sees nothing but dollar signs."

Flaven muttered something, then started up the ladder to the loft with Diane behind him.

Rosie and I glanced at each other self-consciously. I said, "Let's get some fresh air."

Rosie and I meandered towards the front yard of the house. The thick grass was damp. I looked at the sky and said, "More stars than I ever get to see where I live in Cleveland."

"Yeah. I missed them when I lived in Chicago."

"Loyola?"

"Yes. How did you... oh. The sweatshirt I wore the night we met."

We studied the constellations a while longer, connecting in silence.

"You know anything about the stars?" she asked.

"Nothing more than how mesmerizing they can be."

We heard the distinctive sounds of intimate teasing from the barn, looked in that direction, and then at each other. "When I knew Flaven in high school, he was not a womanizer. Not in the least. Now he's this—

"Letch? Fiend? Dog? Predator?"

"I hope he's not that bad."

"My sister knows what she's doing." Rosie folded her arms, perusing the house. We were only a few feet from the front door. "It's not haunted, is it?"

"What if it is?"

"I'd still want to see the inside."

"Well then, let's get you inside."

"I thought you'd never ask! Is it empty?"

"Except for the memories." I unlocked the door and pushed it open. "No mattresses. I promise."

She chuckled.

The only light inside came from the reach of the floodlight above the barn doors, casting a noir atmosphere. I clicked on the lamp I brought for the desk, giving the space enough light for me to deliver the same standing tour I'd given Sally two months earlier. Pointing to each area, I said, "Kitchen. The new bathroom. We're standing in the living quarters. And—"

"Let me guess. The area with the sleeping bags is the bedroom."

"Brilliant deduction, Sherlock!" We laughed. "It's somewhat spartan staying here, but a motel every weekend would add up."

"Smart."

"It was *really* primitive before Flaven added the restroom. The outhouse was my only unpleasant memory of this place."

She began walking the perimeter, sizing up the space using her hands to frame different angles. "It's the interior designer in me."

"Any ideas are welcome," I said.

"Have you and your wife decided to keep the farm for yourselves?"

"Sally wants the money. She'd tear the house down if it increased the property's value."

"Which you would oppose?"

I froze. Something in Rosie's eyes sent my brain into a tailspin.

"Jack?" She touched my arm.

I shook my head and shoulders. "Sorry. You touched a nerve I didn't know existed. That car has really complicated things." I walked out into the yard. She followed.

A thin layer of clouds high above muted the stars. We wandered a few steps toward the barn. I tucked my hands in my pockets and did a slow spin around.

"Something about this place. A kind of nostalgia. I didn't have a father growing up, so Grandpa tried to fill in and brought me out here. I keep hearing our conversations. And now there's this mystery."

"Your ambivalence shows."

I looked at the ground.

She took my hand. "It's not wrong for you to feel this way."

"The visits weren't that frequent. And I'm realizing now how little I know about my grandfather. I should have spent more time with him."

"At least you know that you've got issues needing to be resolved."

I gave Rosie an appreciative half-smile. She squeezed my hand.

We turned toward the barn. It seemed we might be thinking the same thing. "It might be fun to roust the horny teenagers out of the loft," I said.

"It would be, but . . ."

"Yeah. Would you like me to drive you home?"

"I don't know." She looked at her watch.

"He was an all-state high school athlete. They could go all night."

She snickered. "Oh, hell. Why am I hesitating? She's got a key to the car."

ON THE WAY INTO TOWN, we tried to put together a limerick. It started with "Doug and Diane up into the hayloft, and couldn't keep their hands off. . ." is as far as we got. But our silliness went down a soothing antidote to the embarrassment we felt from Flaven's and Diane's hormone-infused teenager antics.

"FYI, Diane wouldn't have gone into the loft with him if she couldn't handle him in that situation. She wears big girl panties."

Rosie directed me to a parking space behind her café. I put the gear in the park and left my right hand on it. "I live right up those stairs," she said and placed her hand on top of mine. "Thanks, Jack. You're a good guy. And you have got a hell of a project going for you."

The darkness of the alley couldn't black out her sweet eyes. Then she blinked, glided up the stairs, and disappeared behind a door.

I took in the moment and backed out.

FALL 1998

The restoration was paused due to the heat and little more to do with the funds needed.

The tall trees all around Cleveland had leaves turning yellow and orange, the color of the day because it was also the name of a southeastern suburb. With a reputation for excellent schools, the sprawling city drew a high socio-economic class of residents. To me it meant we had no reason to be there.

Most schools had been in session for a few weeks, and already Halloween decorations were popping up.

Sally and her sister knew a couple who had moved to Orange and praised the community. So here we were, inside a large contemporary colonial house with an acre of yard. After an initial tour with the realtor, we went back through and talked about the place in private. We paused in the first of three bedrooms upstairs. I leaned on the window ledge and fixed on the forest-like backdrop to an extravagant swing set built of lumber that matched the deck.

"Nice view," I said, "but way more room than we need and too much money."

"Maybe. But I thought we should at least check out one house like this. You know, we need to consider the future, too. Not just the present and where we've been."

I suppressed the twitch in my stomach. "Good point."

"And you know that the price was more about the location than square feet." Sally had dressed for business with black designer slacks, a white blouse, a blue blazer, and makeup. A thin gold chain with a cross adorned her neck and brass loops hung from her ears. In contrast, I was unshaven and wore a Cleveland Brown sweatshirt and sneakers.

"Besides," she added, "if that car of yours gets us what you say it could, we'll be able to make a big down payment and have an affordable monthly mortgage. We could buy the house outright if we get a million dollars after restoring the old car. Right?"

"Only if I put way more into it."

Sally went ahead of me to the middle bedroom. Her sudden reversal on the Bugatti felt like a mental whiplash. She wouldn't have done the research on her own. Someone among her friends or maybe her sister must have enlightened her.

I caught up in the master bedroom. Someone she trusted must have gotten through to her about the real potential of the restoration. I scanned the room, which was twice the size of our apartment bedroom. Otherwise, the hardwood floors and the original off-white walls looked the same. The doors and windows were framed with oak. Nothing in the mini-mansion appeared altered from the developer's blueprints.

Sally said, "Whatever. The main thing is that money wouldn't be a problem if we fixed up the car and sold it."

"That's a real turnaround," I said. "But if you're planning on the big bucks for the Bugatti, remember two things. First, we'll need a lot of money upfront. Money that we don't have. And second, we'll be paying big taxes on that income. I'm guessing thirty-five percent or more."

"So, *you* can dream big about restoring that car, but I can't dream big about what we do with the money by selling it?"

Maybe her sister, whose husband worked in banking, wised her up to the situation. Why was I experiencing a bout of acid reflux?

"Honey," she said, "don't forget who's the business professional in this marriage."

Did she just say, *check and checkmate*?

Back on the main floor, she ducked into the third lavatory between the kitchen and living room, flushed the toilet, and watched the water swirl. "Nice. Excellent pressure! And you know schools here get a top rating."

To be a good sport, I said, "How many points does that add to your scorecard?"

She ignored it and moved into the living room with its fireplace and picture window. I followed behind like Eeyore, the downer donkey in *Winnie the Pooh,* juxtaposed by her Christopher Robin-like energy. She flung her arms open wide and exclaimed, "Isn't it just *fabulous*?"

Right on cue the realtor appeared, echoing Sally's exclamation. "Absolutely!"

I slowly circled the space as the two of them huddled. A few minutes later, and after a couple failed attempts on my part, we finally departed.

I couldn't get into the Honda, parked in the pristine double-wide driveway, fast enough. Armed with a detailed, three-page listing and business card, Sally detoured into the middle of the manicured front yard and stood admiring the brick exterior. Like the sad-ass storybook animal, depressed and pessimistic, I sat and thought about getting used lawnmowers for the farm.

As we traveled homeward, Sally jabbered on about it being the perfect home for when we have kids. I got the feeling she wanted to work on conceiving the first one in the parking lot of our apartment building.

November 1998

Over Thanksgiving weekend, we visited Sally's sister for the feast and the football. Carole was older by two years and didn't share much of Sally's Hollywood looks. She had married only a few months before us but now had two school-age kids: a boy in kindergarten and a girl in first grade. Both were going to a Catholic elementary school in neighboring Shaker Heights.

Their house was a 1930s clapboard Dutch colonial that showed its age. The only apparent upgrades were the kitchen and an adjacent bathroom. From top to bottom, the rooms were small. The best convenience in the kitchen was a doggie door to the fenced backyard for their Sheltie.

Sally had once told me she'd never live in a house like this, finding flaws in everything. Nonetheless, the place fit Carole's husband, Kent, and the kids well.

Football on TV kept the husbands in the living room. The women enjoyed wine in the kitchen while the turkey baked. Fully charged as if on caffeine, the children were all over the house, often with the dog chasing them. They would pause to attempt dog tricks in the living area, obstructing our view of the game, but neither of us minded.

The sisters were conversing about house-buying with the requisite subtopics of schools and mortgages. As a stay-at-home mom, Carole envied Sally's prospects of living in Orange with its superior public schools, but Sally told her sister she needed to return to earth.

Kent and I didn't talk much during the game. We'd comment on great plays and poor calls by the refs. He worked as a loan officer at one of the local banks, earning enough to make ends meet and sock some dollars away for the kid's college fund. The car commercials on TV prompted Kent to mention how he wished he could get a new car, but Carole's minivan was all they could afford.

The subject of cars made me think Kent knew about the Bugatti. Sally must have talked with Carole about my discovery, who would have leaked the story to her husband. And Kent was a source Sally would trust. He could have enlightened Sally about the benefits of restoring my vintage wheels.

On the drive back, Sally defended telling her sister about the Bugatti. Because I trusted Kent's discretion, I didn't mind. Now six people knew about my discovery, plus my lawyer and the people in the loop for the Bugatti title search. The total didn't sit well with me. Could the tipping point be near?

THAT NIGHT, Sally became frisky and jumped on top of me in bed for lovemaking. As our sexual activity had tapered off over the years, I was all for it. I rolled her over for some wholesome breast action. She seemed to be disengaged from it.

Then Sally said, "Weren't those kids adorable?" My head went up. She was still at her sister's house. I resumed. "They're at that right age: out of diapers but still so cute and fun to play with."

I suppressed the urge to joke about breastfeeding and kissed my way to her lower belly button instead. She reached for my lower parts, rushing the foreplay. I reversed direction, kissed her face, and nibbled her earlobe, then neck. She spun me over and was back on top.

If she intended to mix things up, my blonde beauty succeeded. She leaned forward, rubbed her breasts into my chest, and whispered, "Come on, Jack. Let's make a baby."

"Practice makes perfect," I said, playing along.

After more foreplay, she said something about how the effects of the pill, after taking it for years and years, can delay pregnancy for a very long time.

I stopped fooling around. "Are you telling me you're off the pill?"

She looked away and twirled the ends of her hair—a familiar "tell." I rolled out from under her. She tried to snuggle into my backside, kissing my neck. Then she eased a leg over my waist. Being rejected for sex was new to her.

I took a breath. “If you would simply answer me—”

In a cooing voice, she said, “I want to get you off.” She reached for my cock.

I leaped out of bed and reached for my boxer shorts.

“Goddamn, Jack!” She huffed, sat up, and folded her arms over her breasts. “I don’t believe this. You’re frustrating the hell out of me!”

I stared down at her. Unconsciously, my hands formed fists. My entire body felt clenched.

Her eyes switched signs from loving to raging. She slammed her fist into her pillow and pulled the sheet over her body. “Get out! Now!”

I snatched my T-shirt and said, “As you wish.”

“Other wives, and even husbands, do what I’ve done.”

“Deceived their partner about bringing a life into the world?”

She didn’t know how to reply.

“How long have you been off the pill?”

“A week.”

“Not right, Sally. So not right!” I took my pillow and left.

WINTER 1998

GOING to The Gap's annual holiday party felt like penance to me. Conversely, Sally loved to party and relished any opportunity to suck up to her superiors. She floated into the gathering as if ascending into heaven. The reception room at Cleveland's downtown Hilton was the right size for the employees attending from over a dozen stores in northeastern Ohio.

Sally had been angling for a general manager position for the last two years. I played the role of the supportive husband. She wished I were a better actor, but it had been only two weeks since the bedroom fight lodged us into a state of tolerance. We were sharing the same bed again, albeit with an invisible wall.

I wanted to address Sally's birth control maneuver the next day, not bury it or, worse, drag it out as we had before and cause a visit to a marriage counselor. Our differing views about starting a family had gotten too intense.

Like most couples seriously dating, the subject had come up but just in passing— just part of the getting-to-know-you banter. I think I'd said something like "undecided." Our counselor characterized us as being in a rudderless boat. Our compromise at that time was to agree to a maximum two-year delay in deciding. That was four years ago. Such are the limitations of couple's therapy.

Her clumsy and foolish deception that night had backfired, and she regretted it in the morning. The next day of work was critical for her job—Black Friday! I tried to block out the too-obvious omen.

Come Sunday morning, we talked a bit over breakfast until it became a rehash of the things we had said before with the protection of a counselor. Sally brought up her biological clock, but she was only thirty-five. She told me she hoped to have three kids and that starting now would take her to her fortieth birthday.

I thought about her miserable childhood with alcoholic parents living on food stamps and occasional drug dealing. She had escaped to the city hoping for a better life and became embedded in a party life instead. Getting married brought her the hope of getting back on track.

Now she had the fantasy of a suburban life. Being raised by a single mom gave me caution about any make-believe worlds, least of all a McMansion bursting with cheerful kids and parents betting on a Bugatti bonanza.

So, here we were at The Gap's employee holiday event on a Sunday evening before Christmas when the stores closed. The seven p.m. to ten p.m. block made it easier for the staffers to flip the OPEN switch the following day. As the assistant manager, Sally had to be one of those early birds.

The sound of Whitney Houston's newest hit, "All I Want for Christmas," signaled the room with the party. Most employees showed their team spirit by wearing the finest Gap clothing that would flatter their figures. The better sales clerks knew how to do this well. Dresses and skirts dominated, while those cheeky enough sported topline Gap jeans with flashy accessories. Most men had their idea of business casual: sport coats with dress shirts open at the neck. Some opted for sweaters.

The obligatory decorations graced the space on the walls and around the banquet tables. They offered the usual hot and cold appetizers and desserts. High cocktail tables and bar stools were scattered about. A decorated Christmas tree stood in the corner opposite the DJ, with a table for Secret Santa gifts between them. Complimentary beer, wine, and soft drinks were served from two portable bars at opposite ends. From experience, I knew I could get a real drink in the hotel lobby bar. I didn't mind the marked-up price.

Most of the men, either husbands or boyfriends of the employees, were drinking beer. For the female workers, the wine proved the favorite. Those who drank spirits appeared to be administrative types.

I didn't mind playing the dutiful spouse following Sally around. Usually, that required less thought, fewer decisions and, mercifully, less kibitzing. She always wanted to work the room and network with other managers to see where the next promotion opportunity could happen. Sometimes, I'd join a conversation, and she'd get annoyed and tell me to give her some space.

Tonight I thought it would be great if she introduced me as "just a graphics guy," as she had in the past. And then I could say, "Yeah, but I own a freakin' Bugatti!" Now, *that* would put some grist into a group gab. But I couldn't, so I popped that fantasy bubble.

Out of the swelling crowd appeared none other than Doug Flaven, wearing a stylish jacket and tie. He spotted me and approached with a shit-eating grin.

"Hey, Jack!"

"Doug. What brings you here?"

"I heard about it from the sister of a lady customer I once dated. The sister works at one of the Gap stores but didn't have a date and sort of talked me into bringing her. But really, I'm just here for the *free* food and drinks!" He held up a bottle of Michelob. "Cheers!"

"Where is she? What's her name?" asked Sally.

"Oh, Amy's around here somewhere."

"What store is she with?"

"The one down in Parma. I met her last summer when installing ceiling fans in her sister's house. She's divorced with no kids, but Amy is more my type."

"And what type is that?" said Sally, circling the rim of her glass.

"Oh, sexy blonde, well-built, gorgeous. Gee, that kind of describes *you!*"

"Only kind of?" asked Sally, grinning.

The young woman in question appeared. "I've been looking for you," Amy said to Doug. Her appearance wasn't quite up to Flaven's high standards. Her voice sounded Jean Arthur quirky and she wrinkled her nose nervously. "I thought you might be ditching me."

He held up his beer. "I've only just begun. Then I saw these friends of mine." He turned and introduced Sally and me.

"Nice to meet you," said Amy. She reached out to shake Sally's hand but without the enthusiasm of a social climber.

As soon as Sally and Amy got into shop talk, Flaven and I set out for another round of beer and wine. When we returned, the fiftyish, bald Midwest VP for Operations was into his planned remarks. He ended his unremarkable discourse by declaring "Secret Santa" time.

A ten-dollar limit for the anonymous gifts meant a lot of decorative knick-knacks, fancy kitchen utensils, and finer chocolates. Bottles of wine and gift cards were easy to detect and disappeared fast. To appear gracious, Sally waited for the younger employees to get the first choice. She picked up a small package that turned out to be the high-end garlic press she always wanted.

Thinking it had to be a gag gift, Flaven laughed.

I said, "I'll bet you don't even know what that tool is!"

Sally covered for him. "It's what you've always wanted," she said, dropping it in my hand.

Flaven chortled.

While the guests swapped presents, hotel workers cleared the food tables. Then the DJ switched from Christmas tunes to dance music, leading off with a Backstreet Boys number. Sally took Flaven's hand and pulled him into the dancing pool. The music volume went up, as did the energy in the room. They danced as if they were in a scene from *Saturday Night Fever*.

I retreated to the lobby bar and ordered a whiskey and soda. Knowing how motels jack up the price of booze, I was glad to see Jim Beam as their "well" whiskey. The bartender mixed the proportions just right. The first sip was delightful.

A woman's voice behind me said, "Taking a break?"

I turned to see Flaven's date, Amy, who had departed just before me to use the ladies' room. "Company parties can get a little weird," I said.

She pulled up her green and red plaid dress and sat one stool over. Reaching for a bowl of snack mix, she said, "I try not to eat the food at events like this. Don't want to spray particles at someone important."

"Smart," I said. "Want a drink?"

"No, I need to keep my wits about me."

"Good idea, given you're with Flaven," I said. She raised a crooked smile while munching. I paused a moment. "Are you one of those not looking to increase your chances for company advancement?"

"No, just escaping boredom. Think I'm in the minority?"

"The career climbers seem way too obvious," I said. "Including my wife."

"Then she's picked the wrong partner!" said Amy.

I lifted my drink toward her. "To those looking to fill a gap at the Gap!"

Amy groaned.

"Yes, a pretty lame pun," I said. "But I deplore gaps in party conversations."

"Maybe I need a drink after all," she said, pivoting toward me. "Am I not holding up my end?"

"To the contrary. Your end is just right."

"So, tell me. How long have you known Doug?"

"I knew him in high school. Not a guy I hung out with. He was big in sports, so most kids knew him."

"Why do you call him by his last name?"

"He was a fierce-hitting linebacker and guys started calling him Doug Flatten, which was shortened to Flatten. I compromised with just Flaven."

"I get that. So, how long have you two been working on the Bugatti?"

My mouth fell out of sync with my hand, causing pricey whiskey to dribble down my chin. I put the glass down and wiped my face.

"Am I saying it wrong? Bugatti? The antique car you found?"

"You're pronouncing perfectly," I said. "But how did you know?"

The brightness in her face melted. She cleared her throat. "I think I said something I shouldn't have." She averted her eyes and brushed snack crumbs off her lap.

"What did he tell you?"

"My sister and I were talking about this party. He stepped in and convinced me to let him be my date. Awkward, given that they had dated. He said you and your wife would be here and were good friends. Then, on the way, he told me how you and he were restoring a Bugatti."

"I'm a partner with him?" I swallowed more whiskey. "Did he ever mention that this is a highly confidential project?"

Noting the tone in my voice, she guardedly answered, "No."

"Un-fucking-believable."

Slinking off the stool, she added, "I... um, ...need to get back. I'm sorry."

I fixed my eyes on the amber fluid in front of me. A profound sense of disappointment set in. The average person wouldn't understand the situation, but Flaven knew. No doubt about it. So what was his game? He knew about the car, its value, and the vulnerability of the barn.

The last of my bourbon went down and I ordered another. Waiting, I imagined Flaven appearing with a flushed face and tail between his legs. My second whiskey arrived. With an eye on the hallway, I stirred the ice, sipped, and swallowed.

Finally, Flaven strutted out towards me, relaxed and confident, unlike my fantasy. He signaled the bartender. "I'll have what he's drinking, no ice, and bring another for my friend here. The way he likes it." When the drinks arrived he knocked his back, put a hand on my shoulder, and squeezed it. "I don't blame you for being pissed. I'm sorry, Jack. It was a slip, that's all."

I stared straight ahead. The echo of dance music with the murmur of partiers drifted into the lobby. His discomfort grew. Finally, he said, "Come on, buddy."

I took a pull on my drink. "I'm guessing you didn't slip, Doug. You bragged."

"Okay, if you say so. I've never been a humble guy. This is the biggest thing I've been into since our football team made state. But honestly, it just popped out."

"How many times? Who else knows about it?"

He hesitated. "One or two others. But they're people who I trust with my—"

I looked at him stone-faced. "You're off the project. I can't trust you."

"Come on, Jack. Please."

I took a stoic posture, closing him out.

Flaven emptied his drink, paid the bartender, and marched to the party room.

My ears were burning. I took a slow, long breath. His taking off so burning mad baffled me. Was he projecting how I felt, anger for anger?

After a few minutes to shake off the confrontation, I returned to the party. Sally and Amy were flanking the former linebacker in the middle of the crowd. When Flaven spotted me, he grabbed Amy's hand and swept her away.

Sally showed a poker face that seemed out of place. I told her I wasn't in the mood to stay any longer.

"I'm not finished networking. Besides, I'm having too much fun." Pure sarcasm. "I'll get a ride from someone else. Go!"

"Why are you angry with *me?*"

"Just go!"

My eyes were fixed on the road straight ahead while my mind spun in circles, trying to sort out what had happened and why it had set me off. I parked in our space next to the apartment building and headed straight to bed.

But sleep escaped me. Events of the last nine months played randomly in my head. I started counting Bugatti parts instead of sheep until Flaven interrupted, naming all the women he had nailed. Then I tried to recall the beautiful sunsets I'd seen at the farm.

When I finally nodded off, I dreamed I was in a basketball game out in front of the barn. People in my life were tossing the ball over my head in a game of keep-away. Flaven stood under the basket and finally slam-dunked one in my face.

I awoke to see Sally creeping into the bedroom. The bedside clock said 1:38. I faked sleep as she slipped into bed. The party should have ended two hours ago. I thought she must have had a bar-closing nightcap with one of her Gap pals, who brought her home.

The sun came out next and she departed for work. I thought I'd get an explanation later that day, but she avoided the topic.

Two days later, I brought it up over dinner. I made one of our routine meals of baked chicken thighs, peas and carrots, and a packaged rice dish. When Sally walked in, the food was ready—a benefit of having a caring husband who works from home.

"Who gave you a ride from the party?" I asked.

"Doug and his date." She paused. "You really shook them up, so we hung out at the hotel bar until it closed. I didn't want to be out that late, but—" I poured two glasses of white wine and gave her one. "She was a mess and Doug was really pissed off at you. Thought you treated him like shit!"

"Really? I said very little to him."

"He was insulted!"

"Sounds like you're siding with him, and you weren't even there." Putting dinner on the plates, I spilled peas onto the counter.

"Just the same, I could see it. You've gone berserk over a goddamned car!"

"A car you are counting on to get your dream house!"

That brought us to a dead end. We entered the living room with our food and turned on the TV for the evening news.

Afterward, we put our plates in the sink, and I tried to put some closure on the argument. "Loose lips about the Bugatti could draw unwanted attention, which Mickey warned me about."

"I don't care what your car guru said. You need to apologize so Doug will keep helping you."

"Sally, Flaven compromised the security of the Bugatti. The barn isn't a vault, and I'm only there on weekends. I'm not letting Flaven back in."

Her eyes fixed on me. I drank the last of my wine. "I don't get you anymore!" she cried.

"Have you ever?"

A more potent beverage was called for. I reached for a bottle of Jim Beam, poured myself three fingers, and tossed in some ice. "There are other factors in my decision. Mickey told me I needed someone with actual restoration experience. Besides, Flaven seems more interested in scoring with the local women."

"Fine. End of subject!"

“Oh, yes, and I received an invoice from him. Five hundred dollars in labor for the bathroom in the farmhouse. Another reason I can’t trust him.”

“He did the work, didn’t he?” She refilled her wineglass and pounded the cork back into the bottle.

I leaned against the sink. “Okay, so here’s a fresh new subject. What do you want to do about Christmas cards this year?”

“Ugh! You send yours and I’ll send mine. How’s that?”

“Works for me,” I said, then knocked back some bourbon.

Sally set her drink down and folded her arms. “You know, there’s just no joy in Christmas anymore, especially without—”

“Kids?”

“Okay, Jack. I’m calling off Christmas this year!”

"Just for us, or for the whole world?"

14

SANTA SENT us a surprise two weeks before the holiday that Sally had so boldly canceled. Not the positive pregnancy test Sally wanted; that would have been impossible, at least having come from me. Our marriage was in lockdown, frozen for an undetermined period of confined alienation. She tolerated it better than me. I missed the intimacy of sex. So, I was usually the one caving in.

No, the surprise came from my mother. She and my stepdad, George, were coming to celebrate Christmas in Cleveland with us.

There had been years when we traveled to Arizona and vice versa. They preferred coming to Cleveland Heights when in the mood for snow if we had it. My folks would fly in and stay at a fancy hotel. Our yuletide get-togethers with Mom and George were only in Arizona when Cleveland's weather was hazardous.

The first time Mom offered to pay for our flights to go down there, I resisted, thinking about all the years money was so tight for us. If George made the airfares his gift to us, I accepted. Eventually, that became automatic. Their decision to come to us this year was later than usual. Mom's reasoning for a Midwest Christmas seemed suspect, considering we didn't have any snow yet.

While waiting for them to arrive at our place, I worried that our marital tension would spoil the occasion. I asked Sally not to get into any of our problems in front of them. She gave me a *think I'm stupid* look.

On Christmas day, our doorbell rang at eleven a.m. I scooted down the one set of stairs to greet the folks. Their arms filled with wrapped gifts, Mom and George chimed, "Merry Christmas!" He stood almost a foot taller than her, making Mom, wearing a Santa cap, look like one of his elves. I relieved her of the packages and led them up to the apartment as we bantered about the weather.

Sally's enthusiastic greeting in the doorway seemed over the top. She took Mom's coat, revealing her brown V-neck sweater with holiday images over a white blouse and black wool slacks. Then they discussed my mother's freshly frosted coif.

George appeared ten years younger than his seventy years. He wore a Stetson hat, a bolo tie with a silver and turquoise clasp, crisp blue jeans, and cowboy boots. I always thought he had a 1940s movie star presence with his glowing tan. The pencil-thin mustache and trim body helped.

Both were bright-eyed and energetic from having arrived the day before, as planned. We drifted over to our hastily erected Christmas tree and arranged the presents. Next, Mom and Sally went to the kitchen to prepare for an early afternoon meal. I took George to my office to show him pictures of the farm and the Bugatti on my computer display.

After ham, yams, and the usual sides, we took a break before having cherry pie for dessert. We lounged in the living room for the rest of the afternoon and started opening presents, moving at a snail's pace to stretch out the fun part. Earlier, Sally had lit candles scented with pine and cinnamon to counter the smell of her cigarettes. I appreciated how she always tried to hold back when my parents visited. Eventually, George offered everyone a glass of the Glenfiddich he had brought for the occasion.

Mom and George sat together on the sofa. Sally and I sat on the chairs at both ends. I soon saw the look in Mom's eyes, the one I'd seen for many years that said, "Let's get down to business." She folded her hands in her lap and used her voice of authority. "So, here we are. All together for the first time since Dad's funeral. I would love to hear how your plan is progressing with the farm, and... what's it called again?"

"Bugatti," George and I replied.

I cleared my throat. "You know it's out of the barn cellar. We cleaned up the parts, cataloged them, and aligned them with the chassis."

"Quite the find, Jack. Downright amazing!" said George.

Sally inserted, "Jack's friend, Doug, helped. And built a bathroom for the house."

"Very basic," I said. "But compared to the outhouse—luxury!" Everyone laughed. "Which reminds me, Mom. Do you recall how often Grandpa took me out there to the farm when I was a kid?"

"Oh, I'd say about half a dozen times," she said. "Once a summer, from when you were about five to twelve years old. That's when you got more interested in baseball and discovered girls." Mom giggled, George shot me a grin, and I winced.

"Seems more often than that," I said. "I love going out there. My memories are so vivid, like dreams coming alive."

"Your grandfather wanted to get you out of the city. He felt the need to fill in for your father. So, he'd use most of his vacation time from the factory to take you out there and do Boy Scout types of things. Those outings were special to him." She turned to Sally. "Have you been out there since that first time?"

"I've been so busy with work," she said, then drank some wine.

"It's like returning to summer camp," I said, "but without the other kids. I remember riding a horse, fishing, and shooting at tin cans with Grandpa's Winchester .22."

"He borrowed the horse from a neighboring farmer," Mom said.

"The rifle he used to get rid of the varmints. Whatever happened to it?"

"It's in storage down in the basement," I said. "I've been meaning to take it out there for that same reason."

"Before you came along," Mom said, "Dad would retreat alone. Said it reminded him of the old country."

"Back to the car," said George. "Is there any more restoration you could do yourself, or are you pretty much at your limit?"

"At my limit." I shot a look at Sally to pre-empt her from bringing up Flaven again, and she pursed her lips. "And I don't have the tools or funds to outsource the more complicated things. I'd like to do more. Maybe because I did metal sculpture in college, and I want to do more on the car myself. Mickey Mishne talked me through different options and estimates."

"I wouldn't mind working on that car myself, son, but that's not likely to—"

Sally interrupted. "I'm dying to get out of this tiny apartment and into a house. We can't have both."

"Each month, any extra goes into the house fund, ignoring savings—"

"And you're not touching that fund, Jack!" Sally snapped.

"—which I would not even think of doing," I said, leering back at her. "Nor will I take out a loan if I could get one, which is doubtful according to your brother-in-law." I drank some scotch. "So, for now, it's just one lottery ticket at a time."

George scratched his jaw. "Sounds to me what you've got here is a cash flow problem more than anything." His low, resonant voice commanded our attention. "Your limited resources are reserved for a house or for emergencies, as well they should."

He and Mom looked at each other and then turned to us. "We would like to see you two in a position to move on with your lives," said Mom. "We will help financially."

"That would be so awesome, Mother!" Sally said.

George said, "Your mother and I are in a fortunate position with investments—"

"We feel it's the right thing to do," Mom said, finishing his sentence.

Sally embraced Mom in the center of the living room. George and I stepped around them and shook hands.

"This Mickey Mishne," George said. "He sounds like an interesting fella. I'd like to meet him someday."

"Come back this summer for the *Bugatti* exhibition, and I'll arrange it," I said.

"Sounds good. I'll call you after the holidays to follow up on the financing."

Sally said, "We've interrupted the opening of presents long enough." She pulled a Target bag out from behind the sofa with the gifts we'd got for the folks once we learned they were coming. In the later hours, I wondered if Mom had conspired with Sally or vice versa—prompting the most substantial gift of the day—and what their terms had been to close the deal.

GRAY SKIES TOP-FRAMED a panorama of the rural Midwest, dominated by barren fields and bare trees. Scattered patches of snow highlighted the winter gloom with a chilling bleakness, yet the anticipation of my Bugatti returning to life tickled my insides with glee. I pushed back the external drabness by focusing on the billboards that dispersed color along the highway.

Many people despise outdoor advertisements for littering landscapes with crass commercialism. Yet creating them is a rare treat for graphic designers like me. When done well, they can liven up an otherwise dull repeat journey.

Most of my clients can't afford billboards if they want to add them to their marketing mix. The cost to rent and produce them, plus a designer's fee, adds up and puts them out of reach. Once I designed a thirty-sheet poster 10 feet high by 22 feet wide. That it publicized a gun show that bothered me, but not so much that I turned down the job.

The key to designing outdoor advertising is keeping the message simple. If a car is going 75 m.p.h., you've only two to three seconds to get a person's attention with something notable. The emphasis is on a catchy image with limited words. Most clients want to include too much. Imagine a racecar driver on a straightaway and glimpsing a sign from his pit crew.

When possible, I like to have the days between Christmas and New Year's for relaxation and playing with new toys from Santa. But a desperate marketing person might call me for an urgent Valentine's Day promotion, and so I'll be on standby at that time. Can't afford to turn down any work this year.

Enough sunlight seeped through the clouds to highlight the thin white blanket on the ground and on the bushes surrounding the farmhouse. Because the forecast said freezing temperatures, I had packed the trunk with bundles of firewood.

I brought in a couple to start and loaded one into the potbelly stove. "Need to keep you full, Bertha. Going to be living with you for a few days. Hope you don't mind the extra work."

As the house warmed up I transferred groceries and other supplies, including a small microwave and cooler. For this round I had brought a wooden stool for the kitchen counter. Once I got the coffee brewing, I set up my laptop at the counter. The fit was too snug for my legs, so I moved the computer to the desk by the front door.

With a fresh cup of coffee, I settled in for bookkeeping and invoicing. The kitchen window looked westward to the barn, but the view from the desk allowed me to see vehicles traveling the county road.

Before long, the expanse of the countryside grabbed my attention. The sun brightened the snow, reminding me of a rare winter visit with Grandpa. I had loved trying to identify the fresh animal tracks. Rabbits were the most common, and squirrel trails. Discovering deer prints was a real thrill! I followed them from the front of the house to the back and into the woods. Grandpa wouldn't let me go in alone.

I found some unfamiliar tracks near the forest and showed them to Grandpa.

He said they could be from a bear, but they didn't come around much. "They remind me of footprints I saw when I was your age." His accent became stronger, telling stories of the old country. "My *papa* said it was the foot of a werewolf."

The only image of a werewolf I had seen came from *I Was a Teenage Werewolf*, which seemed goofy. I laughed. "No such thing."

"Not here in America, but over there in the black forests..." His voice darkened. "My old man said he kept a silver bullet in his rifle at night, just in case."

He must have seen enough fear in my eyes that he eventually told me the story was one his grandpa told him. And that, personally, he didn't believe in werewolves, either. Then he tickled me until I laughed.

His best stories came from European folklore and his family. Besides a brother and sister, he had cousins in France. Among them was Rene Dreyfus from Nice, France. He and his brother, a driving partner in the early years, would visit Grandpa's family farm whenever in Antwerp. That's how Grandpa got interested in cars and learned to be a mechanic.

Rene's success on the European Grand Prix circuit made him a legend, or so he said. Beating Germany's dominant Mercedes-Benz and Auto Union Grand Prix race cars, especially the "Silver Arrow" in the 1938 Grand Prix, made him a hero. When the Nazis occupied Paris, they tried to destroy his car and the official record of the victory.

That was all I remembered. My stomach growled, so I slapped together a peanut butter and strawberry jelly sandwich and washed it down with milk from the cooler.

After lunch, I took my computer and the stool to the barn. Mickey had given me a thumb drive with a file of photographs and schematics of the Type 50 model he collected. As the laptop booted up, I moved one of two electric heaters to the space under the bench. I started paging through them, looking to match up my Bugatti parts with the research he provided. Many had a number stamped on them. Some of the written material and notes were in French and my high-school class skill wasn't enough to keep the process from slogging.

Flaven wouldn't have been any help with this. When his bill for the restroom arrived, he had inflated the cost. I mailed him a check for the total amount, considering it a pay-off to disentangle myself from the bruiser. Sally's defense of him still infuriated me, even after she made a lame apology. Maybe I blew the situation out of proportion. And maybe I felt a little jealous watching them dance at the holiday party. Of course, perhaps I *am* a dumb fuck.

Imagining each piece of the car looking new and fitting where it belonged made the matching game less tiresome. In the end, I knew my renewed Bugatti would be the envy of antique auto enthusiasts everywhere. Plus, there was the mysterious past. Why did I have moments on the farm like this that sent my mind on unreal musings?

I aimed to have a complete list of missing parts separated by those usable, fixable, or needing reconstruction. That would give my pro mechanic and restorer a jumpstart as soon as March. Foremost, I needed the phone meeting with George for the cash.

Blurry-eyed after three hours, I clicked over to the next page and saw the T-50's iconic radiator rounded at the top. I eyed the upright eroded one on the floor, resembling a gravestone! The common belief is that a horseshoe inspired the design, given Ettore's devotion to horses. Others saw the influence of his artistic father, Carlo, who emphasized the oval shape in his work. Neither factor explained why a gravestone came to mind.

I recalled what Joe at Pastimes had said: "The Phantom Belgian!" What was *that* about? Nine months into this momentous discovery, each question only led to another.

On the walk back to the cabin, I thought about another old Belgian and his daughter. Inside, I opened ol' pot-bellied Bertha, tossed in a chunk of wood, and took my cell phone out.

"Hi, Rosie? It's Jack. Yes, *that* Jack. How are you? I'm out at the farm, alone.

"Seems like a long time to me, too."

I pitched another log into the furnace. "Glad you liked my e-mails. Anyway, I know it's New Year's Eve, so it's doubtful, but I still have to ask if, by some miracle, you might be available tomorrow night? No, I didn't forget what it was. I'm just caving into a brazen impulse to be with a kindred spirit. You will? Well, uh, excellent! I didn't bring any 'evening out' clothes, but the shower works fine!"

16

THE OLD TRANSISTOR radio I brought to the cabin became my morning companion as I woke up over coffee and mealtime. Fort Wayne had an oldies station I could also rely on for the local weather and news. It said an inch of new snow had fallen overnight, which is how I knew the animal paw prints outside were fresh. The soothing voice of Mother Nature called out to me for a session with her winter habitat to ease my troubled mind.

I bundled up and ventured into the forest.

From the back of the house, I trekked toward the western edge of the woods about fifty yards away. The thick layer of fallen leaves and branches covering the ground crunched under my feet. Two squirrels pranced about while a half-dozen crows cawed high in the trees. Deeper into the woods, and still no wildlife sighting. The bare trees let plenty of sunlight in, giving me a clear view of the terrain.

Every few yards, I saw fallen trees with trunks of varying sizes. I spotted a cluster of rocks, the largest one as high as my waist. It made me wonder what had been here in ancient times.

I heard gurgling sounds and then saw a small creek along the other side of the rock formation. I recalled exploring this part of the woodland with Grandpa. He had said the rocks and brook were likely the reason this section of land escaped clearing for growing crops.

As I returned to the cabin, I embraced the *déjà vu* of the experience. Yet, what seemed like a significant forest back then was much smaller.

Inside, I had a breakfast bar with a glass of milk and more coffee. I reflected on my failing marriage and how my Bugatti was like that rock. Most of the time, all we did was tread water. Sally wanted me to be more ambitious like she was. Perhaps because of her deprived upbringing, she desired material things more than I did. We each expected the other to pursue higher living standards but with differing connotations.

In the afternoon I tried to match more parts, but this time with the illustrations Mickey gave me as a reference. I identified some that weren't on my inventory list or on the floor. I'd have to ask Mickey to know if they were critical. Since the Bugattis were hand-built, variations were not uncommon. In fact, even the numbering system for parts, including the frame, was inconsistent.

Later that afternoon, I got ready for my rendezvous with Rosie. All washed up, shaved, and brushed, I studied the limited attire I had packed for this trip and put on black Docker slacks, a light blue dress shirt, and a brown sweater. I didn't know what to expect for a New Year's Eve in Avilla, but no point in worrying about it.

I pulled up near the café at the time Rosie had requested. At the door, a stiff wind pushed me back. A handwritten note taped to it said, "Private event for Jack."

Inside, I felt the same coziness as before. Twigs of holly and pine cones had replaced the red roses on the tables. As I approached the counter Diane appeared, wrapping herself up in a puffy coat. "Hi, Jack. Have you figured out which table is for you and Rosie?"

I looked and pointed. “The one at the front with a bottle of Merlot and two wine glasses?”

“Brilliant,” she said with no inflection. “So, what’s up with Doug these days?”

“No idea. I kicked Flaven off the project and haven’t spoken since.”

“The SOB never called me after that night in the hay.”

“You’re probably better off,” I said, putting my coat over a counter chair. “Flaven’s a jerk and not trustworthy.”

Diane slipped on her gloves. “Officially, we’re closed. Otherwise, there wouldn’t be a bottle of wine on your table. Rosie will be down any minute.” She took a step towards the back door, then stopped. “One more thing. My sister is special. I love her dearly. Don’t be a jerk like your friend.”

I put up a hand. “May God strike me down.”

“Okay. I’m off to Fort Wayne.”

I sat down, reached for the wine, and read the label. Soon I heard the sound of an oven door opening in the kitchen. Wearing her bib apron, Rosie pulled out a covered tray from the oven and brought the tray to me.

“Hello, stranger.”

I stood up, returning the smile. “Hi, Rosie. Something smells good.”

“Nothing special. Some basic nourishment, since I don’t think we’ll find any place for dinner without lines. And I’m not keen on that. So, behold...” She lifted the cover, revealing hot plates of roast beef, baked potatoes, green beans, mushroom soup cups, and homemade biscuits.

“Mm. Smells delicious!”

“Here.” She handed me a corkscrew from her pocket. “Will you open this while I change out of my cook’s garb?”

“Happy to.”

By the time she returned, I had poured the glasses two-thirds full. Without her hat, I noticed her bobbed brunette hair had grown out to her earlobes, with the ends curled up. She still had the bangs I liked. When she sat down, I handed her a glass and offered a toast.

"To the coincidence of all coincidences. You and I together tonight."

We clinked glasses and drank.

She asked, so I explained what had led to my being in the country on the ultimate party night. Her brown eyes reflected the light of the candle. She listened with empathy to the story of my parents' visit.

That opened the door for her to ask me more about my marital situation. I parsed my words and avoided giving too much information. I kept it brief and without pathos. Then I thanked her for changing her plans to be with me on such a night.

"I planned a quiet night at home with my dad after Diane went to a party in Fort Wayne. It's less than a half-hour away, but her idea of a fun night out is most likely not mine," she said. "Then you called, and I didn't want to sound like a party pooper, so..."

"Hard to believe no one asked you out for tonight."

"I got a couple of clumsy offers but not a thoughtful invitation."

"I thought *my* call was pretty clumsy and airheaded."

"It's not just what you say, but your voice. Yours was humble, coming from a kind-hearted victim of circumstances."

We both drank. I took some roast beef. "Mm, good," I said.

"The secret to making a so-so slice of meat taste good...." She clanked the wine bottle with her fork.

"Wine is good with all things in life," I said. "And speaking of life... please tell me something about yours. Have you always lived in Avilla?"

She swallowed, then sipped some wine. "Born and raised here. Then went to Loyola along the lake in Chicago. Like you, I studied art but focused on interior design. When I graduated, I got an apartment with my dorm roommate near the campus. It was right on the border of East Rogers Park and Edgewater. You familiar with the city?"

"Been there twice," I said. "But not in the neighborhoods."

"Right. Well, I liked the people and the energy there and wanted to put my degree to use. I knew design opportunities would be far better in Chicago than here. Meantime, waitressing got the bills paid. I did a lot of interviews but didn't have the experience and didn't know anyone to refer me.

"Finally I got an entry-level office job at a company that makes and distributes restaurant products, from paper napkins to generic works of art. The kind you see on restaurant walls. The job description said *artistic skills are a plus*."

"Did you get to use them?"

"No. A few illustrations. Then I met Dan, a tall, handsome guy, head of the sales department. We dated—"

A gust of wind blowing against the glass facade drew our attention. The corners of the wide window whined and vibrated.

"That's some wind," I said. "You hear that noise much?"

"No." She went to investigate, and I followed. "The last thing I need is some emergency expenses." She examined the lower sides and corners.

With my height advantage, I looked and pressed along the top. We met in the middle, me above, Rosie below.

She asked, "Feel anything?"

"Nothing to do with the window."

We returned to the table and cleared it together, leaving the wine. After sitting back down and taking a sip, Rosie said, "Let's see. Where was I?"

"Introducing Dan."

"Right. So, long story short, we eventually got hitched and lived in the suburbs. By then, I had spent seven years in the city and the change sounded good."

"And you were in love."

"Yes, of course. About two years later, the bastard started cheating on me. I gave him a second chance. That's when I got pregnant. I had the feeling he was cheating again. Losing the baby was a wake-up call. I divorced him.

"My sister stayed with me for a while to help me through it. I also got some serious therapy to help pull myself back together. She had been helping take care of our dad back here. He was retired, living alone, and not in good health. Our mother had passed away a long time before from a car accident."

Rosie took a breath. "That's when we hatched the idea of the café. My divorce came with a decent monthly check that made it possible. So, I came back here and we shared duties with the business and helping our father."

"When was that?"

"A year and a half ago. Almost two. It's been working out okay. I need to stop by and see Dad before we go wherever for the night."

"Is he a native of the area?"

"Yes. He worked on some farms, delivered a lot of grain, and did other things. Mostly, he drove a fuel truck for the Farm Co-op, delivering propane to farmers all over the county."

"I'd be interested in meeting him."

"You're sure?"

I nodded.

"Okay. Well, I need to stop by in about a half hour." She stood up. "I'm going upstairs to change and freshen up. You might as well finish what's left of the wine."

She disappeared through the back door. While waiting, I thought about the parallels and the differences in our lives and why they mattered to me.

Ten minutes later, Rosie returned wearing a short, black taffeta dress over black tights with knee-high leather boots. A gold necklace with blue stones graced a long-sleeved red satin top. She had sparkle make-up around her eyes, teased hair, and cherry-red lipstick.

"Wow," I said. "Pat Benatar in the flesh!"

"I kicked it up a notch. It will get Dad's attention."

"It works for me!"

We entered the brick ranch house from the side door by the garage. I noted a hint of pipe tobacco smoke. Rosie led me into the kitchen, where she dropped her coat and purse on a chair. She yelled out to alert her dad she had arrived with her date, and then we proceeded to a beige living room.

Her father sat in a worn, stuffed recliner next to a window. The opposite wall featured a variety of framed pictures of family and friends, several yellowed with time. His eyes were on an old model TV showing the Lawrence Welk Show.

"Hi, Dad." She kissed him on the cheek.

His eyes widened. "You're all dressed up!"

"It's New Year's Eve. Remember?" She pulled me from behind his chair to stand in front of him. "Here's the gentleman taking me out. Meet Jack."

A stout, silver-haired man with extra pounds on an otherwise middle-weight fighter's frame attempted to stand.

"Please. No need to get up for me, sir." I put out my hand. "A pleasure to meet you."

His body may have been weak, but he still had a hearty grip with thick fingers. "Roger Vermeulen," he said in a raspy voice. He turned to Rosie. "Are you going to celebrate the new year starting or the old one ending?"

"Both!"

"I see." Roger studied me. "What's your name again?"

"Jack. Jack Reinhart."

"He's the new owner of the farm out west of town," Rosie said. "You know, the first one. Sort of looks over a meadow."

Roger rubbed his stubbled chin. "Don't recall any Reinharts around here."

"It was my grandfather's farm back in the early 1930s. His last name was Dreyfus. My grandmother was born in a small town between here and Fort Wayne. They moved to Cleveland after my mom was born. Many years later, she married a man named Reinhart."

"You two continue your chat," Rosie said, "while I check on things."

The old man ran a hand through his wispy white hair. He had deep wrinkles and a square, reddish nose. "Your grandfather's place… it's not much of a farm, as I recall. Never delivered propane out there."

"He had forty acres originally. Because of the Depression, the bank was going to repossess the farm, so he made a deal with a neighboring farmer and held on to a parcel with a couple of buildings. Years later, my Mom and I lived in Cleveland. I'd spend quality time with Grandpa out there on the farm, mostly in the summer. I have fond memories there."

Rosie returned, drying her hands with a dish towel. "Take your pills, Dad?"

He nodded.

"I took care of the few dishes in the sink and checked the fridge. You're all set for the night unless you drink all the beer." He grinned. "Can you think of anything you need other than pipe tobacco?"

He shook his head.

"No? Okay."

"Well, you two have a good time."

"Nice to meet you, Roger," I said, extending my hand. We shook.

"What's that name again? Your grandfather's?"

"Dreyfus. Came over from Belgium between the World Wars."

Rosie took my arm and was leading me toward the back door when Roger suddenly cried out, "The Phantom Belgian!"

I froze. Then I turned around and walked back into the living room. "Did you say *Phantom Belgian*?"

"He lived out there. Not for very long."

"On my grandfather's farm?"

Roger nodded.

"He came from Belgium. But why on earth did they call him a phantom?"

"Some thought he was the one who raced around here late at night. Right down the main street in a car nobody had ever seen before or since. He'd make a cloud of smoke and then disappear like a ghost!"

"Did you see it yourself? What did it look like?"

"Yeah, a couple of times. The car was black and red if memory serves me right."

My jaw dropped. My heart pounded in my chest. I forced myself to breathe.

Roger chuckled to himself. "Haven't thought about that in a long, long time. Some boys drove out there looking for the car after he left and moved out for good. Couldn't find any sign of it."

"Oh, my God... thanks so much, Roger. I will remember you forever for this."

Behind me, Rosie's eyes seemed to have doubled in size. She gave her father a loving touch on his head.

One step outside, I whipped Rosie into a tight circle and hugged her.

"I can't remember the last time his memory triggered like that," she said.

"I guess I struck the right note."

"Yes, you have."

THE JUKEBOX PLAYED the hit song "1999" as we walked into Pastimes. It had been a decade and a half since it was released. It had been re-released not long ago with an update.

It was only a little after eight o'clock and people were already packed in. About half of those at tables and booths were eating a late dinner or ordering one. The rest of them, early revelers in first gear, were playing darts, tethered to the pinball machines, or shoving metal pucks on the shuffleboard. I spotted one lone stool in the middle of the bar, which I gave to Rosie.

Joe's wife, Betsy, was helping tonight, bouncing between tables and booths to and from the kitchen. After jotting down an order for the table next to us, she spotted Rosie. "Oh my, don't you look special tonight! Enough to make a flower shy. You waiting for someone?"

"Yeah. A cute, big-city gentleman. Seen any?"

"This fella right here is better than average."

Rosie slapped her hand down on the bar. "I'll take him!"

The ladies laughed. "I'll signal you when the next booth opens up," said Betsy, and moved on to other customers.

I leaned over the bar to get Joe's attention and noticed an extra bartender.

"I'd like a Heineken, Jack," Rosie said.

"Perfect," I said. "Do you know the guy helping Joe behind the bar?"

"Yeah, it's their son."

Just then, the son afforded me a second look to detect the family traits. He stood as tall as his dad but with half his weight. Same long hair in a ponytail, but light brown. He took my request for two Heinies on draft.

Rosie said, "Quite a few new faces. Wish I could get them into *my* place."

"If you had an advertising sandwich board?" I said. "*Eat at Rosie's.* With images of your baked goods and coffee?"

"Yes! And a salad, soup, eggs, and bacon with a stack of pancakes—"

"Now you're talking about a walking billboard!"

"No. Put breakfast on the front and lunch on the back."

"I suppose you'd want a telephone number and a website, too?"

"I don't have a website yet. So, when are you making one for me?"

"You'd be too tough as a client."

"As tough as they come, mister." She shot me a demure face.

I bent close to her. "You look as mean as a cherub holding a ripe strawberry in your mouth." Slowly, I kissed her soft lips.

"Sorry to interrupt you kids." Betsy stood holding an empty tray. "But I'm about to clear a booth, so you better be close behind."

We did as she said and claimed the most valuable piece of real estate in Avilla that night. Its cozy privacy came just at the right time as Joe Junior arrived with our beers.

I offered a toast. "May the new year bring us both better days!"

We clinked our mugs and drank, leaving foam mustaches on us. We laughed, wiping them away. Then Rosie cleared a smattering of suds on my snout.

"There. Any on my nose?"

I said, "Yours is clean, little lady. Maybe it's an omen for the night."

The jukebox streamed rock, pop, and country oldies. Plenty of Mellencamp. Joe had a college bowl game on the TV with the sound down low. Add the buzz from the packed house and we had a happening small-town party!

"Now that we can talk without yelling at each other," I said, "tell me how the café business is doing."

"It's been about two years. I'm almost breaking even. We could use some of these customers and more, especially from surrounding towns like Kendallville, Swan, and Corunna."

"Corunna? Really?"

"Yeah, it sounds like I'm a drunk trying to say Corona," she replied. "Anyway, that's break even without a regular paycheck for me. Diane gets minimum wage and we split tips. I do it that way because I'm getting alimony. I hate it, but..." She shrugged.

"You like the café business?"

"Funny, I really don't think of it as a business. It's something I enjoy doing. And it keeps me out of trouble."

"Until now," I winked. "What about artistic endeavors?"

"It has a creative side. My favorite is making a palette of frosting colors and painting my baked goods."

"Making note to self: *loves fooling around with frosting*." She smacked my arm. "What about Diane? How does she fit in?"

"We don't always agree or like doing the same things. I'm older, but I don't mind Diane taking charge. She likes doing the books, dealing with vendors, and waiting tables. She knows I'm the better cook. And we share cleaning duties. I've got the kitchen. She does the front."

"Starting a business is tough," I said. "I got lucky that my stepdad helped me. I started freelancing and built a client list. Most were only one-time projects. Now I have a dozen priority customers who give me several assignments every year. They usually start in the first group and then give me more work."

"Do you rent a studio, or—"

"The second bedroom in our apartment."

"That I get a two-bedroom apartment with my building makes it reasonably affordable. So, we're kind of in the same boat."

We finished our beers, so I went to the bar for another round and wished Joe a Happy New Year. I had never seen him moving, gliding behind the bar. "You're like a traffic cop at peak drive time," I said, handing him the mugs.

He put them under the taps and let the beer flow. "One night like this pays utilities for a year. It's a matter of surviving it."

"You deserve a Happy New Year!" I said.

"Same to you!" he said, passing me the beer with foam spilling over.

When I returned to the booth, Rosie picked up where she had left off.

"The thing is, I don't have any grand expectations. No desire whatever to have 'Rosie's' franchises all over the place. Diane is even more old school. Didn't go to college. Had jobs as a cashier for a couple places. She's biding time until the right guy drops out of the sky. If that happens before I discover something better to do with my God-given talents, Rosie's enterprise collapses." She made an explosion sound while spreading her hands.

"What are the chances she finds a guy?"

"Look around, Jack. How many men do you see with a genuine appeal like you?"

"Me?"

"My point is, you can count the number of quality prospects around here on one hand. Besides, Diane is younger and enjoys the single life. You recall how easily she gave up her goodies to Doug in the hayloft."

"Point taken." I glanced at Joe. "He's exhausting himself. Hope *he* doesn't collapse."

The crashing cymbals and organ chords sounded off once again for "1999," much to the crowd's delight. With almost two more hours of partying to go, Rosie suggested we had better get an appetizer before the kitchen closed. She asked if I had any preference. "Food," I said. She smirked and started towards the back.

All the tables and booths were still full, but newcomers replaced many of those having dinner. Betsy continued to make runs back and forth. I could see the empathy on Rosie's face for her.

A few minutes later, Rosie introduced me to a woman she knew in high school who was dressed to stir up the testosterone in the pool of qualified men. She gave me a once-over. Rosie said I was a second cousin from Georgia visiting over the holidays.

"Well, you are as cute as a peach," the woman said. "But I see from your ring that you're married. You haven't got an unhitched brother or cousin nearby?"

With my best southern drawl, I said, "Why, no, pretty lady, I don't. But for the right price, I'll lose the ring and suddenly have amnesia." I sounded so lame.

Rosie looked like she was going to burst. The woman adjusted her push-up bra and disappeared into the standing-room crowd.

Rosie and I both guffawed. When Rosie caught her breath, she asked if I had any siblings.

I explained how I was an only child and how my dad died in Vietnam when I was little.

"How do you feel about kids? Do you have any?"

"No kids. I like them, especially when they're cute little cuddly creatures, but then they grow up. Someone told me once, 'Little kids—little problems. Big kids—big problems."

"Makes sense."

I thought about my fight with Sally about having a baby. It must have shown on my face.

"What is it, Jack?"

"She wants kids, and I don't. Not right now. Not with her, anyway."

The backup bartender delivered our snack. "Hi, Bert!" said Rosie. "Jack, this is Joe and Betsy's son."

"I can see the resemblance to the old man."

"I get that a lot," Bert said.

"Good for you, helping out," said Rosie. "I was about to abandon my date to help your mother myself."

"I'll tell her. But we're good." He pried a grin from behind his goatee and dissolved into the swarm.

The fried mushrooms and nacho chips tasted so good with the beer. Then an alert went on in my head to slow down and share. I once dated a girl who asked me if I was raised by wolves from the way I scarfed down a meal.

THE COLLEGE FOOTBALL game on TV ended, and Joe turned the channel to Dick Clark's New Year's Eve show. A smattering of women applauded. He muted the sound in deference to the music. Before long, Rosie asked for a strawberry margarita to help wash down the salt and grease. I whisked myself away to the bar, hoping to end the talk of kids, and ordered a bourbon and a strawberry daiquiri.

Two sips into her rum drink, Rosie started reeling off anecdotes about certain people around us. She knew some firsthand, and others were tales from what she swore were reliable sources. I'd laugh and say, "Only in a small town." Then she'd say, "That's a fact, Jack!"

I especially liked one about a wedding invitation with a potluck dinner. It's the postscript— Bring meat! And the scandalous Dish-towel Chain Letter! None of them were mean-spirited. I don't think she had a mean bone in her body.

A married couple Rosie knew well came over and asked if they could sit with us to rest their legs, and she welcomed them in. A few minutes later, they left, and two older women came by for the same reason. When one started digging into my background like an interrogation, she came up with a Duesy about me. I was with a mob syndicate out of Cleveland, running a gaming operation at the farm.

Rosie pointed out a high school rival known for her coming on to guys at the get-go. As she predicted, the woman drifted beside me and leaned forward, displaying her plentiful cleavage. When she asked about me, Rosie said I was like a third roommate at Loyola and pinched my cheek. "Look at this doll's face. We had some pretty hot times. You wouldn't believe the money he makes now in Chicago as a gigolo."

With only a glint of doubt from the woman, I gave her a steely-eyed grin. "Don't doubt me if you haven't done me." She held my look, and I said, "I'll meet you any time you want in the ladies' room. I know this trick hanging from the stalls." I nodded my head towards the restrooms in the back and winked. Rosie cracked up, revealing our prank on the woman.

Rosie and I engaged in the shenanigans with natural ease. We had chemistry! And if the local grapevine had a field day, I didn't care. Why not keep them guessing as long as my treasure remained hidden?

AN HOUR BEFORE MIDNIGHT, the party had kicked into top gear. I got another Jack Daniels. Rosie still had half her quart-sized margarita.

Those conversing had grown so loud that they muffled the jukebox. I explained to Rosie my theory that the volume in the room rose in direct correlation to the amount of booze consumed.

She hollered back, "You want another cocktail?" Underlining my point with a grin.

In Indiana, bars could still have smokers if they were restricted to one section of the room. An idiot's compromise, and on a night like this absurdly so. Because I lived with a smoker, the fumes didn't bother me much. That we spent most of our time sitting made the smoke more tolerable.

By eleven-thirty, many of the senior set chose to leave and have their midnight salute at home. This opened the space up enough for a handful of heartier partiers to create a dancing zone next to the video games and jukebox. Prince's song repeated more frequently, and more people joined the refrain, "like it's NINETEEN NINETY-NINE!" The chant became infectious, and Rosie and I were not immune. She took my hand and led me into the crush of dancers.

We bounced and twisted to the pulsating beat. When NINETEEN NINETY-NINE came around again, everyone flailed their arms with a vocal explosion rattling the tin ceiling.

At a quarter to midnight, Betsy came to Rosie and asked her to help serve up a champagne toast. I tagged along.

Bert was laying down rows of sample-size plastic cups. They had opened a case of the beverage behind the bar and Rosie and Betsy started pouring at opposite ends of the rows. I stood guard to deter anyone from snatching the wine prematurely.

Then Joe took out an old police bullhorn and invited celebrants to the bar for a cup of complimentary bubbly. The TV flashed images of the crowds in Times Square and the crystal ball about to drop. Joe Junior turned up the sound.

Most of the Pastime patrons joined the countdown at ten seconds. Then, "five, four, three, two, one, HAPPY NEW YEAR!" the participants shouted. "Auld Lang Syne" played and many sang along. They tossed streamers into the air. Kissing couples surrounding us. Rosie and I looked at each other, shrugged, then kissed lightly. Holding hands, we swayed until the song's end.

Betsy had taken the bar stool nearest the door. As customers entered the chilly night, she and Joe offered thanks and best wishes for the new year. Many they called by name. Meanwhile, Bert took over as bartender for the diehards who were ordering fresh rounds of drinks.

The instant I held my coat, Rosie grabbed my hand and pulled me through the back exit. I tossed my arms in the air, braced my body with winter air, lassoed my coat around her, and pressed my face into her nape. She cooed and rubbed my back.

"Hey, Rosie."

"What?"

"This!" And I landed a full-mouth kiss on her lips. "That's to make up for the trivial smack we resorted to at midnight."

"We?" She retook my hand. "Come along with me, you masher!"

"I will follow you. Follow you wherever you may go! I have complete *thrust* in you."

She giggled. "You are drunk, Jack Reinhart."

"Yeah, the third Jack Daniels did it. Joe makes a generous cocktail."

"For *you* because he likes you."

"Really? Well, I like him for an ex-copper."

She led me toward the back of her apartment. At the stairs, she said, "I caution you, THESE ARE STEPS," she over-articulated.

At the top, I heard the door click. A light flashed on and revealed a kitchen as kitsch as Rosie's cafe. "Welcome to my humble abode." She hung up first her coat and then mine.

She led me into the next room, appointed with throw rugs, warm-colored ruffled curtains, and pillows thrown onto a stuffed chair and a small couch.

"This is the living room," she said. We took a few steps, and she directed my eyes down a short hallway. "At the back, there is the bathroom. On the right is Diane's bedroom. And this—" She swung her arm out. "This is my bedroom."

"May I...?"

"Yes, you may enter."

Original art of varying sizes hung on the walls. The furnishings included a tall, aged dresser, a tiny vanity, a double bed with brass posts, and an old-fashioned quilt. A spicy floral scent delighted my senses. I turned around to face her, my back to the bed, and said, "I like it!"

Feeling tipsy, I draped myself on her for support. We tilted her way, then mine, and then gravity brought us down onto the bed.

We studied each other's faces. I took a slow, deep breath. "Rosie, my darling...."

"Yes, Jack, my sweetheart..."

"May I just lay here for a little while and share your air?"

"Yes. You're in no condition to...."

THE NEXT TIME I opened my eyes, darkness surrounded me. It took me a few seconds to realize I was in Rosie's bed.

I dreamed I fell asleep after making love with her in the hayloft. Familiar voices nearby awakened me, so I turned and saw Flaven on top of her sister Diane, calling out football "hut-huts." She called out an orgasmic, "deeper, deeper, deeper!" Then Flaven turned to me and, with an evil grin, said, "Watch me really nail that receiver!" He fell hard on the girl. When he rolled off, Sally, not Diane, sat up, looked at me, and said, "Rah, rah, rah!"

That's when I awoke. I looked around and rubbed my eyes.

Sunlight came in through a window, prompting me to take another look. It took me a second to realize that I lay alone in Rosie's bed, still dressed. A long crack of lightning banged hard on my head as I tried to sit up. Then more noise that sounded like metalworks next door pounding iron. Peering out of a window, I recognized Avilla's Main Street.

I shuffled the sink next to the toilet, splashed cold water on my face and around my neck, and then relieved my bladder. After washing my hands and finger-brushing my teeth, I looked at the reflection in the mirror.

An old, bloodshot, puddy-faced man looked back. My hair stood up in wadded clumps. "*New wave*, dude!" I said and shuffled onward to the kitchen.

Rosie sat at the small round table by a window that looked out into the alley and beyond. She wore a yellow Loyola sweatshirt, blue jeans, and matching yellow socks as she sipped coffee from a mug with an image of the Eiffel Tower and "City of Lights."

As I inched toward her, she looked up and said, "Welcome to 1999, Jack!"

With a low, hoarse voice, I waved my arms and said, "Hurray for 1999."

"I've had a two-hour jump on you," she said. "So sit, and I'll pour."

Two ibuprofen sat on the placemat next to a glass of water. I swallowed them and thanked the kind woman.

"You are welcome. Now sit." She put a cup of coffee on the mat. "You take cream, don't you?"

I nodded.

She handed me a small carton of Half & Half. I stirred it into the coffee and drank, and then tried to clear my throat. "Do not fear the sound emanating from my mouth. I am a peaceful monster and will not harm you."

She chuckled. "I'm making a little breakfast. Just sit and sip your way back to life."

"The last thing I remember is the view from the top of your stairs."

"Is that all?"

I nodded.

"Then I'm happy to say you were amazing last night, start to finish."

"Doing what?"

She grinned. "Just teasing. I gave you a tour of the apartment, then you passed out on my bed. On top of me. I squeezed out and took Diane's bed."

"It's New Year's Day, right? So why is the factory next door open? That clank-clunk, clank-clunk?"

"Oh! That must have been my coffee grinder. I'm sorry."

"No need to apologize. It's excellent coffee."

She served her favorite "night-after" breakfast—homemade cinnamon rolls with bacon and orange juice. Ironically, my talking skills were coming back, but I couldn't think of what to say next. Feeling a tad embarrassed, I thanked Rosie for everything—the dinner and the breakfast—and said I needed to get back to the farm to clean up and start the day.

She brought my coat out from somewhere. I looked her up and down and said, "Cute outfit, by the way."

"Oh, yes. Go Ramblers!"

"You're welcome to come out later if you'd like. I'm not going back to Cleveland until tomorrow afternoon. I've got lots of firewood to keep the cabin warm."

"Wood fires are nice. Any more furnishings than the last time I was there?"

"A microwave and wooden stool."

"Okay. Did you have anything in mind?"

"Let me think. I could use some interior design advice."

"You said you're selling the cabin."

"Honestly, I like you. And hanging out with a fellow artist might be a good way to start a new year. Oh, and in case I didn't say it last night, your artwork in the bedroom is first-rate."

"You remembered. Thanks." When I opened the door, she added, "Some light snow fell last night, so be careful going down the steps."

I took a watchful step into the white powder, looked back at her, and said, "Just a dusting." Halfway down, I checked to see if she was still watching. She was. We gave little waves.

I took an indirect route back to the farm, first driving by Pastimes and then turning toward the section of town with the Catholic Church, the school, and the playground. The northbound road led me to a crossroads. I turned west into farmland as a picture of Rosie's sweet face kept reappearing in my mind's eye.

WINTER 1999

ON MY WAY back to the cabin from Rosie's, I called Sally as a courtesy—or out of guilt—to tell her I had survived New Year's Eve, Avilla-style. The answering machine came on, and I left a message.

She likely spent last night with some friends at the Old Town bar or with Gap management friends to continue networking. That included male friends. As much as she wants kids, Sally wouldn't have been at her sister's house. And I knew she didn't anchor herself in the apartment to watch a Marx Brothers marathon, which was my regular routine.

The midday sun had already melted most of the snow, but the cabin was still freezing, so I filled Bertha's belly. When the temperature got warm enough, I took a shower. Being refreshed and in clean clothes cleared the remaining fog in my head. My mini coffee pot would brew enough for me and Rosie if she came out. I pulled a sketchpad from my backpack, sat at the desk, and started doodling.

In *Mr. Deeds Goes To Town*, Gary Cooper introduces doodling as something people do when they've got something on their minds. I had plenty on mine. My technique goes further: unpacking a complex project or situation with illustrations, words, and numbers as needed.

My right hand dashed out all kinds of lines and curves. Heavy ones formed roads on three sides. I added some trees and clouds about two-thirds to the top. An abstract of the farm continued to emerge, with the barn on the left and the cabin along the road on the right.

I held the pencil on a slant and shaded in parts of the sketch for texture. The outline of a vintage car then appeared inside the barn. A woman's face surfaced in the center of the page; then a second woman, more petite, inside the cabin.

The aroma of coffee pulled me away. I fetched some, looked at my scribbles, and then gazed outside at the meadow beyond the front lawn. My vision panned out beyond the county road to the sunny landscape of fields and trees before returning to the desk.

Dollar figures came to mind. Under the car I wrote $50,000, then $250,000. Next to the cabin I wrote and circled $12,500, adding dashes to the $250,000 figure.

The outline of a colonial house appeared in the clouds and then linked to the woman's face in the center. The numbers related to each other, so I drew a line of dashes from the $250k to the dream house and put three small "x's" inside the colonial frame.

I put the pencil behind my ear, leaned back, and drank more coffee. The Art Institute of Cleveland emblem on the mug captured my attention. I glanced back at the drawing and then at the AIC logo. I chuckled. "You guys want your degree back?"

These chicken scratches can take a while to reveal my subconscious thoughts. I poured more coffee for a warmup and walked the perimeter of the cabin, tidying up what few things I had.

The drawing called me back. I gave the picture a squint test; then I ripped the abstraction from the pad, crushed the paper into a ball, and tossed it toward the bedroom area. Another mental note: trash container.

The outdoors called to me. With my parka zipped up and the

hood on, I circled the barn, looking again for vulnerable areas. I wondered how far Flaven's slip of the tongue about the Bugatti project had spread and when someone in the media would call me.

An image of Flaven and Sally celebrating New Year's Eve came into my mind. I shook my head and tapped a section of rotten wood at the base of the barn on the west side. Soft, but not big enough to worry about. I focused on adding an interior crossbar to the double doors, a deadbolt lock on the side door, and some kind of alarm. The few windows were too high to consider securing.

Back inside the barn, I scanned the black and red painted steel pieces and the gray iron engine. All appeared to be in good condition. The mahogany dashboard needed considerable work on the indicators and related wiring, plus the edges of the wood itself. The original varnish protected most of it but the cutouts for the speedometer, tachometer, heat, and pressure gauges had decayed.

For the first time, the body parts looked pointlessly scattered around the chassis. I turned on the room heaters and started organizing them.

The front left fender fit over its matching wheel and leaned against the metal frame. I aligned the fender and placed a bolt through the holes in the chassis, roughly connecting them. Easy enough, I thought and moved on to the other three. I attached all but the last one with little effort, then joined the running boards, linking the front and back fenders on both sides. The rear body unit appeared somewhat connected. I wondered why I didn't think of this before.

I heard Rosie's voice calling my name. I stepped outside and spotted her by the house. She stood out in a puffy blue vest over a yellow sweatshirt. I shouted, "Over here!" and waved.

She held a sketchbook under her arm. As she approached the barn, she said, "You better have some heat in there."

"Enough to take the cold edge off for a short visit. Come in and see what I've done today."

I closed the doors behind us. "Hey, you've got a car in here!" she said.

"Yeah, it's suddenly looking like one, anyway. The bolts aren't tightened. This is just a visual exercise. Everything needs to be stripped, patched, primed, and repainted."

Rosie walked around the assembled parts with analytical eyes, and then she nodded. "Nice design lines! The floorboard has a Nike swish kind of look."

"That was Jean Bugatti's artistic touch."

"Are you taking photos to document the stages of the restoration?"

"I haven't been, but that's a good idea."

Vapor came from our mouths as we spoke. She had wrapped her arms around herself. "Are you keeping the same colors?"

"Definitely. My expert, Mickey, is certain they're the factory colors. Faded, of course. Maybe a brighter red, like your nose right now. Come on, let's get you in the house." I picked up the stool before locking the barn.

Even though Rosie welcomed the warmth, she kept her coat on. I gave Bertha more wood and removed my parka.

Rosie began studying the space. "Pretty much as I remember it, but with a few more things. And this…." She looked into the new bathroom. "Not bad. Tiny, but functional." Returning to the center, she said, "I already gave you some decorating ideas. Did you forget them?"

"I have but one excuse. Your stupefying beauty."

She laughed, reached into her purse, and pulled a tape measure. "As I recall, I didn't think you were serious then so I just spouted off a few ideas. That I'm measuring your space is a sign I'm almost serious this time."

"Can I make you some fresh coffee, hot chocolate, or oyster soup?"

"Hot chocolate sounds good."

I put bottled water into an old teakettle, placed it on top of Bertha, and poured two packets of instant chocolate into mugs. Rosie put her pad on the desk. With the metal tape, she measured the living room, kitchen, and bedroom areas and jotted down numbers for each. She also recorded ceiling heights.

The kettle whistled, so I poured, stirred, and handed Rosie the cup. I tried to see her notes from over her shoulder.

"No peeking," she chirped.

"I'll just use one eye."

"You're nutty."

I returned to the counter, sipped some Swiss Miss, and opened my laptop. Rosie ripped a

sheet from her pad, folded it into a paper airplane, and tossed it at me shouting, "Airmail!"

The airplane fluttered and landed at Bertha's feet. The message said, *Get some furniture!* "That's all you got?"

"That's the number-one thing you need to do. Number two involves moving the back wall out a good eight to ten feet. This will enable you to wall off the bedroom and replace the emergency exit door you gave up for the toilet.

"Third, push out the north wall and use one-third of the new space for a utility room with a washer and dryer. Finally, create a real office for yourself in the northeast corner. This will allow you to have a true living room."

"I love it!"

"But do nothing until you decide your future." Rosie spotted my balled-up sketch on the floor and picked it up. "What's this?" She slowly peeled it open and began to read. "Hmm. Developing a website game?"

I acted casual. "No, just some doodling. Need to get a trash container in here."

Rosie started examining it and said, "Looks like you were trying to—"

I snatched the paper back and turned away from her.

"What's the problem? You don't like me reading your trash?" She reached for the paper from behind me, pressing her body into my back.

I used my height advantage, holding it away.

"Let me see what you've got there, mister."

I escaped to the kitchen area. Rosie trailed me like a cat. "Come on, Jacky-boy." The game was afoot.

"No way!" I said, smiling. I darted to the bedroom, kicked off my shoes, and stood on the laid-out sleeping bag.

Off came her shoes as the cute cook slinked towards me. I held the "keep-away" paper above my head as she jumped and swiped to no avail. Then came her surrender. "Okay. I'll stop pestering you for such a personal thing." She turned away and took one step, and that was enough to catch me off guard. Her tackle landed me on the makeshift bed. If not for the air mattress under the sleeping bag, I might've been injured.

Lying on my back, I said, "You pack some power in that petite frame."

Rosie rested her head on my chest. I caught an herbal scent from her hair. She sat up and, responding to the buoyancy of the mattress, said, "Oh! Nice and bouncy!"

I sat upright, too. In teeter-totter fashion, we alternated going up and down as the air shifted underneath us. My weight advantage raised her body off the bed: the law of physics in action. We laughed ourselves into a ball and kissed.

"How did we get so far off track?" she asked.

"I blame myself," I said, and then gave her my doodling.

She sat up in the position of Rodin's *The Thinker* to examine it. "Hmm. Hieroglyphics?"

"Stream of consciousness."

After studying it, she said, “Okay, I think I’ve deciphered your code. Want to hear?”

“Please. I’d like to know what it means, too.”

“You need fifty thousand dollars to restore the car. Then, if you sold it, you could get up to a two hundred thousand net return.” She looked at me. “Really?”

I nodded. “Could be more if it’s restored to ‘show car’ level.”

“Is this house only worth ten thousand dollars?”

“Up to twenty for the whole property.”

“Let’s see… then you apply the quarter-million to a house with a family of three…”

“If *she* has her way. Congratulations, you’ve identified the pieces of the puzzle to come up with a plan. Now, solve it for me.”

She dropped onto her back. I did the same. The sun in the January sky hovered on the horizon, casting amber rays into the room. The burning wood crackled.

“Wait!” Rosie turned towards me. “You have the car making zero to two hundred and fifty. Why the zero?”

“That’s the miracle option. I keep the car, eliminating the quarter million dollar house.”

She was quiet for a moment. “I’m not sure what to say.”

“It boils down to *my* dream versus *hers*. Before this inheritance came along we were having problems, but it was just the usual things. Now we’re at odds over a suburban life with kids versus me and my grandfather’s Bugatti given new life.”

Rosie still had my doodle exercise in her hands. “Your wife looks cute in your drawing.”

“Sally is the one with the long hair.”

“Then who’s the other—? She jumped to her feet. “You must have flunked your illustration class. That’s a lousy rendering of me if that’s—”

“There’s a reason I’m a graphic designer, not an illustrator.”

“I never thought to ask if you had a girlfriend hidden somewhere." Rosie walked away. "Never thought I'd be the other woman."

I wanted to say I didn't go looking for one, but I knew it wouldn't help the situation. Her visit was over. I prayed it wasn't her last.

I NEEDED to follow up with George about the financial arrangement and wondered about introducing the "Rosie factor." My eyes were fixed on the Ohio Turnpike's median strip toward the morning light, driving back to Cleveland.

Then I realized that would be stupid, given her ambivalence. And how would I explain? I guess I had my own doubts about rushing into a new relationship. Besides, we hadn't made love, not sexually. A kiss on New Year's Eve didn't qualify as a love affair. In the 1930s movies, just expressing romantic feelings to a woman was called *making love*.

Did I have romantic feelings for Rosie? Yes, and guilty!

George had been through two marriages before he met my mother. His first one ended in divorce; cancer took his second wife. He would have some understanding of what I was going through. And I liked George. He came from an era when men said as little as possible about their women or their marriages. He told me once, "I never got into trouble by keeping my mouth shut."

Knowing Sally would still be at work when I arrived at the apartment eased my anxiety. I went to my office to catch up on a chamber orchestra project. A yellow sticky note on my computer screen said, "Asshole!"

I was just glad my iMac wasn't smashed. I did the flyer design and print ad by the middle of the afternoon, which was noonish Arizona time.

Mom answered the call. In her chipper voice, she wished me a Happy New Year.

I reciprocated.

She asked me how I was doing.

"Fine," I said. Let me talk with George."

His voice sounded reassuring.

"There was something I couldn't say during your visit," I said. "Sally and I are having serious marital issues."

"Yeah, we figured something was going on between you two."

I explained how we'd been going in different directions. Sally wanted a baby and a big house in a prestigious suburb. I wanted neither. I described how I'd been bitten by the Bugatti mystique.

"Not surprised," he said. *"A lot of men catch that bug."*

"So, the thing is..." I cleared my throat. "I want Grandpa's car. Not to turn around and sell. But to own, if there's any way possible."

"Okay."

"And I won't sell the farm because Sally is desperate for that damn suburban house. Ironically, she knows we can't afford her dream home without selling the Bugatti fully restored. We're even further apart about starting a family."

"I see. You've got marital issues and now you've fallen for someone else."

My heart stopped. Did my stepdad already know about Rose?

"And her name is Bugatti."

"Yeah, that's it. More or less."

"Falling in love with our cars has been a weakness of men since cars came into being. We talk about them like they were girlfriends or lovers. No problem with that as long as you don't do anything foolish."

"Isn't buying a big house, especially one you can't afford, foolish? Hell, it'd be a stretch paying the taxes on the house she has in mind."

"Well, yes, and your mother would agree. But that's another conversation. Now, what about the farm?"

"Right. I realize nostalgia is influencing me. It's the connection to Grandpa and, I suppose, not wanting to let that go. Maybe I won't always feel the same, but that little country place has become my escape. A place to relax and recharge."

After a beat, he said, *"How old are you now?"*

"Thirty-four."

"I was restless and uncertain at that age myself. Thinking about where I was in my career and my life."

"Is that when you got divorced?"

"It was. I had some of the same issues you're having." He paused again. *"Tell you what, Jack. I hear what you're saying. It does change things in my mind. I'm glad you trusted me enough to share your more personal situation. I'll put that into my thinking about our financial arrangement and get back to you."*

He hesitated. *"You know that your mother sides with Sally about the family thing. It's the woman's perspective. But I know you are in her heart. We will do what we can to help you out, son."*

When I told Sally that George needed more time to consider the financing, her nonchalant response baffled me. The urgency she'd had back in the spring had disappeared. I decided to treat it like a racecar driver who continued under the caution flag, alerted to a crash ahead. I'd simply hold my position for the time being.

When George called me back, he said, *"How are you feeling?"*

"To be honest, a little anxious."

"Okay. Well, here's the deal, Jack." He told me they would invest up to thirty-five thousand dollars in restoring the Bugatti with a

share in ownership. He expected me to do as much work as possible to keep within that budget.

After the restoration, the car would be mine until winter. Then George would hold the car for a few months in Arizona. That lets him show it off in the southwest while saving me the hassle of storing it during the harsh weather here in Ohio. I would have it the rest of the year in Cleveland. After three years, he would revert complete ownership to me. If, at that point, I decided to sell it, they would get ten percent of the net with a cap of fifty thousand dollars.

"You see where I'm going here?" George said.

"Yes. The Bugatti is separated from my other issues."

"Right. I figure three years is plenty of time to resolve your marital situation. You can tell Sally we approached this arrangement as a business deal, but not for a profit. Frankly, this is now a deal between two vintage car fans: you and me."

"And Mom's okay with this?"

"I wouldn't have called if she wasn't."

"What if she gets wind of my—situation?"

"I can't stop her from talking to Sally or to anyone else. Last thing I'll say, Jack, is that moms can be mighty good listeners concerning matters of the heart."

I got a twinge in my gut. "This is the second time you've invested in me."

"Setting you up in your own business was risky, without any collateral. I'll be coming after your Bugatti if you fold on this one. Understood?"

"Loud and clear."

WHEN SALLY GOT HOME LATER that day, I tried to tell her about the update from George but she cut me off. "Just shut up and let me talk! God, everything's not always about *you*, Jack!"

"I'm sorry. Bad habit."

"Okay. Well, today the top brass at the GAP made me a General Manager!"

"Congratulations! You've wanted this for a long time. I'm happy for you."

"It's about damn time I got promoted! I'm getting the store in Parma. The one out in Orange would be better. Still, it's a nice salary plus commission and benefits."

"Good deal!" I said. She had this in the pipeline, which is why she didn't care about the delay from George.

Instead of hugs and kisses, we tolerated an uncomfortable few seconds.

"We need to celebrate by eating out," I said.

"Damn right!"

LITTLE ITALY WAS a row of restaurants and shops on a hillside street between Cleveland Heights and University Circle. When Sally ran out of words, I updated her about the financing deal George and Mom offered and she listened intently. "George has become personally interested in the Bugatti and wants shared ownership in it."

She paused for a moment to digest my words. "So, we won't get to sell it for three years?"

"You need to think of the funds as collateral."

She took a drag on a cigarette and let out the smoke. "I see."

The wheels in her head were spinning. I didn't want her digging deeper into the plan, so I said, "Anyway, tonight is about you, celebrating your new job!"

"Hell, yes!"

Inside the restaurant, she asked the middle-aged waiter for one of their best red wines and how the lobsters looked. He returned to our table with the bottle of wine, opened it, and tried to hand me the cork. I gestured to Sally. "She's the boss here tonight." Sally approved and he filled our glasses.

I offered a toast. "To the beautiful woman on my right, cheers for a well-deserved promotion. May there be more in your future."

We clinked glasses and drank. Sally showed a broad smile, which I hadn't seen in a long time. "It's nice to see you happy," I said. "I've missed it."

"I'll drink to that!"

Over dinner, she rambled through a list of things she wanted to do with the increased pay. Some were the tiny, almost silly items a person puts off when feeling poor. Then she said first on her Big Tickets list was a new car, which seemed ironic. But we had talked about it before. The annual repairs on her old beater made it a smart decision and, in light of the new job, a practical one.

She became talkative on the way home and recounted her day, starting with the call from the regional office and her colleagues' reactions to the news. When we got inside, she called her sister and retold the story.

Not a single sour word was spoken all evening. And I slept without a single nightmare.

20

Clevelanders know Parma as the home of pierogies, the potato-stuffed pasta. The city received national attention when Bill Clinton stopped there during his 1992 presidential run.

The Parma shopping mall is several miles south of Cleveland. Most consider this a blue-collar town because of the presence of GM and a major Ford manufacturing plant nearby. Sally's commute became a little longer and more complicated than the straight shot she'd had before, but now she had a new Ford Taurus to take her there. And when she arrived, she was the boss! I hadn't seen her this high since her thirtieth birthday at Old Town, with me serving her drinks all night.

Two weeks into the new job, I showed my support by taking her to lunch. At noon I parked near the main entrance and started through the wide walkway lined with retail stores. I saw the Gap's ubiquitous logo halfway down the hall and walked in.

From behind a rack of dresses, a sales clerk approached me. "Hi, need any help?"

"Not that you've done anything bad, but I'm here to see the manager."

"Aren't you Sally's husband?"

"Yes."

"We met at the Gap Christmas party last year. I'm Amy, the one who—"

"Right. With Doug Flaven. Sorry about how I behaved with you that night."

"Water under the bridge. Let me show you her office."

We entered the backroom, where the raw smell of shoe materials and cardboard boxes filled the air. I followed her through a narrow path to a windowless door that said, "General Manager." She lifted a fist to knock and stopped.

"I'll let you knock," she whispered, and walked away.

I did. A familiar voice barked, *"Come in."* Upon entering, I said, "Surprise!"

Sally sat behind a desk too big for the office, covered with folders and computer printouts. "Jack! What are you doing here?"

"Hi. I thought we could have lunch together."

"Gee, I'm juggling a million things. Lunch is out of the question. Sorry."

"Aren't you the boss now?"

"I am, but I still have a supervisor and he's expecting me at the regional office in..." She checked her watch. "Damn. I'm going to be late!" She picked up her purse and hurried around me. "Another time, maybe."

"All right." I looked around and then examined the title plate on her desk.

Sally Reinhart
General Manager

I muttered, "So, this is your dream job?" I stepped out of the storage room onto the store's soft carpeting. I took two steps on the mall's polished cement floor when someone tapped my shoulder. I turned around to see Amy.

"Hi," she said. "Are you in a rush?"

"No, I don't even know where I'm going next. Maybe you could point me toward the food court."

She indicated left. "If you take your time, you might see her there."

"Sally? She's got a meeting at headquarters."

"No, she doesn't. Hold on a second." She spoke to the salesperson behind the checkout counter and returned. "I haven't much time. Will you walk with me?"

"Sure," I said. We headed in the opposite direction of the food court, then slowed to a stop. "So, what's up?"

She looked around and said, "It's about Doug and your wife." My eyes locked on hers. "Did you know they've been seeing each other since the company Christmas party?"

"Seeing each other?"

"I assumed you didn't. I'm convinced they are having an affair. That night at the Hilton, they really bonded after you left. We were having drinks in the lobby and, being totally ignored, I insisted Doug take me home. Sally insisted on sitting next to him in the truck. As I got out, they talked about going to another bar.

"Not long after that, my sister saw them at a bar on New Year's Eve. When your wife started working here as my boss, I spotted him more than once waiting for her at lunchtime, but he never came into the shop. I suspected they had a rendezvous today."

This time, *I* looked around. "I'm not surprised they were together on New Year's Eve. She's a party girl. I was in Indiana doing the same thing."

"When I recognized you," she said, "I just had to say something."

"What else is there? I mean, proof."

"I'll be honest." Her face turned to stone. "I hate working for her. I don't like her. On her way out just now, she asked me to stall you. She's hiding something and it's not just enjoying lunch together. She's never been back in an hour."

I thought, *friends with benefits.*

"She's the worst manager I've worked for. And Doug is a prick and a crook. He dumped my sister with an e-mail implicating me as one of his reasons. Then he stuck us with a bill twice his estimate!"

"Yeah, he did that to me, too. Thanks for letting me know. I won't say anything."

"Good luck," she said and then returned to the store.

My desire for food went away, so I ambled toward the exit. Amy's report on Sally and Flaven seemed genuine and very convincing. Thinking back, sometimes I'd had my own suspicions but had brushed them off as a fantasy driven by my insecurity.

An image of Sally in bed with Flaven popped into my mind and my blood pressure shot up. Sometimes, a gut feeling is spot on. Amy reminded me of this one. Mindlessly, I put one foot ahead of the other, not knowing what to do or where to go next.

Approaching the exit, I noticed a floral shop with its doors open. As I got closer, the fresh, scented air and colorful arrangements drew me inside. The boutique's ambiance felt like an elixir, both calming and invigorating. Five minutes later, I walked out feeling lighter with a single, short-stemmed rose.

Driving back to the apartment after lunch, I recalled Rosie's "other woman" issue. I wondered if Sally's having an "other man" would make my Avilla girl's concern disappear.

21

I HUNG UP MY COAT, placed the flower into a small glass of water, and set it on my office bookshelf. As the computer booted up, my attention turned to several projects due by the end of the week. Time to focus on work. I started a fresh pot of coffee and spread some cream cheese on a pumpernickel bagel.

Designing the newsletter for an animal shelter took me the rest of the afternoon. Sally usually got back home from work by six p.m. I wondered if she would have anything to say about lunch. For me, avoiding the subject is much easier than lying. We'd had some fierce arguments in the past, but none with the stakes we were about to face. And this one could not be dodged.

While I started making dinner, I recalled the time I was driving on the Ohio Turnpike, where exits were far apart. Looking in the distance of the flat terrain, I spotted a massive storm flashing lighting and pounding rain on the small town four or five miles ahead. With no exit, all I could do was brace myself. When I reached it, the storm wasn't nearly as bad as it looked.

Tuna casserole is one of my go-to comfy foods and is easy to fix. I pulled the ingredients from the kitchen cabinets and lined them up on the kitchen counter, starting with a can of mushroom soup.

Fifteen minutes later, I strained the egg noodles, mixed them with other ingredients and spices in a baking dish, and put them into the oven at 350 degrees.

Now, how to occupy my mind for the next forty-five minutes without thinking about the oncoming storm? I poured myself a beer and got back to work on the computer. Next on the project list came print ads for the Chamber Music Society's spring concert series. They had programmed their spring series on romantic themes with works of Mozart, Beethoven, and Debussy's *Clair De Lune*.

The classical part of my music collection was only so-so, but I had this one and started it in my CD player. Slow and often haunting, the piano suite with phrases of fluttering keys soothed me at first. It reminded me of the movie *Frankie and Johnny*, where a couple with different personalities have a tumultuous relationship with intense intimacy and heated arguments. It hit too close to home. Out came the Debussy CD and in went Vivaldi, whose flowing baroque melodies got me back on track.

The client had sent me too much copy for their small newspaper ads. This wasn't uncommon. It put me in the awkward position of trimming away with my best instincts. I decided this client would appreciate my edits.

The ads were all finished when the oven timer went off. I pulled out the casserole and placed it on the stove to cool. I enjoyed the smell, but not Sally, who preferred I substitute the tuna with chicken.

Back in the office I sent e-mails to my clients, attaching the artwork. They always wanted changes, a tweak here or there, so refining them would be a waste of time. All of my work required flexibility, especially with the arts organizations. They had the strongest opinions, just like Sally.

She entered the apartment, remarking about the lake-effect snow that had accumulated and how well her new car handled it. When she detected the smell of her least favorite dish, she frowned but didn't complain. I had a glass of wine at the ready.

We ate, as usual, watching TV, this time a sitcom rerun. Afterward, I returned to the computer for the fourth project on my work agenda. Later that evening, her sister called and they chatted for almost an hour. I couldn't make out what they were saying and didn't want to.

I COULDN'T BRING myself to confront her about the affair that evening or even the next day. I didn't know why, other than the timing didn't feel right. Perhaps, on some level, I wanted to get ahead in my work because there was no telling what my state of mind would result in.

It happened on the third day. We were watching the TV news during post-dinner drinks when the weather reporter referred to Valentine's Day coming up. I asked her if she wanted to do anything for the "lovers' holiday" or if she and Flaven had already made plans.

Her body stiffened. No response.

"I know what's going on between you," I said. "And I'm filing for a divorce."

She clenched her jaw, grabbed her glass, and sauntered to the kitchen. Instead of wine, she poured herself a vodka, added a splash of tonic, and parked at the kitchen counter. "What are you talking about, Jack? Have you heard rumors?"

"Might be rumors. Likely based on fact. I believe them."

She took a slug of vodka. "You want to divorce me because I tried to get pregnant and I want a nice new house!"

"All the above and more."

She put her drink on the coffee table to get a cigarette and light up, blowing smoke toward me. I grabbed the remote control and clicked off the television.

"I can see their faces, my family and friends when I tell them *you divorced me over a fucking old car*!" Her last words spewed in full fury, chest heaving, face burning red. The eruption of frustration and anger must have been building up for ages.

Adrenalin burst into my veins to the end of my limbs. My heart pounded. Oddly, my left leg started trembling. I had to stomp more than once to stop it. Deep in her own hell, Sally wouldn't notice any of my physical reactions.

"Tell them the truth!" I shouted back. "The passion in our marriage has been slowly decaying to where we simply go through the motions. We haven't anything in common anymore. We tolerate doing things together. Then my inheritance, the farm, and the Bugatti specifically brought us to this breaking point."

"Bullshit! You fucking gave up on me, Jack!"

I thought about that. A police siren echoed in the darkness from somewhere. "Guilty. I've been slowly giving up, compromising with indifference. And now I'm done bargaining on my quality of life. We are finished!"

Her face was still red with rage. She hurled her cocktail glass at my head. I ducked. It crashed into the wall.

"I hate you!" she said, oozing venom. She tore into the bedroom and slammed the door.

My hollow body stood motionless at the center of the room, my head spinning flashes of violence and mayhem. My hands and knees felt like blocks of ice. With concentrated effort, I moved toward the kitchen. Was this how zombies walked?

I spotted my whiskey, half-filled a glass, added ice, and shuffled my sour feet into my safe space: the office. Unconsciously I checked my e-mails on my computer, like beginning a new day. Nothing I saw on the screen brought me out of my frozen state.

I gulped a mouthful of liquid spirit, repositioned my chair, and pushed the button on the CD player. The gentle piano notes of *Clair De Lune* wafted into the room. After several bars played, I went to my easy chair by the window and sank into it.

Drink. Debussy. Repeat.

THE SOUND of the front door slamming shut woke me at seven a.m. I found a note on the kitchen counter: *Moving in with my sister.*

22

A SNOWSTORM SWEPT across the Great Lakes area from Illinois through to Ohio. The conditions weren't so bad in Cleveland as in northeastern Indiana, where they reported up to three feet of snow.

I called Rosie to see how she and my Avilla friends were coping. She said they were okay despite schools and businesses all shut down.

When she asked how I was doing, I fought the urge to spill about the blowout with Sally. So, I went into how Cleveland's "snow belt" could experience enormous amounts because of the effects of Lake Erie. I lived on the cusp of the belt, hence, rarely got the worst of these storms. Only a foot fell. I added that the city's street department had an excellent record of clearing the critical pathways. All of which was said to detour our conversation from where my gut wanted to take it.

The next call was to my inheritance lawyer to get a referral for a divorce. He recommended Mike Temkin, adding he wasn't a bargain basement legal counsel. Quite the opposite. Based on the potential return, it would be worth it. Better take out a superior insurance policy, I concluded.

I made an appointment with Temkin, and then I begged my friend Tom Anderson to have lunch with me.

We met at Bon Appetit II, a restaurant near Tom in University Circle. They had excellent food and what I wanted most right now: a full bar. The artsy ambiance, with original paintings on the walls and classical or jazz music playing in the background, was like entering my own private club. Its proximity within blocks of the art museum, the Cleveland Orchestra, and the Historical Society made it a hotspot for arts patrons.

Sally didn't care about it.

Tom's personality made him a decent surrogate shrink, and I needed a session. He knew much about my situation from our visit to the car museum and the farm. I told him about the last fight with Sally and the decision to get a divorce. He picked his moments well, asking questions or giving me feedback.

I opted for an Irish coffee after the meal. As Tom drank his coffee straight, I confided about Rosie and my plan to keep a distance, given her "other woman" reaction.

"I wouldn't avoid her," he said. "Sounds like she's become a naturally close friend, given her personality and your mutual interests. If you began with a frenzied one-night stand, that would be different." We sipped our coffee. "Did it?" Tom flashed his eyebrows and grinned.

"Did it what?"

"Start out with wild sex?"

"No."

"Then, for all you know, her 'other woman' response wasn't actually her *feeling* but a thought."

"You mean an intellectual response?" I replayed the scene in my head.

"You're overthinking, Jack. The "other woman" is mostly a female thing. I have never heard a guy say he worried about being the rebound man!"

As sexist as that sounded, I couldn't argue.

"Only she can deal with something like that. Respect her feelings. Oh, and Valentine's Day is coming up. Don't get lured into all that fabricated romantic stuff."

Tom took off for work, and when I paid the pricey tab, it seemed reasonable for the session.

THE AIR OUTSIDE had that fresh snow taste. I took a few deep breaths and gazed into the white-capped park-like setting. Since I had no pressing work, I decided to go to the art museum and stroll through a gallery or two.

The Asian collection always gave me a sense of calm despite the dizzying overload of masterpieces in the overstuffed gallery. The museum planned to expand its gallery space, mainly for this highly rated and undervalued section. My approach had always been to pick a few pieces to focus on and scan as I went from one to another.

A mesmerizing, ancient Chinese metal sculpture called the *Raft Cup* captured my attention.

The silver object depicted an old bearded man sitting in what looked more like a small boat than a cup, with an elaborate handle as the mast. The label explained that the bearded traveler was looking at the heavens for direction. He sees two stars, the Spinning Maiden and the Herdsman, with a minor star moving between them.

He goes to the Spinning Maiden to ask what the sighting means, and she gives him a rock to guide his next trip. The back of the *Raft Cup* shows a verse that translates to:

You sailed to the heavens, and all you brought back was a stone.
Why did you not seek some of the heavenly maid's brocade?

As is often the case with ancient Asian art, a riddle held the meaning. Still, the image and the existential message resonated with me.

Back in the apartment, I listened to a voice message from Sally. The serenity I had soaked up in the art museum evaporated. She and Flaven were coming over to move her things on Saturday morning. This made the clock slow to a turtle's pace for the following two days. I much as I did not want to be there when they arrived, I had to guard my belongings.

As I waited, I pondered her decision to move out so swiftly. The short stay at her sister's place didn't surprise me because the house was too small, and Sally never had a good word for it. She grew up in Zanesville, part of Ohio's Appalachian region. They were poor, the conditions of her schooling were deplorable, and her bickering parents didn't provide any relief. Her only ambition in life became escaping that world. I knew she would not be going back there.

She had male friends who were drawn mainly by her sultry looks. The depths of their feelings centering on lust. Her female friendships appeared shallow to me. Hence, it had come down to her new boyfriend coming to her aid. Common sense, one of her better traits, would guide her to the logical and most economical decision for lodging during the divorce transition. How he would hold up did not matter to me. However, I took some pleasure in Flaven doing me the favor of extracting her from the apartment. The timing was right for both of them.

My eyes were on the computer, trying to focus on work, when I heard the distinct sound of Flaven's pickup truck pulling up to the building. The palpitations in my chest perplexed me at first. Then I put it together: First time seeing Sally since the showdown. First time seeing her with Flahen as her defacto male pal. And the first confrontation with him since kicking him off the restoration.

We kept our distance. Sally's Dark Knight appeared nonchalant and cocky, like the winning rooster. They moved quickly, loading his truck in half an hour. Negotiations over items we both wanted were resolved rapidly, some like biting into a lemon. Her stoicism with me didn't bother me as much as the lovey-dovey moments she forced on Flaven. He merely tolerated it, making these moments cringe-worthy.

I'm not sure why I stood on the curb and watched them load the final box, only that the clunk of the truck's tailgate closing delivered instant relief. No goodbyes or waves would've made the departure any less painful. Yet, relief came. Perhaps that's what the first taste of liberation brings.

Inside the apartment at the kitchen counter, I poured some bourbon into a tall glass with ice. Never mind that I never drink before noon. When I walked into the living room to spread out on the sofa, I had to laugh. Sally's muscleman had just taken it away.

It took three nights to achieve REM sleep without bizarre, nerve-sparking nightmares. Eventually, the re-energizing sleep came.

I had an early morning walk and then prepared for another trip to Avilla. It included a short call to Rosie with a heads-up of my arrival despite the snow. Once on the road, my mind freely wandered. The route had seeped into my subconscious. No need for that magical rock for guidance in the art museum's "Raft Cup."

I stopped for a wholesome meal at a family restaurant. As I would arrive in the late afternoon, that would be my lunch and supper. Fortunately, I resisted having a slice of their famous pies. It hadn't dawned on me until the Auburn turnoff that my farm lane would be covered by three feet of snow. I pounded the steering wheel in frustration. Why didn't I think of this before I left Cleveland?

Reaching the city limits, the dusk already set in, making it dark by four p.m. But the mounds of white snow everywhere gave streetlights twice the illumination as usual. The roads were neatly cleared. I parked at Pastimes, figuring Joe would know someone with a snowplow.

He had one hand leaning on the bar, looking up at the news on the TV. The sound of the door drew his attention. "Look who's crawled out of the city!"

I shook off the cold like a dog drenched in water and unzipped my parka. I ambled to the bar and told Joe, "Miller Light, a shot of whiskey, and ... a snowplow, please."

He chuckled and said, "There's only one person around here who does that kind of work. That is my son, Bert."

"Yeah, I met him on New Year's Eve. Do you know if he's available?"

"He's at work at the Home Depot in Kendallville until five." He set my beer down and poured the whiskey before me. I paused for him to finish and took a pull of beer and a sip of whiskey. The moment they blended in my mouth always warmed me.

"But you don't need him," Joe said.

"How's that?"

"He's already been out to your place," he said. "Rosie arranged it."

"Well, I'll be damned."

"No, you'd be one lucky son-of-a-bitch to have that girl as your friend." He gave me a look that I'd expect from the girl's father.

"I couldn't agree more!" I replied. "Is Bert short for Robert?"

"Herbert."

I chortled. "You named him Herbert?"

He gave me the patented cop stare. "After John Herbert Dillinger."

"Right," I said sarcastically.

"In truth, it was Betsy's father's name."

Ragged Red came through the door wearing a thick lumberjack shirt, tails out, and a scarf. Without a word, he sat in his usual spot.

"Aren't you cold without a coat?" I asked.

"Nothing a double whiskey won't take of. With my beer, Joe."

"You are wise in your years," I told him and then watched Joe pour the drinks.

There are times when a boilermaker works for me, slowing the clock while warming your insides. Now that my worries about the snow blocking me out were over, I embraced the time to unwind. Relaxing at Pastimes, away from the city, had become automatic, but being here with the surroundings buried in snow added contentment.

I thought about Joe's background as a policeman, his reference to Dillinger, and the Auburn Car Museum's story. "Hey, Joe. You have any stories about Dillinger I haven't already heard?"

He raised his eyebrows, picked up a beer mug, pulled a premium draught beer, and put it in front of me. "On the force, we called him Jackrabbit Dillinger."

"Jackrabbit?"

He picked up the Jack Daniels, poured a shot, and held it. "Have you heard the one about his enormous dick?" He stressed the last word and knocked the whiskey back.

I chuckled, "No!"

"The story was that J. Edgar had it severed, preserved, and stored in a secret place to show his most deserving agents and VIPs."

I laughed so hard that I started coughing. Joe, straight-faced, sipped more beer. I drank what remained of my whiskey and chased it. Joe refilled my shot glass. "On the house," he said.

"Thanks." I glanced at Red, gazing into space.

"They say the rumor probably started from a photo of him in the morgue after the FBI agents supposedly gunned him down in Chicago. It appeared in all the newspapers. I've seen it myself. The lower part of his body was covered with a sheet with this huge bulge in the center. In the background are these guys looking amused or astonished."

"Really!" I said, playing along.

"You know how newspaper photos were fuzzy in those days."

"Right. But how could a corpse have a woody?"

Joe grinned. "Rigor mortis!"

"Of course," I said, suppressing my laughter. "And the head of the FBI kept the dick as a trophy?"

"Right. Well, the theory was that J. Edgar's boys managed a way to covertly sever his member as payback to Dillinger for making the FBI look like idiots. Public Enemy Number One had so many escapes. After he broke out of the prison with a phony gun he carved from wood, Jackrabbit did four heists—all in these parts. Worst was his last, a bank in South Bend where a cop was killed. The President called Hoover and gave orders to put Dillinger down by any means as people were calling him a hero."

"Like Capone in Chicago."

"Many folks believe the Feds killed a guy, but not Dillinger," Joe said.

"Legends don't easily die," I said.

My glasses were empty. I thanked Joe for the extra shot and the tall tale and exited a bit high.

THE FRONT WHEELS of my Civic spun a few times going up the lane, but I landed without too much difficulty. Once inside, I called Rosie to thank her. Voicemail clicked on, so I gushed with gratitude on her machine, joyfully intoxicated for a cleared path home.

With a fire started, I unpacked the car while the cabin warmed up. The heavy lifting came when I carried in a mini fridge—just what my home away from home most needed. The bottle of whiskey I brought was already cold from the car. I twisted it open and took a shot to warm my insides.

To meet the needs of an extended stay, I brought a small CD player, which I set up on the desk. Among the CDs and books, I packed Fogelberg's new *Wild Places* album and a paperback of *High*

Fidelity by Nick Hornby that I picked up at Half-Priced Books. The only thing missing was an overstuffed chair by the window fire.

WHEN I CALLED Rosie from Cleveland, we agreed to avoid the potential pitfalls of getting together on Valentine's Day. Besides, all the good restaurants would be booked solid. Instead, we'd meet for a dinner date the next day.

I reached the back of Rosie's place around five thirty p.m. At the bottom of her stairs, she had stapled a note onto the handrail: *Beware of icy patches!*

The steps creaked as I walked up. Rosie appeared in the doorway. "Welcome, wayward wanderer! And de-ice."

I stepped inside, holding a bottle behind my back. "You got my voicemail?" She nodded. "To *show* you my gratitude, I brought this for you." I handed her a bottle of vintage wine.

"You didn't need to, but thanks all the same."

Our eyes locked on each other for a moment, and we hugged.

She helped remove my parka and combed her fingers through my tangled hair. "You've let your hair grow. And have you lost some weight?"

"A little, maybe."

Pulling a corkscrew from a drawer, she said, "I'm not ready yet. Why don't you do the pouring?" Then she disappeared into her bedroom.

I did as instructed and went into the loveseat. Rosie entered wearing a red brushed cotton vest over a white turtleneck sweater and garnet earrings. High leather boots complemented her brown knee-length skirt and thick black tights. A white clip in her hair made me notice how much her bob had grown out.

"Your hair!"

"Yeah. It must seem a lot longer to you."

I lifted my glass of wine. "Here's to, well, to us!"

We clinked glasses and drank.

"I'm glad you came back despite the blizzard."

"My need to escape Cleveland motivated me as much as seeing you." I pulled a pocket-sized box of chocolates from my tweed jacket.

"Godiva!" she said. "Nice. Let's have one now, with our wine." She opened the box, revealing four candies. We each took one and started chewing.

Smacking my lips, I said, "Seems a long time." I swallowed and exhaled. "So much has happened in six weeks."

"We may need to get reacquainted." She loosened my tie. "I like the blue on the forest green shirt." Then she put her arms around me. A soft embrace tightened. She rubbed my back in a circle. A low hum vibrated inside me. As she relaxed her arms. I tightened mine.

"Well, I feel better," she said. "Do you?"

I gave her a firm kiss. "There's your answer."

We did some catching up before driving to a restaurant in Auburn called Giuseppe's. Mandolin music played over the speakers, and the aroma of fresh bread and tomato sauce filled the air. Their tables were dressed in red tablecloths. Wood-framed black-and-white photos of the Auburn Automobile Company lined the walls and partitions. They showed how cars developed from the 1910s to the 1930s and featured a variety of factory workers and celebrity owners.

Our meals came. We were finishing when Rosie said, "You've done an excellent job of dancing around the fire, Jack. You should tell me about it."

I had already told her about Sally's new job. I gave her details of my encounter with Amy at the Parma mall and then about Sally moving out with Flaven's help. "I guess his opinion on marriage doesn't apply to female roommates. She's using him and he's happy to get used by a hot chick."

Rosie thought about my words and, perhaps, the sequence of events. Then she looked into my eyes as if asking if that was all I had to say.

"That's it. No more to tell."

Without a blink, she said, "So. How are you feeling about all this?"

I took in some air through my nose. "Dreadful to delightful, and all points in between. I'm glad I went with my gut and held my ground. The worst thing about prior fights with Sally was the lingering anxiety. Same thing after our marriage counseling sessions."

"So you really tried to work things out before. You took that extra step."

"We did."

As our server leaned in to clear the table, we leaned back. Rosie asked for coffee.

"Me too," I said. "And put some brandy in mine."

"Coming up," the server said and walked away.

"Back in Chicago," Rosie said, "when my marriage was in crisis, I did everything I thought I could to save it. He made the end easy by cheating again, with the same woman, while I was recuperating from the miscarriage."

"It's almost like he tried to make *you* divorce *him* so he didn't have to initiate it."

She took a beat. "That son of a bitch! I never thought of that!"

"You parachuted out, what, two years ago? And now I'm bailing out." I wiped my hands on the tablecloth. "I'm worried about what Sally might try to do. She knows what the Bugatti could bring, so I got a grade-A lawyer. I've set up two new bank accounts, one for me alone and one that's a car restoration account. The first installment of my stepfather's funds just arrived."

"George, right?"

"Yes."

"And your mom's name?"

"It's Kate, after her mother. I think she's really bothered by the news, even knowing about our troubles leading up to this."

"Maybe Sally became a real daughter to her."

"And Sally tried hard to be one. Despite her great looks, Sally had insecurities. She and her real mom didn't get along. My Mom really wanted grandkids." I sipped my brandy.

"She could still get them. It's an advantage men have."

"Thank God for my Bugatti to keep me busy outside of my work. This reminds me: I'm looking for an experienced, trustworthy mechanic, one with restoration expertise. You know any around here?"

She tilted her head and invited me into her eyes.

I looked down and said, "Sorry about my rambling on."

"You haven't rambled, Jack." She put her hand on mine. "You know I have deep empathy for what you're going through. Please don't be afraid to open up to me."

My gut clenched. I took a deep breath. Tears filled my eyes. I held Rosie's smooth, warm hands. The muscles in my back released. It all felt good.

23

CLEVELAND'S TALLEST BUILDING, Key Bank headquarters, is where our first legal showdown took place. After meeting with my lawyer about the terms of the divorce, his long-legged legal assistant took me to the conference room on the top floor. The elevator opened into a glass lobby with a stunning view of Lake Erie, reflecting the morning sun on tranquil blue waves. That was atypical for this time of year. A good omen, I hoped.

The room looked out over the city's eastern shoreline all the way to the University Circle cultural district. It brought to mind my honeymoon with Sally in Chicago eight years ago when, as tourists, we had gone to the Sears Tower observation deck with its panorama of Lake Michigan. The rest of that day, I had strolled the revered Art Institute, packed with masterpieces, while Sally had explored the north end of the same street with its exclusive women's boutiques.

Now, though, a cherry oval conference table with thick veneer overwhelmed the space. Bottles of water and notepads for four were placed at the end nearest the window. I sat down in an end seat, facing the door, just as Sally entered.

Her signature Jennifer Aniston-styled long hair had been rolled and pinned into a tight bun. She wore a black jacket with a matching skirt and a white Oxford blouse, accessorized by a delicate gold necklace with a cross. Her idea of dressing for a legal battle could double for a funeral.

A short, balding man in a poor-fitting gray suit followed her. Sally paused for him to pull a chair out for her and then sat down, avoiding eye contact with me. The guy stretched his hand towards me. "Hello. Jim Lockman, legal counsel."

"Jack Reinhart, husband." We shook.

My attorney entered in a spritely manner, looking as polished as the table in his designer blue pinstripes, cufflinks, and silk tie. I wasn't taking any chance of losing the prize that was hidden out at Grandpa's farm. After shaking hands with the opposition, he took the head seat with my wife left of him. He handed out copies of the proposed settlement and spoke his introductory legal jargon regarding Ohio divorce laws.

"Now, let's review the salient points to see where we are. You both agreed on the cash and noncash assets, like furniture, cars, computers, and jewelry. Do the estimated values appear accurate to you, Mrs. Reinhart?

Sally whispered to Lockman, and he nodded. "Yes," she said.

My counsel looked at Sally. "And you haven't any children or pets, correct?"

She shot her eyes at me and shook her head. "No."

"Now, then," said Temkin. "The antique Bugatti and the farmland with house and barn. Jack holds ownership as an inheritance given to him by his grandfather approximately a year ago. Are you in agreement, Mrs. Reinhart?"

"We agreed to sell the property to pay off any taxes and buy a house," said Sally. "He needs to make good on his promise to me."

"Yes, well, I'll get back to that," said Temkin. "Are you aware that your husband's stepfather is funding the restoration of the Bugatti automobile? And that some of these funds have already been used to pay inheritance taxes?"

She looked at me, at Lockman, and at me again. "No, I am not."

I shrugged. "You must have forgotten. The first part of my parent's investment went into a separate account on February 11th."

"A stipulation in Ohio law," said Temkin, "is that you, as a spouse, had to have expressed specific interest in the property before the bequest was made. Had you, Mrs. Reinhart?"

"How could I? Neither of us knew about the car! His mother didn't know about it!"

Temkin looked at me. I nodded.

Sally shifted gears. "Okay, I see what's happening here. So, let's cut to the dirty details of this thing. He promised me the inheritance would go towards a house for *both* of us. I'm entitled to an even share."

My lawyer turned to me. "Are you willing to sell the Bugatti to divide the net income with your wife?" He knew the answer. This was a formality.

I rubbed my chin and looked squarely at Sally. "No."

"You shit!" Sally barked. Lockman touched her arm to calm her.

"Let me finish," I said. "But I'll give you $10,000 for the farm and $10,000 for the car, totaling $20,000."

"That's hog shit!" She pounded the table.

"Your husband is choosing to give you twenty thousand dollars," said Temkin, "which he is not required by law to do, Mrs. Reinhart."

Lockman held a poker face as Sally's nostrils flared. She folded her arms and glared at me. I knew the expression too well and inhaled very slowly. After whispering into her ear, Lockman said he and his client wished to privately confer.

When the door closed behind them, Temkin said, "I see what you meant about her being a beauty and the beast."

I went to the window and tried to spot our apartment building in Cleveland Heights, just beyond a ridge—our only home in the ten years we had lived together. A line of clouds had moved in from the west, dimming part of the lake. Returning to my chair, I asked,

"What do you make of her lawyer? Capable of mounting a serious challenge?"

"If we go to court, there's a chance we'll get a certain female judge. She's a venerable, no-nonsense type."

"And that'll be good or bad?"

The door opened. Sally stepped in, her brow wrinkled. Lockman pulled a document from his attaché and said, "We know the law appears to be in your favor. However, there have been exceptions." He recited two case numbers and addressed me directly. "Mr. Hartmeyer, did you and your wife agree to sell your inheritance to buy a house for the two of you?"

"Yes," I replied.

Lockman continued, "You found the Bugatti on your inherited property."

"Yes, a Type 50 roadster under the barn," I said.

"And did you confirm your ownership?"

"She has a copy of the notice."

"And after the verification, did you ever specify to your wife that you decided not to sell the Bugatti and the farm as you had planned together?"

"My feelings evolved over the initial weeks."

Lockman leaned back in his chair. "Did you tell your wife the car had a potential value of one million dollars?"

"Yes, after some research."

Lockman leaned towards me. "Therefore, she *is* entitled to half."

"You're reaching, counselor," Temkin said. Then he looked at Sally. "You'll need to face a judge. Is that what you want, Mrs. Reinhart?"

"You're damn right! I'm fighting this!" Sally jumped to her feet and raised a fist. "You're not keeping that *fucking car* if I have to kill you!"

24

SALLY and her lawyer had just exited the conference room atop the KeyBank building. My head dropped into my folded arms on the table. "I blew it. Didn't I?"

Temkin stood and put a hand on my shoulder. "Not completely. But you gave them an opening for a challenge."

I stood and pushed the chair into the table. "I said too much."

"Don't be so hard on yourself," he said.

I went to the window and took in the vastness while he picked up his things and went to the door. He said, "We'll be in touch."

When I looked straight down, I gave myself a potent dose of vertigo. Lessons learned today.

MY URGE TO see Rosie grew each day I was away. It had been a week after the meeting with the lawyers and another week since seeing her on Valentine's Day weekend. I cleared my calendar of Cleveland appointments Monday through Wednesday.

My Honda Civic hummed at 75 mph on the Ohio Turnpike towards Indiana. Upon arrival, I had plenty of time to reacquaint myself with the cabin, unload the usual supplies, pet my Bugatti, and get a good night's sleep.

We had planned to make Monday carefree and spontaneous. After a lazy morning and brunch at her apartment, Rosie suggested we go to Fort Wayne so she could show me around. As one spoiled by Cleveland's "mini Louvre," I thought the art museum there had a decent collection. We spent time with her sister and boyfriend, and then the four of us went to a new restaurant with a microbrewery and enjoyed a leisurely meal.

WHEN WE RETURNED to Rosie's apartment, the clock said 9:15. She put on Celine Dion's newest album and I sprawled on the sofa. Rosie kicked off her shoes and leaned into me for room to sit with her legs curled underneath.

"Have you seen *Titanic* yet?" she said.

"No. I've been too busy avoiding a sinking tragedy of my own. Didn't need to see another."

"The lead character is an artist."

"The movie I'm eager to see is *Shakespeare in Love*."

"Oh, me, too. Let's see it together. Auburn and Kendallville have decent movie houses."

I poured us cordials of Hennessey. "*Merci beaucoup*," said Rosie.

I bowed, we toasted, and we drank. And it seemed almost decadent, cuddled with this classy lady. I felt a kind of elegance even if the furnishings and *accoutrements* came from Target and garage sales.

"Do you remember when I razzed you about your illustration skills?" said Rosie.

"Yes, and I agreed."

"Well, here's your chance to get back at me." She slid off the couch, reached under it, pulled out a sketchpad, and then signaled me to sit with her on the carpet. The tablet opened to a full-page pencil drawing of my face, detailed down to my windblown hair and hungry eyes. She turned it over to reveal a trio of miniature portraits from different angles. The last page showed a color illustration of the farm at sunset worthy of public display.

"I don't know what to say. They're wonderful. You're truly gifted, Rosie."

"You think so?" She took a quick glance at them. "What do you see in the pictures?"

"Hmm. Do I get multiple choices?"

"There isn't a wrong answer. Say what comes to mind."

I swallowed more brandy. "I see a man...somewhat anxious and searching...more handsome than me."

"Don't kid yourself," she said.

"Drawn with a certain romantic flare," I continued. "Bordering on dreamlike."

"Perhaps like a girl with a teenage crush?" She smashed her lips onto mine for a lingering, sensuous kiss.

When she released me, I said, "Hmm-mm! That wasn't any teen girl kiss."

She pulled away with a broad smile and pointed to the last drawing. "What about this landscape of the farm?"

"Ah, yes. Give me a second to focus," I said. "Okay. Somehow, you've captured my feelings about Grandpa's place with a nostalgic Rockwell quality. While showing age, the structures aren't rotted and the scrubland still has life."

"Observant and intuitive!" she said, taking back the sketchbook. She dropped it to the floor, and our lips reconnected.

I came up for air and said, "Drawing class was never like this."

She whispered in my ear. "Follow me for the full-grown woman."

She led me to her bedroom. Our clothes started falling off as we continued kissing. We slipped under the quilt, and our naked bodies entwined. Our passion became all-consuming. My lips moved down her neck. We pushed back the blanket, gasping for the air our pumping hearts demanded. We glided into a lower gear, cherishing the nuances of our senses.

Our bodies connected, time suspended. Graceful, rhythmical swaying began. We breathed deeper and rose to a sublime finish.

Resting on our sides, we let the serenity wash over us. Our heart rates returned to normal.

She whispered, “I sense your thoughts are wandering. Where?”

“To your farmhouse drawing.”

“What about it?”

“I saw us in it together, cozy and content.” I paused. “Is that okay?”

“Okay? The sweetest post-nooky words I’ve ever heard.”

On the road to a meeting at the Auburn Museum, my brain replayed the "teen crush" banter with Rosie. The play-acting seemed to be her way of softening the emotional calluses left by her ex's behavior. In the morning light, I thought about our lovemaking without cringing at our first-time awkwardness.

And I felt in my heart that I had found a genuine artist, simpatico with my own senses.

What joy! Each of us infatuated with the other, triggering unrestrained passion without expectations. And avoiding a slip into shallow love-talk slop. Regardless of what lay ahead for us, I prayed the memory of last night would not fade like the sun's light to pencil drawings.

Damn! I *do* over-analyze everything.

It took only fifteen minutes to arrive at the museum. I hoped to get a few leads on an experienced antique car restorer and clues about how the French-made car ended up on my Grandpa's farm. The museum had many volunteers who were trained as docents to direct visitors and answer their questions. The chances of finding anyone among them with firsthand experience at the factory were slim. Still, the automaker was the largest employer and people were living longer.

"My official title is Volunteer Coordinator." The fifty-ish woman sat across from me in a small café two blocks from the museum. "Everyone calls me Maddy. I talked with our director and curator about what you want. They gave me the names of two qualified restorers. Both are up there in years, but unlike other professionals we've engaged they live in the area."

She passed me a sheet of notepaper with names and phone numbers and explained more about the volunteer group. "They're mostly retired, both men and women, from all backgrounds. They are serious car lovers who take pride in their hometown's legacy. Many are fortunate to own an Auburn-made auto, some passed down through generations." Her face glowed with pride and enthusiasm.

"I talked with the curator about any Bugattis acquired by Mr. Cord in the early '30s, and he couldn't find anything in the archives. Your lawyer or his people must have dug deep for that info. It's an intriguing notion. Given our international business, some of my oldest volunteers thought it possible."

"That's disappointing," I said. "May I have a look at your files? I've been sort of a detective myself with this project. I keep poking around in various places, but the Auburn Museum will most likely have clues. Memos, letters, cables... any correspondence between Cord and Leamy, the head designer."

"I don't see why not. It's a benefit of museum membership."

"You checked up on me," I said. "Yes, I signed up the day I learned about the museum."

The waitress approached with a carafe and refilled our coffee cups. Maddy asked me more about my project. I told her a friend in Cleveland had discovered a Bugatti, and I described Mickey to her. I didn't see any harm in sharing the rest of my story, moving the location to a farm between Cleveland and Akron.

As we walked back to the museum, Maddy explained that the

curator and even the executive director would love to see the Bugatti when restored. "We're always looking to expand our collection. A Bugatti is one we would like to have."

"I'm sure Mickey would love showing the car to you when the time is right."

She showed me the research room in the inner offices and introduced me to two women on staff who helped me access administrative files. While modest, the room appeared like other parts of the restored historical building. The woman handed me a pair of white cotton gloves while the other person went into the archives. A few minutes later, she returned with two accordion folders labeled *Leamy-Cord Correspondence* with slots for each month of the year.

Handling 1930s letters, reports, sketches, and memos from the vault tickled me at first. That had long worn off when, an hour into the perusing, I came upon a memo stuck to the backside of a carbon copy letter. The missive from Leamy to a production supervisor regarding specifications for the Auburn 851 had a handwritten note in the upper corner:

Send over Jacque Dreyfus when convenient.

I reread the scribbled message word by word. My grandpa's name was unmistakably there!

I showed it to the staffers. "Can either of you recognize Leamy's handwriting?"

The older one said, "That's it."

"You're sure?"

"Pretty sure. I've seen his signature and other notes before. He was a big-time designer here before taking off for Detroit. Sad what happened to him."

"What happened?"

"Months later, he died of a rare blood disease from an injection."

The date on the memo was two weeks before the shipping

receipt found in the ownership research. It tied Leamy and Grandpa. I recalled seeing "Jacque" on the farm's ownership documents. It added up. He was new to the country, still a noncitizen learning the language. He Americanized "Jacque" to "Jack."

That's the man I was named after. Right there in the archives of the Auburn Automobile Company, confirming Grandpa did work at the plant!

AFTER THEY HANDED me a photocopy of the memo, I thanked Maggie and the ladies and took another walk-through of the galleries. When I came upon the Duesenberg, I studied the details more carefully. Because I now had a picture of my Bugatti, albeit loosely assembled, I could see some differences.

My Type 50 had a sportier look with sleeker lines accentuated by the slanted windshield. The floorboard formed a straight line to the front and rear fenders, each one curving over the tires, creating a beautiful elongated "S" shape.

The Duesy was more muscular and boxy and had a unique hood ornament: an Art Deco flying goddess. Bugatti cars from the Molsheim factory lacked hood ornaments. The exception was the Bugatti Royale Type 41, with its standing silver elephant sculpted by Ettore's brother, Rembrandt.

MY GRAPHIC DESIGN business had been falling off since I discovered the buried treasure. I serviced current clients but neglected the tasks of landing new ones. Now I needed to make that a priority. I committed to staying in Cleveland until I picked up some fresh projects, especially considering the lawyer fees ahead of me.

Even if I could do most of my pitching from the farm, being there would make it impossible to resist Rosie. Besides, the left side of my brain kept warning me that our second time making love could never be as magical as the first. Hence, not staying would be wiser.

The call to my mother about the divorce was overdue. Procrastination gets me into deep doo-doo with her more than anything. The news was bound to reach her. As if on cue, the call came right after dinner.

"What's this I hear about you and Sally splitting up?" Mom sounded more steamed than I expected. No, *hello*, or *hi, sweetie*? My stomach twisted into a knot. She resumed, "And just who is this Indian woman you're seeing?"

My body went limp recalling that particular tone. Then she shifted from annoyance to lamentation. "I'm your mother. So many years, just the two of us trying to survive on our own."

The guilt crushed me. After a gut-felt apology, I confessed my failures as a husband, easing into how Sally and I had grown apart.

Mom acknowledged that she had noticed the signs but tried not to worry about them, as all marriages have troubles. I didn't have to remind her she and George had both been divorced. Then, telling her about Sally's secret plan to get pregnant brought her over to my side.

After a long pause and a sigh, she said, "So, there's not any chance you two could patch things up?"

"Mom, she admitted to having an affair with the man who had worked with me on the Bugatti." I paused to let that sink in, then added, "I am truly sorry you heard this from someone else. I have no excuse for waiting so long."

"Your happiness counts most."

I took that opening to segue to Rosie, describing her as an artist and kindred spirit who helped me understand myself. I explained our relationship as mutually beneficial without making it sound trite or trying to sell Rosie's many good qualities. In short, I emphasized that Sally and Rose were very different women.

Still, Mom couldn't resist warning me about rebound romances. She recalled the trap she had fallen into, calling it a "false restart" after my father died.

"Mine is a very different situation," I told her. "Especially not having kids. So, tell me: Was Sally your source or was it her sister?"

"Sally called to tell me she was having a garage sale of some old things in the apartment. A couple of them were anniversary gifts from me. She wanted to know if I would mind if she sold them? It sounded so...I don't know what, but I got the story out of her."

"Right," I said, not wanting to extend the conversation.

THE FOLLOWING DAY, I awoke wanting to call Mickey and catch him up on the small steps towards the car's restoration and the investment deal from George and Mom.

He didn't react the way I hoped he would. "Of course, that thirty-five thousand could be enough if you get lucky. You'll need more repairs than replacement parts and hopefully avoid any costly surprises."

"I'll simply have to make it work."

"And I'll do what I can to help. I know you're not looking to showcase it anywhere, like the Concours d'Elegance in California."

"Don't make me weep!" My sarcasm got him to laugh. "Have you found a restoration guy yet?"

I told him about the handful of names I received from the Auburn Museum. I admitted I didn't know what to ask them and asked if he would help.

"Yes, of course. E-mail the info you have. I'll narrow it down and even meet with the finalist out on the farm with you. Be best to show him the car before the hire."

Before I hung up, I said, "Sally and I are splitting up, so now I'll have a clear path—mentally, anyway—to do the restoration and keep the car."

"Can't say I'm surprised," he said, "and won't say I'm happy for you. A divorce can be tough on a person. Beware, my friend, and guard your inheritance."

I HAD ALREADY GONE through the easy ways to get new clients. The time had come to do what I hated most: make cold calls. The evil necessity to gin up business. What I couldn't say, I wanted to. "Saw your ad in the newspaper, and it sucked!" A telemarketer advised me to compliment the prospect, show genuine interest in their company, and smile during the call. Getting an appointment to show my portfolio was the aim. If I couldn't close in person, then always follow up.

Altogether, the process was time-consuming. It also required thick skin, likening the actor who prepares for an audition knowing the chances are slim. While rare, I have turned down a customer, knowing we would be a terrible match. Better to pass than to spend endless hours coping with someone you'll never satisfy. I remind myself that I'm in the business of art and make it subject to individual taste.

My last pitch went to my friend and occasional shrink, Tom. I sent him a friendly e-mail, giving him a heads-up that I'd be calling to see if he had any leads.

He called me back, saying he might have some work for the art museum. "Glad you e-mailed me, Jack. It so happens that with upcoming exhibitions and extra activities for the summer, I'm getting backed up here. So, I've asked for funding to get a freelancer."

"Hey, hey! My lucky day."

"I'll call you back next week."

"Thanks, Tom. Most appreciated."

"Oh, how did things work out with you and Sally?"

"We're on the divorce court's docket."

"Good luck with that. And the girl out in Avilla?"

"Dreamy."

"Sweet. Later."

THE NEXT DAY, Mickey went over topics to cover in the planned telephone interviews. He shared a draft work timetable and reviewed key categories like antique car safety requirements and the limited budget. Assessing the expert's experience and knowledge would be essential. He shrewdly brought up the expression *restomod class,* meaning I'd accept non-original parts to make the car drivable. We asked about ways he would keep the costs low and save time.

One of the two guys interviewed understood right at the top. He said, “You want the car for the road, not a museum piece or a means for a trophy.” With that, Henry Van Kinder, a seventy-something mechanic and body shop pro who had done restorations for the Auburn Museum, clinched the job for himself. He grew up in Auburn and most of his commercial repair equipment was still there.

After I talked one-on-one with Henry about the pay and work schedule, I mailed him a letter of agreement—which he promptly signed and returned. That the restoration would start at long last boosted my morale.

27

The call from Tom Anderson came on the last day of March. He had funding approval to hire me. His design for the Bugatti catalog was complete and in the hands of a high-class printer in Italy, awaiting proofs. There would be no compromising in quality for the documentation of the exclusive Cleveland show; the museum was expected to attract over 100,000 visitors from everywhere. Now the marketing department needed brochures and flyers and all the components of a direct mail campaign, plus print ads for the show set to open in three months.

"I assured them you were the best local freelancer for the job," Tom said, "and someone well versed in the Bugatti mystique." He laughed. "I didn't tell them how or why."

"You're a good friend, Tom."

"Mostly, you'll work with the museum's marketing director. Meeting her deadlines would please her and lead to more projects."

I liked hearing that. Now I had to deliver.

The next day I rendezvoused with Mickey, who volunteered to make the trip to the farm for me. He thought it best we meet with Henry in person to go over a game plan for the restoration, but I needed to dig in on the new job.

Handing a set of keys to Mickey, I thanked him in advance. "I really wish I could be there, but—"

"This is good timing," Mickey said. "While Henry and I go over the game plan, I'll be able to get my hands dirty working on the rare Type 50 myself. It'll be fun!"

"This time, you'll have the convenience of a bathroom on the old Dreyfus estate."

"Dreyfus?"

"Yeah, that's my grandfather's name."

"Hold on. How did I miss that? Your last name is—"

"Reinhart. Dreyfus comes from my mother's side. My biological father's name was Reinhart. He died in Vietnam just before the war ended. My mother married again, twice."

"Any relation to Rene Dreyfus?"

"Cousins. Grandpa's family lived in Belgium. Farmers." I said. "Grandpa didn't talk about him much. Just that Rene got him interested in cars."

"But you said you were Catholic. Dreyfus was a Jew, one of the most famous in sports."

"My mom followed her mother's religion."

Mickey started flipping the key ring in his hand. We were standing between his Bugatti and the Maserati. "Did you know Rene began his racing success with a Bugatti and also raced for Maserati?"

"No kidding?"

"He started with a Bugatti Type 22. Then he bought a Type 35 in partnership with Ernest Friderich, a legendary Bugatti racer."

"Is it true Bugatti cars won a huge number of races back in the day?"

"Indeed. Friderich was head of Bugatti's racing team for years. When he retired from racing, he started a franchise in Nice. That's where Dreyfus grew up and got a reputation as a daredevil, winning consecutive amateur races. Friderich checked him out and took Dreyfus under his wing."

"Did Rene and Ettore cross paths?" I asked.

"They met, crossed, and crashed! I can't say that Friderich consciously got back at Ettore over their falling out. Ettore, *Le Patron* as they called him, could be arrogant, stubborn, and demanding. He was also diplomatic and even charming when he wanted to be. It's more likely that Friderich lost interest after his daughter died in a race."

"What? How tragic!"

"She was a successful driver in female competitions. After her fatal crash, Friderich went out and won his next race, the famous 24-Hour Le Mans. Then he called it quits."

"That's the stuff of Hollywood movies!"

"Your grandpa's cousin had his share of great stories. He competed against Bugattis all the time, often beating Ettore's drivers, who had superior cars and made better money. When Rene asked to join the Bugatti team, Ettore rejected him and said he didn't know how to drive his cars. So, Dreyfus went out as an independent driver and beat three Bugatti drivers in the next Grand Prix. Now Dreyfus was good enough! He drove for Bugatti and also Maserati. That was a long time before they built this one."

Mickey opened his Maserati and sat behind the wheel. "Dreyfus became a national hero for France when he beat Germany's Mercedes-Benz and Auto Union teams in the Million Franc Race in 1937. Look it up sometime."

"I will."

28

SPRING 1999

For two weeks, I concentrated on the museum's marketing materials. Working with a new client required a learning curve and I knew the assignment would be challenging, given their high standards. Each day, my thoughts drifted to my hired hand in Avilla. Fortunately, Henry didn't own a cell phone yet or I would have called him daily with updates.

Finally, the day arrived when I would see for myself.

Driving up the lane to the farm, I spotted a late-model green pickup parked beside the barn. Henry must have heard me pull up because he stood just outside the doors, wiping his hands with a grease rag. He wore an old service garage uniform: a blue denim shirt, navy blue slacks, work boots, and a VFW baseball cap. Except for the Veterans of Foreign Wars cap, Grandpa dressed the same for his job in the factory.

Shaking hands, I said, "Glad to meet you in person at last."

"Likewise," he said. His tenor voice had a high, nasal sound. "Let me show you what I've done so far."

I liked his no-nonsense attitude. He had transformed the barn, adding work lights, cleaning the place, and arranging things to make it into a car surgical studio. The chassis rested on risers, giving plenty of room to work under the carriage. Sections of the car were already in place. The arm of a power winch hung over the engine block, which now sat on a nearby metal bench. The wall above the original workbench in the corner held a pegboard filled with tools of all sizes.

"You and the other guy did a good job cleaning the parts," Henry said. "I attached the functional ones as you had them, like the back and side panels, the doors, and even the running boards, which will still need work. I prefer to deal with cosmetic fixes like rust spots last."

He then took me through the completed work on the chassis. "The brake linings and all the hoses, gauges, and electrical wiring obviously need replacing. Over on the workbench are the parts I can recondition myself. I'll let you know the number of hours it'll take me, so you can decide whether I should repair those or buy new. Some will need to be sent out to be overhauled."

I perused the items on the bench. "Better write out a list for me, and we'll have a conference call and discuss it together. You can go ahead without asking for permission for anything under a hundred dollars. I plan to be back frequently enough to handle the larger invoices."

"Okay with me. By the way, would you prefer I call you Jack or Boss?"

"Boss? That'll sound like you're mocking me."

"Okay, Jack." He cast his gaze at the partially assembled, slightly elevated chassis. "You know I've worked on a lot of old cars, almost all American designed and built. But nothing like this one. The Duesenbergs come closest. This is something else."

I reached for my wallet. "Here's your paycheck for the first two weeks. Make sure it's the right amount. Must say, you've made a great start, Henry."

He glanced at it. "Yeah, it's right." Then he tucked the check into his shirt pocket below his embroidered name. "It's a refreshing challenge."

HALF AN HOUR LATER, Henry compiled a list of things for me to buy at the nearest auto supply store in Kendallville. By the time I got back I was itching for an assignment, one that would get my hands grimy.

We worked the rest of the afternoon. Henry gave instructions well, like maybe he did some teaching in his past. The occasional anecdotes from his life experience, about the town of Auburn or the cars that gave it national stature in its glory days. Contrary to slowing us down, his words complimented the interplay between us, rhythmically stepping up our productivity. Forgetting to call work breaks seemed to be his only flaw.

AFTER I CLEANED UP, I decided to call George. The last time we talked, I told him about Henry. He deserved a report as my primary investor.

"I'm really impressed with what he's done in the first two weeks," I said. "He's transformed the barn. And standing beside him today, I saw how methodically he works. He didn't hesitate to give me dirty jobs."

"Good!" George said. "You said he's a former military man?"

"Army, just before Vietnam. After that, he had some car factory jobs until he decided to work for himself and opened an auto repair shop. Most of his restoration work has been with American cars, especially his hometown favorites—Auburns, Cords, and Duesys. This is his first Bugatti."

George seemed to hang on every word. Then he asked if Mickey was still involved.

"Yes. He and Henry have different personalities, but they respect each other. Henry said Mickey's expertise helped him get out of the gate fast."

George thanked me for the update. Then, being the good son, I asked how Mom was doing. With that, he handed the phone off to her.

So much for a quick call.

ROSIE and I had planned for dinner at Pastimes the next day. She said she had some news but needed to tell me in person.

Avilla's downtown was busier than usual when I arrived, leaving only a side street parking space for me. When I walked around the corner of Rosie's café, I spotted a *For Sale* sign in the window. I peered inside. Everything looked the same.

When I entered Pastimes, Joe shouted, "Hey, stranger! Welcome!" Voices in the busy saloon echoed his greeting. The *Cheers* theme song popped into my head. The place looked about two-thirds full and I realized this was the TGIF work crowd.

I took the last open booth. On the table, a pink sticky note in Rosie's handwriting read: "Reserved—Rosie and Jack." I tossed my Indians windbreaker onto the seat and stepped up to the bar between two stools.

Joe had a bit of a sway in his steps when he came over to me. "Glad to see you, Jackie! Miller Lite or a Heinie?"

"Make it a Heinie this time."

He pulled the tap. I noticed his beer gut had become more pronounced. Had it been that long? Joe limped towards me. Beer foam tipped over the top of the mug. Before putting it down, he wiped away the spillage with the ever-present towel over his shoulder.

"You're walking awfully gingerly, there, Joe." As a habit, I put my credit card on the bar.

He pushed it back. "I trust you."

Back in the booth, I noticed the TV above the bar had the Fort Wayne news on. Typically I paid no attention, but today I was curious. When their sports coverage came on, they noted the upcoming opening of the new baseball season for the Indians. I thought about what might be happening in Cleveland and my divorce case. The lawyers were trying one last time to keep it from going to court.

I had been monitoring the front for Rosie when my eye caught her walking in from the rear. Her shoulders drooped, and her face lacked color.

Getting to my feet, I said, "Hi! You surprised me," and hugged her. "It didn't occur to me you'd come in through the back." I relaxed my hold and rubbed her back. "So, how are you?"

"Oh, I've been better." She tossed her purse onto the table and slid into the booth.

I sat beside her. "So, why the droopiness?"

"Not a good day. Would you get me a white wine, please?"

I went to the bar while she stared at the menu she knew from memory. As Joe poured her drink, I glanced back. Her tired and distant expression was foreign to me, a reminder of how limited our time together had been. Joe poured me another beer and handed me the wine.

When I gave Rosie her drink, she guzzled half of it down.

I asked, "Is your dad okay?"

"He's fine. I mean, not any worse."

"And Diane?"

That brought her to life. "You saw the sign in the café window, didn't you?"

I nodded.

"It's not a catastrophe or imminent doom, but Diane's quitting." She took another full swallow and then sighed.

"When did this happen?" I asked.

"Two days ago."

I didn't want to press her with questions. We were quiet, taking in the murmur and other bar sounds. I wanted to let her racing brain slow to a calmer pace.

Then she spoke. “My sister has stepped up the relationship with her boyfriend in Fort Wayne. She’s taking this guy seriously and is moving in with him. It’s only a half-hour drive, but she’s started looking for a job closer to him.”

“Oh, I see. What’s your opinion of the guy? I mean, in your view, is he worth the commitment?”

“I think so. Living together is a good way for her to find out. We talked about the situation for an hour or more. It quickly expanded to a review of her life and the need to move on.”

Rosie looked out the front window, twisting her purse strap. “It’s made me take a serious inventory beyond the cafe. I suppose it’s possible I could find someone to replace her, but covering the cost is a different thing. Diane and I have had this shared living arrangement. I don’t pay her like a regular employee. We split whatever we have left at the end of a week.”

“What about employment taxes, FICA, and all that stuff Uncle Sam likes?”

“I pay them for myself only. She doesn’t make enough to report income from tips.”

I wanted to help relieve Rosie’s distress. Listening seemed the best option, but she clammed up. Joe had been monitoring us. I might have been projecting, but I thought I saw empathy in Joe’s usual stone face. After a spell, the silence finally got to me. “What the hell, Rosie! You’ve got a situation.”

“Shit, yes,” she said. I gave her a shoulder hug. “I knew my experiment would end eventually,” she continued, and then took a deep breath. “She said she’ll continue working until I find a replacement or she finds a job down there.”

I took her empty glass to Joe for a refill. As he poured, he said, “I wish I could do something for her, but we don’t have a lot of options in this little town.”

"Your businesses complement one another," I said. "What about a merger of sorts?"

"I could think about that."

I went back to Rosie.

"Selling the building is going to be the hard part," she said. "That's why I put up the sign."

"Ironically, "I said, "that might increase your business. And then maybe you could hire someone."

"You're trying to be a glass-half-full kind of guy," she said. "That's sweet." I touched her hand resting on the table.

Rosie continued, "I'd have to trust a new person so much. And the thought of a new roommate...." She shook her head.

"If this is the end of the café, what kind of work would you like to do? Ideally?"

"Interior design," she said. "Fort Wayne has some shops. If they don't have any openings, I could try freelancing."

"I'm afraid my heart got ahead of my head. I was thinking maybe you'd have a better chance of getting design work in Cleveland. Duh!" I said, knocking the side of my head.

We ordered dinner. I decided not to bring up my exchange with Joe. No point in raising false hope.

When we left the tavern, the night was so pleasant I decided a leisurely drive with the windows down would be good. Sally would go nuts if I started just taking off without knowing where we were headed. Rosie didn't say a word.

I let the Honda navigate. After a few blocks, the destination became obvious—Dairy Queen! Is there a better treatment for despair than ice cream? We indulged in hot fudge sundaes in the car while the radio played oldies songs.

After DQ, we went to her place, where we sipped brandy. Two

rounds is all it took before she slumped in her love seat, droopy-eyed. I carried her to the bedroom, removed her shoes, and pulled the bed sheet over her. She fell asleep. I kissed her forehead and turned off the light.

29

I DIDN'T KNOW what to expect walking into the courtroom, except the ones I had seen on TV. This modern version seemed small and dreary with its fluorescent lighting. The three rows of comfortable chairs at the back for visitors were empty.

In the middle were two rectangular tables. Me and my attorney at one, and Sally with hers at the other. She looked much like she did at the KeyBank meeting, except for a royal blue suit. Why did I think it might be a "wear it one time—then return it" number?

We were called to stand for the judge. A fiftyish woman with streaks of gray in her black hair stepped up on the dais. Her face had the chiseled features you'd expect of someone making rulings. Her Honor put on reading glasses, studied the documents, and then removed the glasses to study her subjects.

"From what I see here, Mr. Reinhart, you offer to compensate your spouse beyond the law's minimum. Are you hiding something?"

"No, Your Honor."

"How did you arrive at the amount?"

"It's based on fifty percent of the inheritance I received a year ago, Your Honor. That includes the Indiana farm property, which is a parcel of land with cabin and barn, and the Bugatti automobile we found there."

"And according to the paperwork here," she said, "that comes to twenty thousand."

"Yes."

"The Bugatti car looks like your main point of contention. Is that right, Mrs. Reinhart?"

"Yes, Your Honor," Sally replied.

The judge held the case brief and read it. "The expert who evaluated the car seems well qualified. A member and former president of the Bugatti Club of America. A published car historian and curator for the Cleveland Museum of Art exhibition, including a version of the same car you are disputing: a Bugatti Type 50."

"Your Honor," Sally's lawyer said, "we are not contesting his credentials. Rather, we believe the car's value, once restored, is the basis on which my client should be compensated—not the value of the Bugatti when discovered."

"I see. I'm not a car expert, but it makes sense that a rare car could be worth more than the sum of its many parts." The judge looked at me. "In what condition was the car?"

"Under a tarp, disassembled from the chassis, rusted, and moldy."

"In what condition is it today?"

"Thanks to a loan from my parents that's allowed me to hire full-time help, we've restored roughly seventy-five percent of it. That includes the work I've done on it myself."

The judge wrote a note. "Mrs. Reinhart, have you contributed anything for restoration?"

That caught Sally and her lawyer off guard. They whispered back and forth, and then Sally said, "I can't say that I have."

"Your Honor," Lockman said. "If I may...."

"Yes, counselor?"

"Regardless of how much my client has put into the process, we contend that Mr. Reinhart promised to use all funds from selling the property, including the Bugatti, to buy a house for them to start a family. I believe the two cases I've cited do support this."

I glanced at my lawyer. He didn't blink an eye. Sally's teeth clenched her lower lip while her guy stood at attention.

"The figure you're projecting is an amount only a movie star would pay," the judge said. "I've studied the two cases and I do not believe they support your argument, counselor. The circumstances are vastly different. Request denied."

Sally's jaw dropped.

"Your Honor," Lockman said, "based on your decision, my client requests additional time to consider the previous offer by her husband."

"What's to consider?"

"Instead of receiving the settlement in monthly payments over a year, Mrs. Reinhart wishes to receive it upon signing the agreement."

"Very well. The court gives you thirty-one days in which to sign a new settlement. Otherwise, I will determine a final amount and consider the case closed. Do you understand, Mrs. Reinhart?"

"Yes, Your Honor."

The judge hammered the gavel. Sally's face reddened and she dashed out the exit behind us.

I turned to Temkin. "Why didn't her lawyer try to re-negotiate the amount?"

"Perhaps he was worried that the judge would reduce or cancel the compensation you already offered for the car, given the situation."

"The circumstances being?"

"Your wife reached for the gold—the maximum the car could bring."

"Ah. Greed *can* have consequences."

I SAT among a handful of familiar faces in Avilla's Catholic Church. At the front, Rosie stood next to Diane, whose tall and slender groom had a shaved head and a goatee.

I had arrived from Cleveland just in time. Given how hastily the wedding had been decided, I'd imagined the bride's father holding a shotgun.

The happy occasion had been squeezed into the last available slot on a Saturday at eleven a.m. When Rosie called urging me to attend, half-joking, I asked if she was carrying the man's child.

"You're not the first to ask," she said. "But no. She's just nervous the groom might change his mind. And she didn't want the hassle of moving in with him without the paperwork."

"Guys like Flaven might have influenced her in that regard."

"No doubt."

When Diane started a cashier job at a new Costco in suburban Fort Wayne, Rosie closed the café. She had tried out a young woman and then a grandmother to take Diane's place. Hiring and training them exhausted her. Disheartened, Rosie put the café on hiatus to explore interior design opportunities around the area.

The wedding decision had come during an overnight visit to

Fort Wayne with Diane. "Diane and her guy were drunk," Rosie had told me on a phone call. "I thought they'd sober up the next day and realize that an engagement for six months to a year would be wiser."

She took a breath. "I'm happy for her. I'm just so fatigued by the frenzied pace of life-changing events." My troubles, for which she's been so empathetic, were among them. "I'm her bridesmaid and I'm sure she'll run me ragged!"

The reception line outside curled into a semi-circle. Smokers lingered behind them. When I reached Rosie, I wanted to take her in my arms and land a big-mouth kiss on her lips. I restrained myself. Instead, I took her hand and gave her a peck on the cheek. Decorum above passion.

I did the same for Diane, who gave me a knowing smile and thanked me for coming. From the father of the bride I got a weak handshake. Out of the corner of his mouth, he said, "There's Heineken downstairs."

The church's lower level sparkled like new, as did most of the building. The fluorescent lights spoiled the look. Tripling the flower count would have made a significant difference to the atmosphere by covering up the antiseptic scent.

The meager spread of food made me think they were on a tight budget and prioritized the honeymoon over the wedding expenses. Another party would follow elsewhere. Various sandwiches, chips, and beverages flanked the cake and the bowls of mints and mixed nuts. The cocktail napkins read "Diane and Gil" in the flowery Lucida Calligraphy font.

Knowing what I did about Rosie, she had not been in charge nor had she been influential in the planning. Someone had visited "Weddings R Us" for the package.

I picked up a ham on rye, chips, and a beer, and then sat with Joe and Betsy at a table. They gave me the rundown on Gil, the groom, who had got a recent promotion at the General Motors plant.

"And that's what prompted the wedding?" I asked.

He shrugged.

"Gil also plays in a rock band and makes money for it," Betsy said.

After two bites into my sandwich, Joe revealed that the inner circle would gather at his tavern later. Maybe I'd get more details about the quick wedding there.

Bert joined us and Betsy introduced me. "Yes," I said, "the good man who plowed my lane and fetched drinks for us on New Year's Eve."

"Oh, I forgot you met him already."

The wedding agenda clipped along, perhaps to get another wedding shoehorned in. Every few minutes, I saw Rosie tethered to Diane and the photographer. As the younger sister by only two years, Diane showed the energy of a woman in her twenties.

Rosie's father arrived with two men his age who had served as ushers. He took a seat at the wedding party's table with the in-laws.

I waited for the initial chit-chat to end, then approached him. Looking closer, his wrinkles seemed more profound and his skin paler compared to the man I had met not so long ago. The cynic in me wondered if Diane's share of caregiving duties for her ailing parent might have influenced her marriage decision. Unlike Rosie, who went off to Chicago for college, Diane hadn't had a life of her own. So, who could blame her?

I stepped between the ushers. "Hey there, Roger! Can I get you a beer and some food?"

"No need, Jack. These old-timers will do that." His buddies took off so I could converse with the dad.

"Where have you been keeping yourself?" he asked.

"Cleveland, most of the time. Making a living. So, how does it feel to have the younger daughter married?"

"Just hope the marriage turns out better than Rosie's," he said.

"Too bad about Rosie's Café," I said.

He thought a moment. Then, his voice bittersweet, he said,

"Rosie's Café was a good thing for this town. Their mother would have loved seeing her girls working together." His eyes searched the room. "Wish she were here today."

With a hand on his shoulder, I said, "You know she is."

A rueful smile appeared, and a tear rolled down his clean-shaven face. Then, as if on cue, one of his friends handed him a beer. He held it up and said, "I'll drink to that."

I echoed his sentiment, and we both swigged.

As the other usher gave him a plate of food, I felt a woman's arm reach around my midsection and tug. "What are you fellas up to?" said Rosie.

"Drinking a toast to your mother."

"You guys!" Her eyes filled with tears. "Now, look what you made me do."

I handed Rosie my *Diane & Gil* napkin, took her hand, and walked to the other end of the hall where a volunteer bartender was serving. I gave him my empty and flashed two fingers.

"What was your mother's name?" I asked."

"Dotty. Dorothy."

"To Dotty!" I said. We clinked bottles and drank.

"That was sweet...what I saw you doing for Dad."

"I have a special feeling about dads."

She enfolded her arm with mine." I'm so glad you're here." Standing on her toes, she kissed my cheek.

"You holding up, okay?" I said. "Weddings have a way of coughing up emotions."

"Don't I know. I assume Joe told you about the after-party."

I nodded.

"I'll meet up with you there."

She took a full swallow of beer, tapped her tummy, and burped. "Ah! Hope I don't do that on the in-laws during the photographs."

"Any password needed for the after-party?

"Try, 'Joe sent me'." She broke a smile. "Did you, by any chance, have time to get a wedding present? I'm worried that the gifts table will look pathetic."

"Sure did. A case of beer."

"You did not!" she said, gripping my wrist.

"I couldn't decide between a toaster or a blender, so I got both."

The chatter in the room picked up. I stroked Rosie's back. Her muscles were tight, so I pressed with my fingertips and caressed.

"Oh, Jack," she moaned. "That's...so...good!"

Several folks looked at us to see what felt so good. Then Rosie's eyes locked onto a member of Gil's band about to play for the wedding dance. She handed me her bottle and scrunched up the napkin. Then she uttered, "I love you, Jack," before dashing away in big-sister mode.

My reciprocal "love you back" faded in her tailwind.

Diane and Gil stepped into the center of the room, holding hands. The musician, whom I recognized from the wedding party, began playing his guitar. Rosie had positioned herself to help the photographer select his shots of the scene. The young singer started playing Dan Fogelberg's popular wedding song *Longer*. All eyes were on the bride and groom self-consciously swaying in unison, her hands around his neck, his on her waist. Their action barely met the standards to call it a dance.

After the first verse, the in-laws, younger than Roger, began dancing in proper form. Rosie pointed at them to be photographed. I flashed back to slow dancing with Rosie on New Year's Eve, and suppressed the impulse to take her in my arms in the name of decorum.

Then came the traditional switch off. Gil's dad tapped his son's shoulder and took Diane's hand to dance. The groom took his mother's hand. The photographer clicked away at the two couples and Rosie stepped back into the circle of onlookers. She looked across at me while those around her joined in the dance. We both entered the circle, connecting in the middle.

As we took the dance position, she said, "I thought you'd never ask me."

"To dance? I still haven't asked. The Greek gods above are manipulating us from the clouds and we're just their puppets."

"My Dad worked in the factory. Auburns were darn good cars," Henry said. We were prepping for the final coat of paint. "E. L. Cord saved the Auburn car company in the 1920s. He was a sales genius with interesting ideas, but he wasn't an engineer or a designer. Just a mechanic who raced cars back in Missouri until he went into selling them in Chicago."

Henry took the all-black parts, like the trunk and the S-shaped floor boards that extended over the tires as fenders. I did the cherry red highlights on the hood and the doors. My art classes prepared me well for this step, but the medium now was steel sculpted into angles and curves.

"I remember reading about him at the Auburn Car Museum," I said. "First thing after he got the job, he gathered up all the unsold inventory and repainted the cars in bright colors like yellow, red, and blue."

"And orange!" said Henry, shaking his head.

"Then he covered a city block with them, attached balloons, and hung banners for a gigantic sale," I said. "His promotion worked, and he used the money to restyle and design the next generation of Auburns. Like Bugatti, he wanted his cars to be beautiful and powerful."

"Yeah," Henry said. "And he started a new line, the 810 and 812, with front-wheel drive that lowered the chassis and gave them a sleeker look. They called this design, with the first hidden headlamps, a 'coffin nose.' In the tradition of all carmakers, he named it after himself: the Cord. And he built up the advertising and sales departments. He loved placing the cars with famous people and in movies. Did you see the photo of the Marx brothers in one?"

"Darn! I missed that," I said. "Sounds like he really knew marketing."

"That's the word."

The red paint on the hood formed an elongated triangle pointing to the nose. A line of black separated the hood's top from its red-vented sides and extended onto the doors, where the red formed a stretched oval shape. We had sent the metal frame of the convertible roof off to a company using a particular black canvas with smooth backing. It was classy-looking and durable, thanks to a rubber core.

Henry continued. "E. L. was a real opportunist, like when he learned that the Duesenberg brothers were scraping the bottom with their production line. Their reputation was based on the Indy car engines. But putting a version of them into the new street vehicle cost too much and they kept losing money. Cord cut a deal with them and grouped the Duesenberg company with Auburn Cord."

"Did Cord make money with the Duesy line?

"As I understand it, the Duesy had so much debt they couldn't catch up. Like you said, then came the Depression. With a large backlog of chassis, the Indianapolis plant stopped making them in 1930 and still had enough to keep selling them for years."

"So, other than the Great Depression, which impacted everyone, what ended the company? Others survived. There had to be more to the story."

"Cord lost focus and started acquiring suppliers like Lycoming Engines. He decided that air transportation would take over all other forms, buying large shares of American and Alaska Airlines. Everything went under the new Cord Corporation based in Chicago. He also bought up Checker Motors, the taxi company, and got into a nasty war with Yellow Cabs."

"I remember reading something about that. So E. L. was in on that?"

Henry nodded. "Did you also read about the kitchen cabinet switcheroo?"

I shook my head.

"The thing about the Cord 810/812 was that Cord himself didn't want to build them. The designer, Gordon Buehrig, came up with the concept when he was at GM, but E. L. refused to invest the million dollars to retool and start it up.

"He was living in Beverly Hills after two years in London, dodging the Fed's investigation into all his stock holdings. The workers at the plants in Auburn and Connersville where the Cords were being built needed work. So, the guys in charge convinced E. L. to invest in kitchen cabinetry for Sears and others. Only the money went into the coffin-nose cars instead. That kept the company going for a few more years.

"Cord eventually cut a deal with the Federal government to sell his automotive businesses and other interests. That paid him two million. Some punishment for stock manipulation!

"By 1937, all those employees were out of work and the town turned on him. He had already disconnected from Auburn after his first wife died. His second wife seemed more of a jet-setter with homes in Nevada, Florida, and California. His airline businesses struck it big when he got the U.S. mail contract. How he got that after his troubles with the Feds' is anybody's guess."

"I know something about getting knocked off course trying to please a wife," I said.

"I don't." Henry grinned. "Guess I lucked out in that department."

32

Before Sally and I were married, we took a road trip with another couple. The destination was the Pocono 500 in Pennsylvania. I went to experience an Indy-style Formula One race. Sally and her female friend, Glenda, were going to party overnight. An adult version of a sleepover. Glenda's boyfriend, Ben, worked for a national car rental company associated with the race. He said he had to attend as part of his job.

We drank a lot and came close to being a foursome at the hotel. The event was a mix of long, dull moments in the sun, punctuated by exciting crashes and dangerous moves among the leaders. A couple cars went into the wall and another flipped side over side. When the ambulance took that driver away, the audience submitted to obligatory applause. I don't recall who won the race and I've never seen another since.

Yet I looked forward to the Indianapolis 500 this year. Being a part-time Hoosier with The Brickyard only an hour and a half down the road had something to do with it. The Bugatti education I'd had over the last few months included much about the origins of the sport. Plus, I had a Hoosier sweetie pressed next to me at a familiar place: Pastimes.

The hometown crowd appeared less excited than the two

known Clevelanders, me and Ragged Red. The opening ceremony began with Jim Nabors singing "Back Home Again in Indiana" and Jay Leno driving the Chevy Monte Carlo pace car. Then came "Start your engines."

Given the race was a three-hour event, Rosie and I decided to spend a part of the time with her dad. He was glad for our spontaneous visit after the first thirty laps. We all had a round of beers as we watched. Occasionally, he chatted about Indy races in the past.

Within a half hour of finishing his drink, he dozed off. Rosie turned the TV volume down, took my hand, and led me to what was her bedroom. Now a guest room, the walls were a mixture of posters and family photos. Rosie pointed to a theatrical poster of her high school's production of *Arsenic and Old Lace*. "My poster design," she said with a hint of pride. "I also painted most of the set."

Most of the framed pictures showed Rosie and Diane growing up, and some included their parents and relatives. She identified them and gave bits about certain people and particular family gatherings. I noticed how Rosie resembled her mother.

"You take after her," I said, "and your sister is more like your Dad. Wait... I don't see any boyfriend photos."

"There were some. You know. Prom photos. Diane's pom-pom girl with a football boyfriend. But they came down when we broke up with them. Here's the only boyfriend picture that's survived." She pointed to a photo of herself, about ten years old, with a shaggy mid-sized dog. "Bud. He was my most loyal guy until I went away to college."

"He's a winner! I like dogs. Grandpa and Grandma had one kinda like him."

Rosie plopped on the bed and looked at the ceiling. "I never had the chance to sneak a boy in here because I shared this room with Diane. Until now."

I bent over and kissed her. She kissed me back harder. Then she went to the door, closed and locked it. Pushing me onto the single bed, she said, "Time to change history. Take your clothes off, Mister!"

THANKFULLY, her father was still asleep when we finished making love. My face would've given away what we just did in his little girl's room. Rosie wrote her dad a note and we returned to Pastimes for the end of the race, with some twenty laps remaining.

The bar had standing room only, but neither of us minded. The crowd's energy rubbed off on us. Driver Robby Gordon was out front for most of the closing laps but sacrificed a pit stop to hold the position. Everyone knew he would run out of fuel before finishing, and he did, allowing Kenny Bräck to take the lead. A third of the crowd left the bar for the closing interviews, which opened up two seats at the bar for Rosie and me.

We watched as race officials handed him the traditional bottle of milk. To cheers, Gordon swallowed some and then poured the rest over his head.

"Why the hell do they do that?" I asked Joe.

"It goes back to the 30s when the winner, I can't remember his name, opened a thermos of buttermilk and guzzled it down. He said his mother made him drink it to protect against heat stroke. His mother swore by it."

"And mothers know best," Rosie said.

Impressed with Joe's Indy 500 knowledge, I tested him further. "Do you know if any Bugatti cars ever won the Indy?"

"Bugattis? The real question is, did any even run in it? Some French cars did well in the early years. Italian makes have done much better and still compete. But Bugattis? They were mostly a flash in the pan like so many car builders." Then he sharpened his look at me. "What makes you ask?"

"I know a guy outside Cleveland who owns a Bugatti race car."

"A guy?" Joe said.

"Yeah, his name's Mickey Mishne. He knows a lot about Bugattis and their European race history, but he never talked about them competing in the Indy race."

"Okay, well, then check with him and see if I'm right."

"I'm sure you are, Joe. Don't doubt you for a second."

WALKING BACK to Rosie's apartment, I said, "Joe knows about the Bugatti. I can feel it. I'd sure like to know how."

"Come on, Jack. An ex-cop like Joe? He hears things, sees things, smells things."

"Do you think others around here know?"

She stopped and took a breath. "It's been a long afternoon, Jack, and I'm tired now."

Her reaction caught me off guard. We continued to the stairs and then she stopped again. "Since the wedding," she said, "your visits out here have gotten longer. People get curious. It's human nature. When I get asked about you, I give them your standard line about fixing up your grandpa's old house. People have eyes and see no activity around your house. It's just the barn. Then I hear, *is that all?*"

I followed her up the stairway. "Maybe Henry said something accidentally."

Rosie stopped two steps ahead of me, turned around, and looked down. "You're not listening to me, Jack. So hear me now. You are turning paranoid! And I don't like it. If you distrust your friends here over whether they know something, how can you call them friends? They will turn away!" She hesitated and then said, "That includes me."

She continued up the stairs.

A grenade went off in my stomach. I knew the day would come when I would do or say something that didn't sit well or flat-out pissed her off. Perhaps my being an only child had not prepared me to face intense anger. I took a breath. "It's not really distrust—"

From the landing, she said, "Okay, then. Call it big-city cynicism. That doesn't fly with me, either. I tolerated it in Chicago, but now I guess I'm halfway back to being a small-town girl." She stepped inside and turned around. "Isn't your car mostly finished?"

I stood one step behind her, sweat on my forehead. "Yes."

"And then what?"

I didn't know what to say. Her eyes searched mine. Answers swirled in my mind. I couldn't be flip. Utterances substituting for words stumbled out.

"Your immediate reaction—silence—said it all." She shifted her stance and cleared her throat. "You know, Jack, maybe you haven't noticed that I'm struggling with problems, too. I think we need to chill for a while." She shut the door.

The drive back to Cleveland was a long one.

33

SUMMER 1999

THE CLOCK KEPT TICKING for the art museum project. The elaborate direct mail brochure for membership sales, a monster part of the assignment, was completed and approved. Next came the print ads. The marketing director kept tight reins on every aspect of my designs. Maybe because we hadn't worked together before, she insisted on face-to-face meetings for each stage of revisions. So, I was at the computer screen in my apartment office instead of my laptop in the cabin on the farm.

How things ended with Rosie in Avilla kept distracting me at the gut level. That Joe had pieced together clues surrounding my real purpose on the farm rattled in my brain like a loose Bugatti bolt. Then Rosie's call for a cooling-off period festered in me. Since his arrival, Henry's presence at the farm has been reassuring. I sensed in him a protector. Also reassuring, if word-of-mouth did spread, was how the average person hadn't a clue about a Bugatti's pedigree. (Ettore had called an early model his *pur sang,* or "highbred.")

Still, my anxiety persisted on my first night back. Whiskey became my relaxer. I did the same the following evening. Then I realized my nervousness had more to do with Rosie than the car. And somehow, sorting out those two things helped. I finished the job by the end of the next day and hoped the marketing director would give her final approval so I could get on the road.

Her office was on the first floor of the museum. Mercifully, she gave the artwork her blessing.

With the project finished, I decided to see Tom. His office was on the third floor. I exited the elevator and saw him in the hallway with his assistant.

"Hey, Tom! Sorry to interrupt, but I'm in a hurry. I just got a sign-off on the last portion of the job you snagged for me, and I wanted to thank you again."

"How did you like working with our marketing department?"

"Between you and me, that woman is one hard-nosed client!"

"Welcome to my world. I'm glad I could pass along the work. You plan to spend the weekend in Indiana?"

"Longer if things work out. We're giving the car its first test drive."

Sleeping in the cabin on the air mattress had long lost its novelty camping spirit. My restless night finally ended when a sharp crack of thunder shook me onto the floor.

An eerie glow seeped through dark clouds hovering over the eastern horizon. I had to turn on the kitchen light to see the coffeemaker. Rolling thunder accompanied a spectacular lightning show as I awaited my first cup. Recharged air from the storm wafted in from the window and seemed to push the fog from my head. The gurgling last drops fell into the carafe, mixed with sounds of rain on the roof.

Twenty minutes browsing the Internet and two cups later, the sun blazed through and sprayed abundant sunlight over the land. I opened the barn to see how much rain had leaked in. The car and workbench areas were dry except for puddles in the usual places.

Before long, Henry pulled up in his old, well-preserved truck. "Morning, Henry," I said. "Did you get the rain I had here?"

"Not as much. It'll dry up soon enough."

"Did you get the parts we've been waiting for?"

He stepped out with two smallish boxes in his arms. While I opened them, Henry put on his shop apron. I sorted through packing peanuts and pulled out the "ammeter" with its original face but new workings. The other package held a regulator, also for the old electrical system.

He examined them and said, "These should do it!"

With the screwdriver in one hand and the gauge in the other, he lay on the car's floor and reached behind the dashboard. In less than five minutes he was back on his feet. Like the surgeon to the nurse, he said, "Regulator." I placed it in his hand. He picked up the Bugatti wrench Mickey lent us and leaned under the hood. He grunted a couple times and said, "There."

"Finished?"

We were still behind schedule, but not by much. Working with Henry had paid off.

"Okay, Jack," he said. "You get in, turn it over, and I'll watch."

The steering wheel on the right side still felt a little awkward, but the scent of the reupholstered black leather seats was delightful. "Should I pump the gas pedal?"

"Good idea."

I pressed twice and turned the key next to the steering column. The engine cranked but didn't turn over.

"Hold on," Henry said. He picked up the red and yellow plastic gas can with an extended spout, opened the hood, and dribbled some into the carburetor. "I poured most in the tank but saved some for this possibility. He took a step back. "Okay, try again."

This time, the engine sputtered, but still no go.

"Stop," he said and put more gas in. "Okay, now."

The engine coughed and then started running.

"Rev it up!"

I did. The eight cylinders ran high, so I lowered the choke to calm it down. The windows and convertible roof were down. I noticed a thin cloud of exhaust fumes enfolding the car, drifting into the hayloft.

"How's this?" I said.

"Good. Now, ease it into first."

The 4.9-liter, eight-cylinder, 300-horsepower beauty was the fastest Bugatti production car. Its supercharger was the first for any of his vehicles. In London it sold for 1,225 pounds, similar to a Rolls-Royce Phantom II, which had a bigger engine and carried much more weight.

With my left foot, I pressed the clutch pedal to the floor. Then, with my left hand, I pulled the gearstick back and eased off the clutch. The Type 50 crept forward a few inches. I gave it some gas. It lurched like a bucking bronco out through the barn's double doors! I turned right onto the path toward the lane, braked, and clutched again, putting it in neutral.

Henry came to me, laughing.

"What?" I said.

"Your expression." He laughed. "You ever ride a horse? The idle needs adjusting."

"Jeez!"

Henry opened the hood, a screwdriver appeared in his hand, and the engine decelerated. "There you go."

I listened and touched the gas pedal. "You sure it's not too low now?"

"Could be," he said.

"That does it! You're driving 'til you get the kinks worked out."

The veteran scratched his whiskers and lowered the hood. The stick shift was too high to climb over, so I got out, ran to the other side, and said, "You've listened to her heart, doctor. Now *this* baby needs a more experienced handler."

As he settled in behind the steering wheel, the gray clouds broke above us and released direct sunlight. The rest of the sky was a mush of cotton balls separated by splashes of blue.

Henry released the brake and gave it gas. The rear tires spit out a few crushed rocks under us. We strolled down the lane and stopped at the county road.

Henry said, "You ready?"

"Wait! I forgot the license plate."

"It's a test drive," he said, brushing me off. "Let's see what this Bug can do."

No sooner did he turn left, away from Avilla, that he needed to shift into second. Mickey said Ettore thought of first gear as nothing more than a walk. When Henry accelerated, the roadster leaped into a gallop to 70 kph, which was about 45 mph.

Bugatti's Grand Prix engine, the most powerful he had put into a road car, sounded rich with an overtone buzz. Our speed jumped past 100 kph—about 70 mph.

Henry shifted into third but before we could go much faster, he needed to slow for a wide ninety-degree turn to the north. He down-shifted, missing the lower gear at first. We drove by a country church and another farm before curving back toward the west into a straightaway.

Henry put it back into third. "All clear," he said. "I'm going all out!" He raised his voice to be heard above the motor and wind noise.

I gave him the "okay" sign.

He punched the pedal, a piece of steel not much bigger than a matchbox. The car sped up to 120 kilometers, which was 75 mph. I reached for the seat belts that weren't there. *Maybe we advanced to the test drive stage too soon.* The noise and vibration intensified at 145 km—a full 90 mph.

Just then, a pickup turned onto the road a half-mile ahead. He tapped the new brakes.

We trailed the truck for about three miles and entered the

outskirts of Albion, where an auto body shop had done some specialty work for us. Farther along, a teenage boy on a mountain bike did a double-take as we passed him. At the town's only stoplight, where Road 8 intersects with Road 9, Henry pulled into a gas station, put the gear in neutral, and set the emergency brake.

"Okay, that's enough for me. You're up. I want to monitor the drive from the passenger side."

We changed places. Henry said, "The engineering on these old cars hadn't allowed for the body leaning in the turns. Did you notice it back there?" I nodded. "Any speed 45 or more, remember to let up early into the turns if you don't want to flip."

I gave him another thumbs-up as I settled behind the solid wood steering wheel. I released the brake, shifted into gear, and eased the clutch. At about 20 mph, I fumbled into second. We approached 45 mph, exiting the town, and I slid into third. The speedometer went from 45 mph to 65 and coasted.

That took an edge off my nerves. I started appreciating the view of the farmland when it occurred to me that Henry might have made up an excuse to share the thrill of this first drive.

My body tightened the instant I saw a car approaching us in the other lane. "We've got to install seat belts!" I shouted to Henry.

"Don't slow down!"

He was right about my easing up on the gas as the car got closer. So I picked up my speed. I braced myself when the car finally swished by us.

After a beat, Henry said, "You can breathe again."

I did.

My driving coach signaled to pick up the pace. As the speedometer climbed, he noted something on the gauges. At 90 mph, the chassis trembled. With the top down, the wind whipped around us with marked velocity. I decided to stay there. My Honda would still be quiet and smooth, but I rarely drove faster. Why press my luck with the old bones below me?

Henry shouted, "More gas!" I sensed he wanted to see if the car would do the equivalent of a hundred miles an hour. The gas pedal wasn't on the floor yet!

The speedometer inched up to 95. My blood pulsed through me a hundred times faster. Then the engine growled. My foot came off the accelerator. My double-cam roadster might have done more, but I couldn't push any further.

"What happened?" Henry asked.

"You tell me! Didn't you hear that sound?"

He was quiet as the car slowed to 70 mph. The noise descended. Henry leaned toward me and said, "I'm sorry, Jack. I got carried away monitoring the rpm. Measuring it at 100 mph is—"

"Then why didn't *you*?" I said.

"A pickup truck pulled out ahead of us. Remember?"

He spoke like a father trying to calm his hysterical teenager. When we reached the farm lane, downshifting into second was a struggle again. Henry put a hand on mine, nudging the gear into place. I'd have to repeat the action soon.

"Okay, Jack," Henry said. "The shifting action starts in your shoulder. Just relax the arm and your grip."

I pressed the clutch, then glided the stick cleanly into first. No grinding! We coasted to the barn and put the gear in neutral.

Henry jumped out. "Keep the engine running," he said and went to flip open the hood. "Ahh, dammit!" he hollered painfully, jerking his hand away.

I killed the engine and dashed to him. "You okay?"

"Yeah, think so," he said, shaking and blowing his hand. "I should have known better."

"I'm getting you ice." I sprinted to the house. He trailed after me.

Inside, I grabbed the ice tray from the mini fridge, pulled some cubes, and put them on his burn. Clenching the cubes, he grimaced and then moved his hand over the sink. This tidy mechanic wasn't going to let water drip onto the floor.

After putting the ice tray back in, I grabbed two cans of beer, popped them open, and handed one to my partner.

"Thanks," he said. "They taught you well in Scouts."

"Sure did. Always grab the coldest beer!"

We guzzled several swallows simultaneously. I let out a belch and looked out at the Bugatti. We were quiet for a while. Then I said, "So Henry, in your estimation, how did she run?"

"Better than how we drove it," he said. "By the way, you forgot to connect the horn."

"No, *you* forgot!" I said with a grin.

"Don't kid an injured old man."

"Did you notice a high, crackling buzz sound at high speeds?"

"Mickey said most Bugatti engines have a unique sound, especially at racing speed. But I never heard one before."

"Speaking of Mickey, he'll want a full report about the test drive. Preferably, mechanic to mechanic."

"I'll call him tomorrow."

We replayed parts of the drive as we drank. When Henry smiled, I said, "What?"

"One hell of a ride, man! Almost as good as... no. Have you considered a name for her?"

I nodded. "The Phantom."

Henry finished his beer, removed his VFW cap, and rubbed his forehead. "That's not usually considered a woman's name. I'm old school."

"You're suggesting Rosie? I considered it, but don't want to jinx what I've got going with the real woman." I pulled two more from the fridge. "So, you going to finish that sentence? You said she was almost as good as—as what?"

He drank and took a breath. "I've driven only one other car that compares to your Bugatti."

"What's that?"

"Not important. You really should name her Rosie or just Rose.

That way, whenever you need help, I can say, 'Always a pleasure to work on your Rosie."

"Hey, man!"

Henry guffawed. "You can always get another girlfriend, Jack."

"Not one like her, old man," I teased back. "She's an original. The real deal. A kindred spirit and muse rolled into one."

"Man, oh man! You better get her to the church."

"I wish I could, but it's way too soon."

"Okay, Jack." He put his cap back on.

I had never seen him so loose and liked him more this way.

He asked, "You got a half-hour to spare?"

"Sure do."

"I'm going to take you for a ride in my truck."

HENRY WENT BACK to his quiet self as we headed towards Auburn. Not far from the downtown area on a tree-lined street, he pulled into the driveway of a brick bungalow. Next to the house was a double, maybe triple-sized garage. This was where he worked on cars for a living. I was here once before when I assisted him in transporting his floor jack to the barn.

He glanced inside a side window. "Don't see the wife's car. She must be out partying with her girlfriends. Follow me."

We walked to the back of his property, out to the original wood garage. He punched some numbers into a covered pad next to a back door and after a beep, I followed him inside.

I could make out the shape of a car. He flipped on a set of incandescent spotlights.

My jaw dropped. The pride of ownership showed on Henry's face.

"I'm speechless," I said.

"High praise coming from you."

We started a turtle-paced walk around the noir metal sculpture.

"It's a 1935 Auburn Eight Supercharged Speedster," Henry said. "Uses a 4.6-liter straight-eight Lycoming engine. Only one hundred and forty-five were made. And get this: Some say this Auburn was built to take on European cars like Bugatti."

My head jerked back. "My God, how could you not tell me about this after all these months? Why keep it a secret?"

"Same reason you've tried to keep a lid on your Bugatti. That and..." He hesitated, rubbing his chin.

"What?"

"Well, let's just say I never lost a job because I showed up my boss."

"Ah, discretion."

I noticed a streak of fine lines in red along the body of the car. Four chrome exhaust tubes protruded from the mesh on the side.

"Leamy designed this car before taking a new job in Detroit," said Henry. "Then Gordon Buehrig modified it with this boat tail at the back."

"That's a racecar styling feature, isn't it?"

He nodded. "Just like your Type 50, it's supercharged. Known to do more than 100 mph. The engine doesn't look as impressive as yours, but the horsepower is about the same. The vehicle has a single casing for its three-speed transmission and Columbia dual-ratio rear axle, which creates six speeds."

"Woah! If I only understood any of what you just said. Still, I'm damned impressed."

"I've reached 105 miles per hour in it."

I asked him how he had acquired this fantastic machine.

He said his father passed it on to him. "Dad said he won it in a poker game with some Indy 500 big shot. I was about twelve. My mother and I were both skeptical. So, I ran to the old garage and saw that his Studebaker was missing. Poker, my eye! Maybe poker-faced when making the trade deal."

Henry's father *could have been Avilla's infamous racing phantom!*

That's what I was thinking about back at the cabin. It was a good thing we had Roger's eyewitness account from twenty years earlier.

I made the call I'd procrastinated on all day. "Hi, Rose. How's it going?"

"As good as I can expect. You back in town?"

"For a while. The last parts arrived today, and then we had the test drive."

"And you wrecked your Bugatti," she said, joking.

"It actually went very well. What am I saying? It was thrilling! Like going on a new ride at the state fair!"

"Did you ever go to the state fair?"

"No," I said. "I was sixteen and took a date."

"Well, I'm glad your car's all restored and working."

This was not the perky, charismatic Rosie who won my heart. Something in her had changed beyond our fight over my paranoia. It could've been bad news about her ailing father or her sister's departure, not to mention closing the café and career issues.

Add to this list some crazy Clevelander getting tethered to her. The last issue is the only one I could do anything about. And I could start by not annoying her.

"So, anyway," I said, "I'm thinking tomorrow night the stars might be perfectly aligned for the return of the Phantom Belgian in his Bugatti."

She didn't respond.

"You think the patrons at Pastimes would get a kick out of that?"

"They might, if it's done right. If not, they'll think you're an arrogant asshole from the big city."

"I deserved that. Now, if I only knew a creative person who understood the local vibe. Someone I could trust to advise and guide me."

"Okay, you maniac! I'll do it."

THE NEXT DAY, my divorce lawyer called. *"There's a problem,"* said Temkin. *"Your wife hasn't signed the paperwork yet. Her attorney is about as frustrated as we are.*

"Does Sally know I'll make all the payments in half the time?"

"Yes. The timetable for getting the money doesn't seem to be the issue. But you know her better than anyone. Any idea what's going on?"

"Other than stubbornness? Does she know she's jeopardizing the whole deal?"

"Lockman said he told her as much right after the trial and in follow-up voice mails."

"She's got a boyfriend now. He could've put some ideas in her head."

"You should try to get her to sign for her own good and your peace of mind."

I hung up and called her cell phone right away. No answer, so I left a message.

Then I tried her store. The person who answered said she was off for the weekend. So, I asked for Amy and was told she had quit working there some time back.

When Sally got the manager job, I knew her weak spot would be coping with the staff. I saw how she would snap at co-workers and gripe about them constantly. Sales and sucking up were her strengths, not managing personnel.

I wondered how things were going with Flaven. Was he influencing her recalcitrance? She could be a basket case with the job, the divorce, and her new guy if they're still together.

Henry walked from the barn to my front door. I waved him in.

"Morning, Jack. I made those adjustments we talked about. And I reinforced the connection for the exhaust pipe," he said. "Here are the keys."

"That went fast. Tell me, Henry, honestly: Do you think I handled the car well enough today for a solo drive?"

"Believe you can, especially without me pushing you."

"Good point. Thanks ... for everything."

"You'll see me again. And my Black Beth, too, now that she's out."

"Is Beth your wife's name? For the Auburn?"

"Yes, both."

As soon as he left, I e-mailed Sally at her work and personal addresses. Then I looked into getting a vintage car license plate for "Phantom" or "Rosie." The names were so contrasting! Must decide.

Insurance for antique cars is less expensive, given the expected low driving miles and the extra care an owner will take. From what I read at the Indiana DMV, adding the Bugatti to my regular car insurance as a rider was the most convenient and least expensive way to go. I called my agent in Cleveland and gave her the info to get my Bugatti insured for road action.

Pastimes was not my preference for lunch. I still missed Rosie's Café. But today, I didn't feel like driving into Auburn and had nothing to eat at the farm.

Joe asked me if I wanted a beer. Instead, I took a Dr. Pepper for the caffeine.

"So, what's happening, Jackie?"

"You remember when I first started coming in here, and you told me about the *Phantom Belgian*?"

"Yeah, you were here with the other guy," he said, shelving clean glasses. "I introduced you to Rosie and Diane."

"Well, that other guy just might be coming back."

He stopped with the glasses and strode over to me. "What are you telling me, Jack?"

"You've probably deduced some of this already, given your keen cop skills."

"Spill it."

Joe listened to my telling of the Bugatti discovery, the abridged edition.

"That's quite the tall tale if it's true," he said.

"You'll see for yourself tomorrow because I'm going to drive the roadster through town at midnight. Rosie is coming along with me."

"Drive it or race it?"

"Both."

Contemplating my words, Joe said, "I knew you were on some kind of mission. Then you dropped the Bugatti name." I braced for a wisecrack. "Tomorrow night, huh? Want me to fix it with the Avilla cops so they don't crash your party?"

"You would do that for me?"

"Mostly for Rosie's sake. And you're okay, too." Joe smiled, flung his towel from one shoulder to the other, and ambled away.

Betsy came in just as my sandwich arrived. She sat by the cash register and yawned.

"Long night, Betsy?"

"They had me doing inventory in the store last night."

Joe put an iced tea down for her. She took a drink. "Rosie stopped by—" Betsy raised her lined eyebrows. "She's going through some tough times."

"Yeah. Wish there was something I could do."

Betsy gave me a moment to eat, then asked, "What's the word on your divorce?"

"Three words." I said. "All but signed."

"What does that mean?"

"My weird wife is AWOL. The judge will probably throw the book at her and declare me free." I raised my glass of soda and finished it. Joe gave me a refill.

Betsy said to Joe, "You tell him yet?"

"I was about to when you walked in."

"What's up?" I said.

"I've seen your ex-partner around town lately, more than once," Betsy said. "Black Ford pickup, elevated, right?"

I nodded.

"He stopped for gas once, so I got his license plate and gave it to Joe."

"Yeah," Joe said. "So, I called in a favor and did some checking. His name's Douglas Flaven of Cleveland, Ohio?"

I nodded. "Did you know your mechanic friend has a record?"

"No."

"Three arrests and one conviction. No time served. Two for assault and one for burglary. He got off with a fine and probation."

"Not surprised by the assault. Flaven would flatten guys on and off the football field. And he worked as a bouncer at a couple roughneck bars in Cleveland. But burglary?"

"Construction equipment, mostly. Could be worse, I suppose. But we don't know what things the badass has gotten away with."

I SPENT the evening in the cabin. My watch said eleven thirty p.m. Thanks to Cleveland Sports station WSPR having what they called "a clear channel frequency" on 1500 AM, I could listen to the Indians' game. I couldn't have had a better distraction, along with a bottle of Irish whiskey… the comfy companion who doesn't talk back.

A waning crescent moon had surfaced in the east. After opening the barn doors wide, I flipped the switch to pop on the incandescent lights. That produced a ghostly shimmer on my Bugatti.

Gazing upon my Phantom Rose, I reflected on the life-altering angst and joy that came with her. The gut-twisting death of a declining marriage and the discovery of a loveable kindred spirit. The fear my beloved grandpa Jacque was a car thief, or worse, and teaming up with two enigmatic male father figures in Mickey and Henry. And the mind-numbing conflict between my chosen profession and art avocation. Old friends versus new ones.

It pestered me that I had minimal experience driving this French car with the steering wheel on the right and gears center requiring my left hand. I had zero time driving the Bugatti in the dark of night. The last thing I wanted to do was mess up the Phantom's return to Avilla, especially with Rosie.

Time for a practice run.

It fired up instantly. A good sign. I turned the headlights on. The instruments on the dashboard glowed. We coasted down the lane, turned left to go away from town as Henry had done, and followed the same test route. Changing gears seemed easier, perhaps from being relaxed from the whiskey.

When I finished the test route, I went straight into the village. The clock on the dash showed both hands straight up. The dead of night.

I didn't want to be recognized, so I pulled into the closed Marathon station, unfolded the rooftop, and hooked it over the interior compartment. The engine in first gear seemed to pierce the silence in the darkness.

Once past the cemetery, the road veered to the left. That gave me a good look ahead, well beyond downtown. No cars in sight.

I slowed for the red when I approached the only stoplight intersection a block away from the abandoned Rosie's Café. While stopped, I did a 360 check of the scene. One car parked in front of Pastimes. I could see some guys still in the back through the front window. No vehicles were approaching.

I lightly revved the engine, awaiting the green light. The night was so quiet I heard the stoplight box click to yellow. My foot pressed the gas pedal to the floor as I released the clutch. The new Dunlop tires squeaked before gripping the blacktop.

I zoomed to 60 mph in maybe ten seconds through the green-lighted Old Route 3 intersection. The posted speed limit was 45. As I didn't see any flashing lights behind me or taillights out in front on Route 8, I gave the engine what it needed to reach 80 mph and held it for several miles.

Approaching the ramp to Interstate 69 outside of Auburn, I slowed, turning onto the southbound lane toward Fort Wayne.

The right-sided steering wheel and tall stick shift heightened my driving awareness. I merged onto the freeway, sliding into third gear, and soon reached 70 mph. The only headlights I saw in the rearview mirror were distant. Ahead I saw a pair of red dots, maybe a mile away. I convinced myself the chances of a state trooper being out had to be lower than low. That I even gave the cops any consideration showed how programmed I am toward caution.

Mickey had explained to me how the Type 50's double cams sucked in more oxygen, lifting the torque to boost the roadster like a rocket. Despite his competitors' success with the innovation, Ettore Bugatti didn't adopt it for his racecars. He believed using the device was cheating. Without telling his father, his son Jean decided to put the twin-cam engine into a new production car, making the Type 50 one of the fastest cars on the road. Ettore saw the results and made them standard for all his racecars, starting with the Type 51.

Phantom Rose tipped her needle over 80 mph. Air whistled between the rooftop hooks. As my knowledge of physics could fit into a thimble, I wasn't sure if I should roll my door window down to divert the air seepage from above. Or would that only enhance wind force and rip my brand-new custom-made convertible top into shreds? I let go of the window handle and focused on the climbing tachometer. The gap between me and the car ahead closed while the top rattled.

The speedometer hit 160 kilometers, translating to 100 mph. I pictured Henry in his Auburn Speedster next to me, grinning.

Suddenly, the car in front appeared to be crawling only three lengths ahead. I turned into the passing lane and zoomed past a white Toyota Camry with a silver-haired couple. What were Grandpa and Grandma doing out at this hour? Or was it Grandpa cavorting with another woman?

Still dreading that I might be ruining my new rooftop, I took my foot off the gas. At 75 mph, the rattling ceased.

The Union Chapel Road Exit came up fast. I entered the ramp into the suburban north end of the city. The back roads seemed to be the wiser route back. I turned west onto Coldwater Road North.

On Gump Road, I pulled to the side, collapsed the roof, and rolled the windows down. Thankfully, I had already visited Fort Wayne with Rosie to see her sister and her sister's new husband, so I knew a safer return route via Old State Road 3.

The sky offered a resplendent celestial view. The moon was now at about nine o'clock high. Recalling the art museum's Raft Cup traveler, I put the car into second gear, a comfy pace for star-gazing my way home.

DEEP SLEEP ELUDED ME. Events of the journey towards this day flashed back in anxiety-fueled nightmares. Grandpa's gift had tossed my life like a pair of dice in a craps game.

I went for a long walk around the farm. There seemed to be no better way to tame the jumble of thoughts whirling in my grey matter. I fixed on each step, took pauses in every moment, and consumed nature around me. I looked up through the tree branches and thought of Grandpa looking down. Would it be one of everlasting fulfillment or frustration?

After a shower and minimal breakfast, my design muscles took me to the new project for the Akron Art Museum. The marketing director there noticed the newspaper ads I did for the *Bugatti* show and hired me for one of their upcoming exhibitions.

Meanwhile, Rosie had the routine check on her father and chores related to his needs. An appointment with the real estate agent handling her building came later. Her arrival at the farm would come in the early afternoon.

When I saw her driving up the lane, I went out to the front doorstep and waved. She honked and parked at the side of the house. The sun hung straight above and the temperature sat in the mid-80s. I tucked a hand in the back pocket of my pale blue jeans and met her halfway to the front door. We stopped with about five feet between us. She wore khaki shorts, a white summer blouse, and sandals—ideal for the weather but too plain and simple for her. I sensed her tenseness by how she clutched her purse. My powder blue golf shirt was chosen to deflect my own nerves. It didn't seem like seven days had passed since we were last together.

"Nice summer look, Rose, especially your bobbed hair."

"Thanks," she said. "It's sort of a seasonal thing."

"Brings me back to the day we met. So much has happened."

"For both of us."

A nearby robin chirped. I held out my arms. She walked into them. In the embrace, I whispered, "This night would not be right without you beside me."

"I'd be pissed as hell if you did it without me." She pulled back. "I hope you haven't any plans for the rest of the afternoon."

We went to a vintage clothing shop in Kendallville, where she helped me select a fedora. She found a black cloche and a burgundy silk scarf with colorful Art Deco patterns for herself.

The town had a sprawling park with a lake at the south end, designed for hanging out on a day like this. While cruising, we spotted a Tastee Freeze. I hadn't seen one of these since childhood and so parked for dinner. Our standard order of hamburgers, fries, and root beer was taken by a cute teenage girl who delivered it with a smile five minutes later.

We topped off the nostalgic interlude by sharing a vanilla and chocolate Twister ice cream cone. Rosie impishly tipped her swirl of ice cream on my nose. I returned the gesture, and then we exchanged nose kisses to clean them up. It seemed surreal, two thirty-somethings flashing back twenty years, seemingly without a care in the world.

Driving back to Rosie's, the sinking sun crafted shadows on the rustic landscape, stirring my dreamy consciousness. Faded images of Salva Dali's melted clocks appeared on barns, hills, and roadside. I thought how Father Time had been messing with me since that first drive to the farm, the images of Grandpa living there, coping as a migrant, ensnared in a ploy with an awe-inspiring automobile, and suddenly escaping to Cleveland, wife, and baby in tow.

INSIDE ROSIE'S LITTLE APARTMENT, the anticipation of the main event became a bit much, so she popped a DVD into her player: Tom Hanks and Meg Ryan in *Sleepless in Seattle*. Later, Rosie had me open a bottle of Italian Pinot Grigio while she put on Shania Twain's newest album. Girl's apartment, girl's choice of entertainment. I didn't mind in the least.

AN HOUR LATER, the time came to get ready for the Phantom's return.

The night brought a line of cumulus clouds above the western horizon. The temperature hung in the mid-80s with some humidity. As we strolled towards the barn, I realized Rosie had never sat in my new sports car. "You've got the patience of a saint," I told her.

"I do?"

"Even though I've had the reupholstered leather seats installed for a month, you've never asked to try them out."

"I told you I wanted to save it for the complete experience, like riding in it straight from the Paris dealer's showroom."

"An Avilla, Indiana barn is a long way from that."

"Ah, but it's the mysterious barn of Avilla!"

I wondered what monikers might be assigned to this rare gem once out for the media to write about. Avilla's Unearthed Bug? The Dreyfus Type 50? Or simply the Phantom Bugatti.

Rosie ran her hand over the black leather passenger seat and sniffed the fresh leather. I opened the car door for her. She sat and hummed with approval. We put on our period accessories. My black felt Fedora fit a bit snugly, which I would need when driving with the top down. Around her neck and shoulders, Rosie's Art Deco scarf added a graceful touch.

Like last night, the engine fired up with one turn of the key. VROOM! VROOM!

"Woo!" Rosie yelped. "That buzzed my bottom!"

With the headlights on, I dropped the stick shift into first gear and, without touching the gas pedal, let the engine purr as we coasted down the lane. Rosie marveled at the dashboard's instruments aglow against the panel's enriched wood texture.

I imagined how Grandpa felt at this moment, driving an automobile designed for the upper crust of society with his true love next to him. Did the car's sporty elegance and power impress her? Or did my future grandmother laugh nervously, anticipating the bold thrill ride she had cajoled her boyfriend into?

And how did he feel? Bursting with pride like I'm feeling now? Cocky with confidence like his cousin Rene before a race? Or fretting about the consequences of being apprehended by authorities and ending his grand illusion of life in America?

The road to town was three miles. Plenty of room to give Rosie a taste of the Type 50's speed. I pushed it into second gear, flooring the gas and making the car leap forward to 50 mph. Even with the limit posted at 55 mph cars often sped up to 70, so I engaged third gear and hit that mark with little effort. We coasted there at the low end of the tachometer until the Marathon gas station came into sight. I eased down to 45.

The clock with new inner workings said eleven fifty-seven p.m. A faint glow from the downtown hovered above the houses and trees. After five or six residential blocks, we could make out people gathered on the sidewalk. Nobody followed us, so I slowed to a crawl. Rosie untied her scarf to cover her head. I tugged on the front of my chapeau.

I'm guessing the initial mysterious vehicle event took place with very few observers. But someone deduced the driver had to be the young Belgian immigrant tenant farmer. Tonight, over a dozen spectators stood out in front of Pastimes spread out in both directions.

As we approached, the streetlights brightened the shine of my black and red beauty. I put the car in neutral and I revved the eight cylinders.

"Hang on," I said to my partner and slid into first gear while flooring the pedal as I had rehearsed last night. The rear tires squealed and the car lunged forward.

Rosie shrieked, the sound tingling my spine. We streaked through the few business blocks in a blur. I let up a quarter mile farther away at 75 mph, tapping the brakes to ease down to the maximum.

"Look," Rosie said, holding an arm out. "I've got goosebumps!"

The sprint ended. The people under the bright lights became distant in the rearview mirror. Rosie kissed me on the cheek.

I said, "Think we deserve a curtain call?"

"Yes! Oh, yes!"

Just before Old Route 3, I made a quick turnaround at a small shopping strip. We were both silent on the drive back, hoping the crowd hadn't fully dispersed.

But no worry. The spectators had awaited our return and were still abuzz. The event may have lasted seconds, but the crowd's energy held. Applause and cheers greeted us. Some chanted, *"Phantom, Phantom!"*

"Let's roll down the windows!" said Rosie.

"Definitely!"

The crescendo of the chants climaxed as I pulled over to the curb out front of Pastimes. People reached out to touch the car or Rosie's extended hand. One couple came into the street to greet me on the driver's side and have a look inside the vintage two-seater.

Rosie waved her scarf out the window like a victory flag. "Boogatti!" she bellowed, delighting the onlookers.

I pushed back my hat. Joe approached and said, "Congratulations, Jack! This is an amazing set of wheels!"

Rosie chirped, "Hi, Joe!"

"Now, if you two would kindly move on, I might sell a few more drinks before closing. Even better, park legally and come inside for drinks on the house."

"Yes, officer," I said with a grin.

"Oh, not yet!" Rosie pleaded. "We need to do an encore!"

The crowd approved with more chanting. Joe took a step back and waved us ahead. I eased forward.

A small group on the next block cheered as we passed by. When I glanced at them, I noticed the whites of two eyes glaring at me from under a black hoodie. Something in the silhouette seemed familiar.

I asked Rosie if she had seen the figure, but she hadn't. Then she said, "Gee, I wish Dad could have seen us tonight."

"I thought I'd bring the car to town at a reasonable time tomorrow. Take him for a spin."

She planted a powerful kiss on me. The woman really loved her father.

We drove a little further. I convinced Rosie not to do an actual repeat, burning rubber and speeding. Instead, I would take down the roof to openly bask in the applause.

I pulled into the gas station and folded the top back. From the passenger side, I asked Rosie, "Would you like to drive this time?"

"Oh no. I'd be an utter failure without some practice. But I appreciate your generous, if reckless, offer."

Unlike cars today, the Bugatti's gear shift stood alone, closer to the dash. Maybe an inch separated the two front seats. Rosie snuggled up next to me with an arm over my shoulders. From behind, we looked like a two-headed driver. She stayed glued to me as we waved to the smaller group of people who lingered outside. One guy hollered, *"Viva la marquee!"* which I recognized as the slogan for the Bugatti Club.

36

Wispy clouds filled the western sky, approaching a bright three-quarter moon above the farm. Its rays outlined the black truck creeping up the lane. The broad-shouldered man behind the steering wheel had a blue-eyed woman beside him. Neither saw any cars by the darkened house. With a low purr, the Ford continued to the barn and then backed up to the doors.

Flaven and Sally, dressed in black hoodies and jeans, got out of the pickup. She watched the house while he took out a long-handled bolt cutter and applied just enough pressure to snap the loop of the padlock. The sound cracked into the humid air, making them both freeze.

Still no signs of life from the cabin.

Flaven opened the door closest to the wall-mounted alarm a few inches and squeezed through. With a pocket flashlight, he disabled the unit. He opened both barn doors wide, sat in the Bugatti driver's seat, and put the gearshift into neutral.

He went to the truck's bed and removed the thick chain he had used to pull the chassis of the prized French car from under the earth over a year ago. Sally stood nearby as Flaven connected it to his bumper and then whispered, "Signal when it's tight."

She shifted her focus from the house to the limp chain as Flaven returned to the truck and eased forward. The links tightened, and she waved a hand in the air. Stealthily, the Type 50 emerged from its habitat. Once clear of the doors, Sally waved to her accomplice again. He jumped out of the pickup to check the connection, and then both culprits stepped back for a full view of the roadster in the moonlight.

Sally seethed. “The goddamned devil that cursed my plans and ruined my marriage.”

“Yeah,” Flaven said. “Gorgeous, isn’t it? You’re really sure we can take it?”

Sally spit at the car. “For the last time, yes!”

Back in the truck, Flaven eased the shift into drive and moved forward, figuring to cut across the lawn to the lane. Above the cabin’s front door, a motion-detecting yard light flashed on, blinding them for a second.

As their sight returned, I stepped out the front door into their path and pointed my grandpa’s Remington .22 at the windshield. “Stop right there!” I shouted.

Flaven hit the brakes. Sally slapped his shoulder and commanded, “Go on! Drive over the son-of-a-bitch! He won’t shoot. He’s a wussy.”

Flaven tapped the gas. The 4x4 lurched forward. I shot a round at the front grill. The bullet pinged off. The former linebacker howled and sprung from his seat.

My heart pounded as I cocked a second bullet into the rifle’s chamber. Flaven’s face flared, charging at me. I shot at his feet. He halted.

Sally got out from her side of the pickup.

“I’m warning you,” I said. “I’ll shoot the first one who takes another step toward me. You’re both trespassing.”

The humidity of the hot July air still hung in the air. Sweat broke out on my forehead.

I pointed the Remington at the linebacker just a few feet from the barrel. My eyes darted to Sally an arm’s length from him. Where there once was blue in her eyes, I saw fire. Flaven raised his clenched fists. Behind his fury, I saw a glint of hesitation.

Sally took a step towards me as a dark smile appeared. "You wouldn't hurt *me*, Jack, after all the adoring sex we've had together. The loving we shared." She took another step.

Even attempting to yank the gun away from me would give Flaven an opening. I decided hooting her would probably stop both of them.

"Take another step, Sally, and I swear you are getting an awful scar on your face if you survive."

Her comeliness evaporated and the witch returned. "You'll put that rifle down or else!"

"What'll you do with the car? Try to sell it or drive it into Lake Erie?"

"Both excellent suggestions, but you'll never know."

"You are totally unhinged, Sally. You need help."

"I still have a right to be here. I'm not trespassing."

My head went back. "That's why you haven't signed the divorce papers." I shook my head. "Sally, it's over. Ask your lawyer."

"Him? What a dud he turned out to be. Impotent, just like you!"

"The divorce was final at midnight. You had an irrevocable deadline. I tried to reach you in every way possible."

Flaven glanced at her and relaxed his arms. The wheels in his head looked derailed.

"Unchain the Bugatti, Doug, or the next shot goes into your windshield."

Sally screamed. "Your Bugatti! Your *goddamned* Bugatti!"

"I'm unhitching it," Flaven said, retreating.

"No, don't!" Sally shouted. "He's tricking you!"

I heard the chain landing on the bed of his pickup. With his hands in the air, Fahaven inspected the grill. "Fuck!" he said, feeling a gash. He turned to his accomplice. "You lied to me! We're finished here. Get your ass in the truck!"

Just then, Rosie appeared under the yard light over the front door and waved. "Hi, Doug! Diane sends her regards. She's happily married now."

Sally scowled at her. "The whore who stole my husband!"

"You lost him, girlie. He's a free man now."

Police sirens echoed in the distance. All eyes turned toward the county road.

"Goddamn!" said Flaven. He jumped behind his steering wheel, revved the engine, Putting it in gear, the tires spun on the grass.

I lowered the .22 as the pick-up passed by. When he reached the lane, the tires spit gravel behind.

Sally jerked back her hoodie. The long strands of golden hair she pampered were hacked off below the ears. A demonic screech spewed from her. She lunged at me, wielding a lethal six-inch hunting knife.

I held the rifle out across my chest to deflect the blade as it came down at me. It glanced off the barrel into my right forearm, opening a three-inch gash under my elbow. Rosie, standing ready, jumped at Sally as a distraction. I tossed the rifle at the ex-wife and took her wrist. Adrenalin-pumping rage had given Sally new strength. Weakening, she kicked at my groin, and I flung my bleeding elbow backward at Sally's jaw. She fell to the ground, releasing the knife.

Rosie seized the knife and straddled her deranged rival. "Now you don't want to mess with an expert self-taught chef!"

I whipped my T-shirt off and started wrapping my wound. An Avilla squad car with flashing lights pulled onto the lane, blocking Flaven. An officer with his revolver drawn shouted, "Police! Exit your vehicle, hands behind your head!"

Flaven obeyed.

A tall, mustachioed man emerged from the cruiser's passenger side. By the truck's headlights, I recognized Joe holding his megaphone. "You guys all right?"

Rosie waved and hollered, "Get up here quick. Jack's wounded needs attention. And I'm holding the one who did it. She needs the looney bin!"

WE WERE SITTING on a pair of lawn chairs in the long shadow of the barn, watching the sun's orange and red rays streak over the landscape. The humid late July air carried a hint of the tiger lilies around us.

Rosie had come out at my invitation to relax over wine spritzers. I'd arrived around noon after several days of working in Cleveland.

"That's what Joe told me," Rosie said. "Red became Flaven's mole back in March. That's how he and Sally knew when the restoration was complete and about the debut outing."

"How did Joe find out?"

"Need you ask? The day after he helped bust your ex and Doug, it was all over town. When Red entered the Pastimes, Joe detected something in his behavior immediately. He caught the scent and made him spill."

"What was in it for Ragged Red?"

"Yeah, you'll like this. Your old buddy and ex-partner gave Red a certain Cleveland address and password for a *good time*."

I laughed. "Flaven got Raggie Red laid?"

She nodded with a broad expression.

"I shouldn't be surprised, but I had no idea Flaven trafficked in the underworld."

Once in a while, I heard a car drive by on the county road beyond the meadow. The prairie grass had grown so tall I couldn't see them passing. None had the distinctive sound of a Bugatti.

"The breeze feels nice," she said.

"My trip out here today felt different. I was thinking about you and us and the last pieces of the puzzle that started my long journey here."

"You found another piece?"

"Yes. And I shared it with Mickey, who agrees it fits. The car arrived at the farm in the first place because Cord, Auburn's hotshot owner, wanted his head designer, Leamy, to study it up close. I'm guessing Cord wanted him to capture the design spirit for their roadsters. Maybe in the next Duesenberg." I looked at Rosie. "If you were the successful head designer, how would that make *you* feel?"

"Damned pissed off!"

"While insulted, Leamy felt dutiful. He enlisted a part-time welder at the plant to get Cord's surprise, but he didn't dare open the package at the factory with witnesses around. So he told Jacque, a cousin of a Bugatti racecar driver, to hold the car right here on the farm in secrecy. Then Leamy bolted to another car company in Detroit and, shortly after, died. And here's Grandpa, not even a citizen yet, with a dream car in his hands but no paperwork!"

Our panoramic view had cross-faded into twilight. Stars appeared in varying degrees of brightness. Mosquitoes found our flesh.

"We need to retreat to the house for cover!" Rosie said. She stopped and tilted her head inside the doorway, scanning the interior.

"Reassessing the arrangement again?" I said.

The furnishings were no longer piecemeal or used things. Because Mom and George were visiting in July, I decided to splurge at the nearest Target store. With Rosie's advice, I picked up a loveseat with an ottoman, an end table, a small bookshelf, and two padded wooden chairs. The cabin now had a complete sitting area for four in the living room, color coordinated in what Rosie called raspberry and gray.

Having already had a 90° day, I mounted a window air conditioner in the bedroom. Just as important, I purchased a full-size bed.

The Cleveland Plain Dealer broke the story about my Bugatti discovery at the same time the exhibition opened. The show was a hit! And as Mickey now had time to come out for a day to check out the roadster, he accepted my invitation to come out at the same time as the folks and make it a party.

He arrived early for a private viewing of my Phantom Rose. After his critical review, he praised the Type 50's overall appearance. I started it up for him while he looked under the hood. His desire to take it out on the road was palpable.

I asked him, "Can you imagine doing a rally on a Grand Prix-style course?"

"You were reading my mind, Jack!"

"Let's go out and carve a make-believe route from the Indiana countryside." That brought out a rare broad smile from him.

I started him out on the test drive path Henry used. Mickey then augmented it with a couple of winding roadways. Then Mickey ran the car all out through its paces. His confidence in navigating turns, shifting gears, and braking convinced me he had raced his Bugatti many times. Still, I practically peed my pants on the tightest turns.

As we pulled into the farm, he said, "The engine, transmission, and brakes all tested well. That Henry really knows his stuff!"

"I'll have to get you two together on a track to race my Bugatti to his Auburn."

MOM AND GEORGE arrived at the Fort Wayne airport, rented a car, and checked in the night before at the Holiday Inn Express in Auburn. Mom had forgotten what the farmhouse looked like, but the whole property seemed small to her now. She appreciated that Rosie had come out to join us. I credited Rosie with making the place presentable, at least on the inside. Mom was almost too effusive about Rosie's artwork, now framed and hanging on the walls.

I took George to the barn and introduced him to Mickey, who relished talking my stepdad and investor through the restoration process. George impressed me with his questions. After he sat behind the wheel, he asked for the requisite ride. He didn't want to drive it himself, so I insisted Mickey give him the Grand Prix treatment.

Upon returning, the youthful vigor on George's face was priceless. Investment resoundingly approved!

Mother looked relieved to see George back in one piece. She resisted his initial effort to go along with him for a "little, very tame ride." But she conceded. Mickey gave George a few essential tips and they were off.

Before the party ended, Mickey and my folks made plans to meet at the Cleveland Museum of Art where he would give them a personal tour of the Bugatti exhibition. I sensed they would also take time to see Mickey's backyard museum on their next visit.

That was a week ago. I'm only now feeling settled down from the grand gathering.

Rosie realized she needed to stop fussing with the cabin's interior arrangement. "It is what it is," she said. "Maybe you should think about other improvements next."

"Like what?"

"Like before winter, you need to replace that potbelly stove with a propane fireplace."

We were sitting on the loveseat. "Send Bertha to the ironworks?" I said.

"Although she has a good character, you'll be happier and healthier with clean, thermostat-controlled heat for winter stays here. My place won't be an option when I get a buyer."

"What about your idea of converting the café into a decorating and design shop?"

"Only a backup plan. I'd much rather do projects for an established business than start my own again. Spend more time on the creative side, like the projects I've picked up from the Fort Wayne stores."

"I can't blame you," I said. "This is about when I'd be watching a ball game, and a TV would fit nicely in Bertha's spot."

When I went to a preview party for the art museum's *Bugatti* exhibition at Mickey's invitation, he autographed my copy of the catalog. That's when he told me he was the person who shouted, "Viva marquee!" that night in front of Pastimes.

Rosie reached for the book on the ottoman and flipped through the thick, glossy pages. Then she read from the foreword: "*Forty-five objects designed by Carlo Bugatti, two-thirds furniture and works in silver. Twenty bronze animal sculptures and two human figures by Rembrandt Bugatti. And six automobiles by Ettore and Jean Bugatti.*"

"These photographs are amazing!" she said. "I'm dying to see this. When are we going?"

"How about next weekend?"

"Excellent!"

I stepped into the kitchen and poured the white wine and club soda into the tall glasses. As I made the spritzers, I told Rosie about a call I got while in Cleveland from a guy in Hollywood. He asked me to contact him when I knew the whole story about Grandpa and the buried Bugatti.

"No kidding? Woo woo!"

"Yeah, like that's ever going to happen."

I dropped ice cubes into the glasses, handed Rosie hers, and walked to the desk with mine. "Do you remember the housewarming gift Mom brought? I need your help to figure out the best place for it." I reached into the center drawer and removed a small, framed wedding picture of Grandpa and Grandma in front of a church.

Rosie joined me. "How sweet! They're so young."

"And wild in their day."

"How so?"

We returned to the couch. "Being back here on the farm sparked Mom's memory. She remembered Grandma's story of when they first met. It was in what used to be a speakeasy in Fort Wayne. Prohibition had just ended, so she and her sister decided to celebrate legal drinking together."

"Good for them!"

"Grandpa drew her attention as the only man wearing a blue beret and speaking with a Belgian accent. They thought it odd that such a pleasant-looking young man was sitting with two gangster types."

"Intriguing," Rosie said, snuggling next to me.

"It gets better. Young Grandma and Grandpa started seeing each other. He had been picking her up in an old truck, which embarrassed him. He really liked her and was afraid he couldn't keep her if she thought he had nothing. So, one night, after a few drinks, he took her to the farm to prove he had land and to show her something very special in the barn."

"And she fell for that old line?"

"Yes, but it wasn't a haystack. Turned out to be a beautiful French-made roadster. Naturally, she was impressed and convinced him to give her a ride. And he drove her through Avilla, showing off its power and speed."

"Oh my God!" Rosie said, jumping to her feet. "You've pieced it all together!"

I stood and enfolded her with my arms. "It just makes sense."

"And my Dad witnessed it."

We kissed and kissed again. She pressed her pelvis into mine.

"There's just one more thing," I said. "Why Grandpa buried it."

"Oh, yeah."

I took an opened business envelope from the desk. "One night a long time ago, Joe mentioned an incident involving Dillinger in Nappanee, Indiana. It came back to mind when Mickey was here, and we brainstormed for an answer. I contacted the Warsaw Historical Museum. This photocopy of the newspaper account just arrived."

Rosie skimmed the clipping. "The Nappanee bank robbery? You can't grow up around these parts without hearing Dillinger stories, but I don't recall this one." She read aloud:

"Dillinger's daring robbery at the First National Bank of Warsaw netted the gangster $28,000. He fired shots into the ceiling and ran out with his accomplice to a getaway car, a black Ford sedan. It raced away to pick up one of the gang members standing watch a couple blocks away.

"According to an eyewitness, a red and black roadster came around a corner at high speed. It hit Dillinger's man as the getaway car approached. With police on his tail, Dillinger drove around the body to make the escape. The Nappanee police captain said, "We know nothing about the roadster or who was driving it. So anyone with information about this person needs to contact the station at..."

Rosie looked up. "Your grandfather?"

I nodded. "Grandpa could never drive that car again after that night. He didn't even want to risk selling it for fear of getting caught and deported."

"Besides, he was in love and wanted to get married!"

"Naturally!" I said.

We were quiet. Then Rosie said, “So that’s it. Now that you can put it to rest. Write it all down in detail.”

“Note to self: Write out provenance for the Phantom Rose.”

“I’m flattered my name is part of your car’s name, but why?”

“Henry convinced me it’s a she, so it had to be you.”

“Well, *this* she thinks it’s something we need to sleep on.”

Epilogue

The day after Labor Day, I woke up in Rosie's bed, not knowing when I'd be back. My busy season had arrived, and I needed to be in Cleveland. Doing the work long distance wasn't possible until maybe Thanksgiving.

When I walked into the kitchen, she was checking messages on her laptop. I kissed her and poured a cup of coffee.

"I found something of interest online," she said.

"What's that?" I sipped some coffee and sat across from her.

Quoting, she said, "The Auburn Auto Museum posted a notice for a part-time graphic designer. Salary with benefits." She turned her computer around to show me and then reached over to close my mouth.

I read it. "I'm not dreaming, am I?"

"Want me to pinch you?"

"You think an experienced graphic designer who owns a Bugatti would have an advantage getting the job?"

"Might. Then again, it might also move your resume to the reject pile."

"How so?"

"They might get the idea that you're out of their class. A Cleveland dude who owns a valuable Bugatti wouldn't be content living on a part-time salary in rural Indiana, would he?"

"I've got an answer for that."

"Yeah?"

"There's this woman here. My muse and soulmate. I have nowhere else to go."

"Gosh," she said. "You're hired."

NOTES

The exhibition about the Bugatti family at the Cleveland Museum of Art in 1998 made me a believer in the Bugatti mystic. The curator for the automobile portion of the show was, in fact, Mickey Mishne, who lived south of Cleveland. Without Mickey, this book would not have been written. As hard as I tried to come up with a fictitious name for him, it was impossible. He and the exhibition referred to in this novel could not have been made up in my mind. Hence, the story blends many facts including those historical, with characters and events out of my imagination.

In truth, *The Phantom Bugatti* was supposed to be the secondary plot of a historical fiction about the Bugatti family of artists: Carlo, Ettore, Rembrandt, and Jean. It was initially written in the form of a screenplay and received positive responses from all three of the exhibition's curators. When a Hollywood agent told me the story needed an "American hook," I already had one in mind.

That was 2001. After the tragic "9-11" event, many lives were changed, including mine. I left the Cleveland Museum of Art for a theatre management position in Kansas City. As I adapted to a new job and city, Mickey and I still communicated about the Bugatti screenplay. Then the unthinkable happened. My advisor and friend Mickey had his life taken away in a brutal murder. The shock, along with life changes around me, put the Bugatti story on hold.

Flash forward to 2021. I had experimented with converting a play I had written to the novel form and eventually published it. From that experience, I felt prepared to return to the Bugatti project as a novel. As I wrote the "American hook," the characters took over my creative self and became the complete stand-alone novel, *The Phantom Bugatti.*

For those wondering, the only Bugatti cars I own are 1:32 scale models of the Type 50 and a Bugatti race car. I am more fortunate to have acquired a Rembrandt Bugatti bronze sculpture, The Puma, which, like some of his brother Ettore's cars, is among the world's fastest animals.

NEXT FROM WP TRUESDELL

BEAUTY AND SPEED

The Bugatti Family Saga

In the vibrant Belle Époque era, the Bugatti family emerges as a beacon of artistic brilliance. Carlo Bugatti, a visionary furniture designer, nurtures his sons, Ettore and Rembrandt, amidst a lively community of artists in 1890s Milan. Ettore's audacious leap into automobile design and Rembrandt's enchanting sculptures capture the imagination of Europe.

Amid their creative pursuits, the bewitching Barbara Bolzoni intertwines with their fates, sparking both rivalry and passion. As Ettore's innovative cars begin to dominate the racing world, Rembrandt's sculptures mesmerize Paris. Yet, the tides of war and personal turmoil shadow their success.

The family's journey through triumph, heartache, and untold passion paints a vivid tapestry of ambition and artistry, echoing through the generations.

For more information, go to www.wptruesdell.com.

www.ingramcontent.com/pod-product-compliance
Lightning Source LLC
Chambersburg PA
CBHW060626310726
48982CB00003B/692

* 9 7 9 8 9 9 1 0 4 3 8 1 6 *